MIMOSAS, MAGNOLIAS, AND MURDER

A GRIME PAYS MYSTERY
BOOK 4

TRICIA L SANDERS

First edition November 9, 2020

Second edition November 21, 2023

Copyright © 2020 Tricia L. Sanders.

ISBN: 978-1-962175-10-4

Cover Design by Mariah Sinclair

This book is a work of fiction. The names, characters, places, and incidents are the products of the author's imagination or are used fictitiously. Any resemblance to actual events, business establishments, locales, or persons, living or dead, is entirely coincidental.

DEDICATION

This book is dedicated to caregivers. Whether you're caring for a family member, volunteering as a caregiver, or are a paid caregiver, please accept my sincere gratitude. It's a difficult task and you are appreciated.

ACKNOWLEDGMENTS

My first thank you is to my dear readers. Thank you for continuing Cece's journey.

Thanks and hugs to my daughter, Amy Kristin Sanders who is riding out this pandemic lockdown with me. If you cook, I'll do the dishes. Love you. Thanks for being here with me. One of these days we'll get to explore Texas.

I love when readers get to participate in helping me create my stories and characters.

Big thanks to Carolyn Schellert for proposing the idea of a wedding for this story. I hope I did your idea justice.

Thanks to MaryAnn Johnson who won the opportunity to name Flick Donovan, the photographer in this story.

Thanks to Natalie Marie Bucco who won the opportunity to name Sasha Withers, the caterer in this story.

To Ava Mallory, your daily sprints made me buckle up and finish this book.

To the writers who join in Ava's sprints, fill up your drink, and let's write. Thanks for being on the journey with me.

My critique group—you know Cece as well as I do. Thank you, Margo Dill, Camille Subramaniam, Sarah Patsaros, Brandi Schmidt, and Grace Malinee. A special thanks to Sarah, Brandi, and Grace for our weekday sprints. You ladies kept me writing through a bleak time.

Many thanks to my ARC team - Meg Gustafson, Mary Ingmire, Lacey Harrington, Michele Wicker, Lee Dunn, Maggie Herrel, and Dee Doub.

To Cayce Berryman at Kingsman Editing Services, your eye for detail impresses me more with each project. Thank you for accepting me as a client.

To Mariah Sinclair Book Cover Design, thank you for your amazing covers and patience.

To my mystery squad, you all make me laugh, cry, and write. Thanks for being there.

To my extraordinary friends, Barb Schmidt, Dixie Dart, Dee Doub, and Deborah Schott, even though we are apart, you fill my life with joy. Whether it's phone calls, cards, or text messages, you each have a special place in my heart.

CHAPTER ONE

"My mother is always looking for bonding experiences for us. The day of my dad's wedding is not the time."
Michelle Cavanaugh

"Mom, don't make me go to this lame wedding," Michelle grumbled. "Dad's gonna be distracted. It's not like I'll get to spend any time with him. Why do they even have to make a big deal out of it?"

I nudged her through the front door of Maggie's Salon and Day Spa where we had an early appointment for facials, manis, pedis, hair, and makeup. Her, for the evening nuptials. Me, because I needed downtime. It was 6:45 a.m. on what promised to be a gorgeous day. The sun was rising in the east, a gentle breeze was blowing, and the forsythia and weigela were in full bloom. Normally, I'd be all over a glorious spring day, but I wished it would rain. Buckets. A torrential downpour. Thunder, lightning, and hail.

"It's your father's wedding. You're going. You don't have to enjoy it, but you have to attend." I, thank goodness, was exempt from the festivities. My ex, Phillip, and his bride-to-be, Willow, didn't send me an invitation. Not that I would attend. I'd rather yank my toenails off with rusty pliers. Instead, I planned to pamper myself and stay as far away from Highland Park Country Club as possible.

"Why do they want me in this lame wedding and not Jessie?" Michelle whined. "Willow has all her sorority skanks hanging around like little sock puppets. She won't miss me."

I felt horrible for Michelle. Phillip put her in an awkward position by insisting she stand up as his *best girl* for his wedding to Willow, the woman who blew apart our marriage. "Your sister is attending the guest book. Willow might not care whether you attend, but your father does. He's counting on you being there for him. And your grandmother would have a fit. Besides, Willow will be your"—I gagged a little—"stepmother. At least try for your dad's sake. You can get through this for him. He's always been there for you. It's one evening. I have confidence you can pull it off. Let him know you're here for him too."

The only reason I could think of to attend this wedding was to see Hazel's reaction. Phillip's mother, the matriarch of the Cavanaugh family, still lorded her queen bee status over Wickford society. She had to be going mental over Phillip's upcoming nuptials to a woman half his age.

Michelle crossed her arms over her chest, much like a six-year-old preparing to throw a tantrum. "Whatevs! Just so you know, I'm doing this for Dad, not for Willow. You can make me go, but you can't make me like it."

That much was true, and I anticipated this wedding would drive the wedge between Michelle and Willow even deeper. The thought of her having a stepmother made my heart ache—especially one only eight or nine years older who might be more of a bestie than a mother figure. Not my finest maternal moment, but my ugly jealousy rose like cream to the top.

"Michelle, I never want you to think you have to choose between me and your dad. If you think going to this wedding will hurt my feelings, you're wrong."

Her face puckered up like she might cry. "I know. I just feel bad for you."

I patted her shoulder. "Go. Be there for your dad. I'm fine."

I saw my hairdresser, Sarah, and waved her over, hoping to head off a meltdown. Michelle and I had been on tenuous ground since her father left last year. She blamed me for the divorce, but we'd overcome some of her hostility a few months ago when I'd almost gotten myself killed. I needed to keep the balance we'd achieved.

"Hey, Cece. Michelle," Sarah greeted us. "Wish Jessie didn't have to cancel."

"She was looking forward to the pampering. She pulled a shift at the last minute," I said.

Sarah frowned. "Will she be able to attend the wedding?"

"Yeah," Michelle said. "Mom gave her the standard lecture this morning about how we have to be there to support Dad. Blah. Blah. Blah." She pretended to stick her finger down her throat and made a gagging noise.

"Come on back, and we'll get you both started." Sarah and my older daughter, Jessie, had been friends since childhood, so she knew when to sidestep Michelle's moodiness.

Maggie's provided a one-stop shop in Wickford for all things beauty-related. With my financial situation in the toilet, as it had been since Phillip left, I had not been frequenting the salon for anything other than an occasional haircut. During my separation and subsequent divorce, I'd opened a cleaning business, which strained my finances even more. I specialized in cleaning in the aftermath of catastrophic events. If my daughter had to endure this wedding, I could spring for a relaxing mother-daughter outing to prepare her and shower her with some love.

Sarah led us to the nail area where two techs awaited our arrival. "Have a seat, ladies. Can I bring you water?"

Michelle and I both nodded.

I turned my phone to silent, slipped my feet into the footbath, and leaned back, eager for a bit of indulgence and relaxation. Home manicures and pedicures were my norms these days, and I did them in a slap-dash manner with no thought to pampering.

The techs placed slices of cucumber on our eyes and told us to sit back and unwind. I had almost dozed off when a woman's voice disrupted my zen. "O-M-G! Phillip's wife is here."

Someone giggled and said, "She's his *ex*-wife."

I sprang up, and the cucumbers slid down my cheeks, bounced off my chest, and landed on the nail tech's head.

My ex's bride-to-be and her cadre of bridesmaids stood before me—each decked out in designer yoga wear in varying pastel shades. Willow wore a wide, white sparkly bride sash across the boobs my ex purchased for her with the funds we'd planned to use for a trip to Tuscany. The other three women wore sashes proclaiming their placement as bridesmaids or maid of honor.

Phillip left me one year ago this month, and this was the first time I had come face-to-face with Willow since he moved out. I had seen her at his office plenty of times before I found out he was boinking her. Then she'd been his airheaded assistant. His words, not mine. I hadn't known her well enough to make that judgment. She'd always made herself scarce when I visited the office. It had taken me long enough to figure out why. I'd never had reason to speak to her back then, and we didn't run in the same social circles.

Except now she'd be Mrs. Phillip Cavanaugh and be socializing with all my former friends—the ones who'd dumped me right after Phillip did.

Michelle removed her cucumbers at the sound of Willow's voice.

Willow wiggled her fingers at my daughter. "Hi, Shelly."

"It's Michelle," my daughter said between clenched teeth. "My name is not Shelly."

Part of me wanted to flee, but the other part wanted to jump up and scratch out Willow's eyes. Wouldn't *that* look pretty for her wedding. Determined not to make a scene and ruin my daughter's spa day, I reached down, retrieved the cucumbers from my nail tech's head, and placed them back on my eyes. Under my breath, I said the ancient Sanskrit word my yoga teacher had taught me to use as a mantra during times of stress. "Om. Om. Om."

Nothingness. Nothingness. Nothingness.

How appropriate. If seeing Willow on her wedding day didn't count as stress, nothing did.

The problem with small towns like Wickford was the lack of services. Maggie owned the only day spa in the county. I knew, when I booked the appointment, we might run into the bridal party, but Sarah assured me their appointments were at noon. She'd promised to have us finished long before their arrival. Not the case. I never dreamed Willow would drag herself from Phillip's bed before seven in the morning.

Michelle touched my arm. "Mom, they're gone."

I removed one cucumber. "As in left the building?"

Michelle sighed. "No, Maggie herded them to the back."

"That's better than nothing." I peeked at my phone and saw I'd missed a call and a text from Alder—Detective Case Alder. Unusual in that, he rarely texted. He hadn't left a voice mail, so I checked the text.

ALDER: NEED TO TALK TO YOU. XO

After Phillip walked out, I'd put up a barrier, determined not to allow myself to depend on anyone for anything. When I met Alder, shortly after Phillip left, there had been an instant connection that I'd fought as long as possible. Alder had broken down those walls. I finally trusted myself to maintain my independence yet be in a relationship with someone who viewed me as an equal—something missing in my marriage.

To say I loved Alder was premature, but I had feelings for him. He had divorced many years ago and had qualms about getting married again, and I had reservations about being in a non-committed relationship. But after my divorce, I threw caution to the wind and chose to have fun. After a little convincing, anyway. Whether or not it ended in marriage no longer mattered. I enjoyed his company, and he enjoyed mine.

I wondered what he wanted. He rarely sent a text message, so I was curious. My fingers were poised to send a reply when I heard a smooching noise and glanced at my daughter who was making kissy faces at me.

"I thought this was our time together," Michelle whined. "Can't you ignore Detective Studmuffin for a couple of hours? First Dad, now you. I guess the next thing is you'll get married."

I rolled my eyes and slid my phone into my purse. She was right. Alder could wait. "Happy now?"

She gave me a thumbs-up.

A harried-looking man with a duffel bag and two cameras slung around his neck struggled through the front door. "Where's the wedding party?" he asked in a loud voice.

Maggie headed him off at the reception desk and led him back to the massage area.

I stared in disbelief. A photographer to shoot a massage session?

Sarah arrived with what looked like alcohol and hopefully

non-alcohol for Michelle. "Mimosa?" she asked, handing one to me. "And virgin mimosa. Don't tell anyone. Maggie swiped them off the tray Willow's caterer is serving. She feels bad but hopes this will help—considering the circumstance."

Michelle waved away the drink. "No thanks. Water is fine for me."

"Willow's having her spa day catered?" I asked, staring toward the back. "With a caterer, a photographer, *and* virgin mimosas?" Non-alcoholic drinks for someone in the wedding party only meant one thing. My best friend, Angie, loved wine, and only one thing prevented her from having a nice chardonnay—pregnancy.

Why else would Willow be serving virgin mimosas? My stomach clenched at the thought that Willow might be pregnant with Phillip's child. I snuck a peek at Michelle and hoped she hadn't come to the same conclusion. It was bad enough her dad was marrying a woman the same age as her sister. If Phillip, at fifty, couldn't keep his girlfriend from getting pregnant, there was no hope for the man.

I grabbed the mimosa and took a big mouthful.

Sarah nodded. "Photographing massages is a first for us. I would have warned you about them coming in, but I didn't know. Willow called last night and twisted Maggie's arm to let them come in earlier with the caterer. I didn't put your appointment on the books, so Maggie didn't know you'd be here. She feels horrible and said to tell you she'll comp your appointments."

I waved my hand. "Don't worry about it." So much for a stress-free morning. "Let's get this finished."

"Maggie said to remind you about cleaning Sunday and Monday," Sarah said.

Word of mouth about my cleaning business had spread, and for the first time, Maggie hired me to deep clean the day spa. Her normal crew booked a previous commitment. Since she always closed two days a week, it gave me and my assistant, Nancy, the perfect amount of time to get this place spotless. "We'll be here nice and early tomorrow morning."

Sarah smiled. "I'll tell her. She left the key at the front desk for you. She also left a gift certificate for another visit, so remember to pick them up before you leave today."

———

We had settled in for our facials—anti-aging for me and aromatherapy for Michelle—when the door burst open.

I opened my eyes and saw Willow standing in the doorway.

"Excuse me, ma'am," my esthetician said to the intruder. "I'm with a client."

Willow wrung her hands. "I'm sorry, but I need to talk to Cece."

I shot to a sitting position. "Are you freaking kidding me? It's bad enough you're marrying my ex-husband; now you have the nerve to interrupt my bit of solitude with my daughter." I wadded up the towel I'd been using as a pillow and threw it at her. "Get out."

Willow recoiled when the towel hit her but stood her ground. "You can be mad. I totally get it, but I need your help. Kayla, my maid of honor, is sick, and I need to know if you have anything to settle her stomach."

"A dozen people in this spa, and you ask me. You've got some nerve. Get a life. And not mine." I scooted off the table and wrapped my robe tighter around me. Out of the corner of my eye, I watched the woman wearing the maid of honor sash stagger across the room and lunge for the closest trash can.

Settle her stomach, my eye. If I had to guess, mimosas at 7 a.m. or the bachelorette party played a part in the maid of honor's *illness*. Hazel's eyes would bug out of her head when Willow and her band of drunken bridesmaids stumbled into the country club. Yes, I would pay money to witness it. And Hazel, my former mother-in-law, accused me of being an embarrassment to the Cavanaugh family. She ain't seen nothing yet.

The other bridesmaids closed ranks on the sick one, shielding her from the prying eyes of the other customers.

My nurturing instinct rose to the surface. Then I saw that the crowd had turned their attention to the showdown between the former Mrs. Phillip Cavanaugh and the soon-to-be Mrs. Phillip Cavanaugh. I squashed my instinct. Rumor and gossip reigned supreme in Wickford, Missouri, and this confrontation was the equivalent of the showdown at the O.K. Corral.

"Why are you all gawking?" I screamed at the onlookers. "Find something better to occupy your time."

Willow flinched but stepped closer. "It hit her so fast. I remembered Phillip saying you used to be a nurse and thought—"

"You thought wrong. Get out before I do something that you can't cover with makeup." I gave her a gentle nudge and slammed the door. As the door swung closed, I saw the mob snapping photo after photo with their cell phones.

Tomorrow morning our daily gossip column would contain at least one photo of me with my head wrapped in a towel, my mouth gaping, and my cheeks flaming red from the hot flash searing through my body. My luck, the photo would be full color. Who knew what the caption would read?

I closed my eyes to collect my thoughts. Embarrassment and humiliation descended around me like a cloak. How did I justify my outburst to Michelle? Several thoughts, defenses, and explanations toyed with my tongue, but none excused my behavior.

Take a breath. Remember why you're here. This day wasn't about Willow. It wasn't about Phillip. It was about me and Michelle strengthening our relationship. It was about me helping my daughter through a tough time. I could do this for her. I could set aside my disdain for Willow and all she stood for and concentrate on my girl.

Screw the gossip column and the rumormongers who wanted something to distract them from their boring lives.

A noise behind me interrupted my deliberations.

When I turned around ready to defend my actions, I saw Michelle sitting on the edge of the bed swinging her legs and clapping. "Way to go, Mom. I thought you were going to punch her. Too bad Jessie didn't see this. Now can I skip the wedding?"

CHAPTER TWO

"Why Phillip has to rush into marriage is beyond me. One would think he'd learned his lesson with Cecelia." Hazel Cavanaugh

After texting Michelle and getting no response, I slammed my van door and trotted across the parking lot of the Highland Park Country Club. The wedding didn't start for another hour and a half, but the wedding party had arrived early for a photo session in the club's garden.

The number of parked vehicles indicated there were more people here than the wedding party. Cars belonging to Hazel and her best friends, Mavis Blevins and Bitsy Harris-Dodd, sat front and center, parked next to one another. Those three were like pack animals. If you saw one, you saw the other two.

Parked under the *porte-cochère*, the *pièce de résistance*, a classic Bentley touring car waited, bedecked with a white-and-pink rosebud-framed JUST MARRIED sign over the rear bumper with trailing pink and white streamers. Angry tears stung my eyes. Phillip was moving on, and I was okay with that, but it still hurt that he had imploded our family to get what he wanted. I swiped away my tears. I had one job to do, and I intended to do it as fast as possible and get out with as little bridal party interaction as necessary.

I entered the front door while Phillip's wedding ring burned a hole in my hand. Not the ring I'd given him on our wedding day—the new one he'd be wearing when he married Willow. Michelle called when she realized she'd left her dad's ring on her dresser. Instead of ripping out my toenails one by one with the rusty pliers, I did what any mom would do. I pulled on my big girl panties and offered to deliver the ring to avoid Michelle being embarrassed or, worse, being accused of sabotaging the wedding. If it had been up to me, I'd have flushed it down the toilet, after I'd flattened it with the rusty pliers.

Blissful silence blanketed the club's foyer. It was too quiet for a Cavanaugh event. My shoes sounded like twin jackhammers on a concrete slab. I nodded to the receptionist sitting at the front desk who stood when she saw me enter. She gave me the side-eye, knowing they had revoked my membership.

"It's okay," I said. "Michelle left his wedding ring. I'm just the ring bearer." I laughed at my lame joke.

"I'll call security and have them take it to her," she said, her voice icy.

"Unnecessary. I'd prefer to deliver it myself."

Geoffrey, the club manager, appeared from his office, summoned by an inconspicuous alert from the receptionist. "Hello, Cece. How can we help you today?"

I held up the ring. "We are taking the groom's ring to his best girl," I said with a heavy dose of sarcasm. "Nothing nefarious."

"Can you contact her and have her meet you up here?"

"Tried that. She's either turned her phone off or left it in the dressing room."

"W-Well, I don't know," he stammered. "Why don't I go get Mr. Cavanaugh."

I wanted to tell him he could kiss a certain part of my anatomy, but I refrained. Even though the club was membership only, weddings and similar events were exempt from the members-only rule. He had no precedent to keep me out.

"I'll be out long before the wedding starts. Trust me, Geoff, I'd rather be anywhere other than here." I rolled my eyes. "You're welcome to go with me."

He glanced at his watch. "You have ten minutes. Don't disappoint me."

"Righto. Be back in a jiff, Geoff." I laughed at my pun and headed down the hallway toward the banquet room, which opened onto the lush garden.

Greta, who owned Oppenheimer's Bakery with her husband, Opie, fussed with a multi-tiered wedding cake on a table in front of the wall of windows.

"That better not be your famous coconut cake," I said as I approached.

Greta looked up, confusion etched on her face. "Oh my. What are you doing here? You know what today is?"

I explained my mission and hugged her. "Have you seen Michelle?"

Greta pointed to the gazebo in the garden. "She is with the older Mrs. Cavanaugh, Mrs. Harris-Dodd, and Mrs. Blevins. But, mind me, steer clear of your ex-mother-in-law. She's in a mood today. Already chewed out the maid of honor, had a screaming match with the bride, and then took a hunk from Phillip's hide. Michelle is the only one who hasn't been a victim of her anger."

At a table near the gazebo, my daughter appeared glued to her dad's side. My insides melted at the scene. She was her father's daughter. In her opinion, he could do no wrong. I wondered what would come of their relationship if Willow was pregnant. Michelle had always been the baby of our family, and Phillip treated her like a princess.

He looked dashing in his tux. His blond hair, with enough silver shot through it, looked like he'd stepped out of a GQ ad. He'd taken to bleaching the tips and wearing it spiky and longer than normal. No doubt an attempt to look younger.

My wedding day ran like a bad video through my head. I'd been the starry-eyed bride embarking on a future of wedded bliss with the man of my dreams. The man of my dreams had been nervous and inebriated from his raucous bachelor party the night before. His buddies at his side all in various stages of hungover. Maybe I should have heeded that warning. Today he looked stone-cold sober. Not even a glimpse of the boy I'd married all those years ago. The buddies who had stood by him then were no longer friends. In fact, the only person in the wedding party on his side was our daughter.

My breath caught when I saw Willow. She looked stunning in her slim-fitted sheath dress, covered in antique lace. All the old feelings I'd thought were dead rose to the surface and threatened to suffocate me. I squared my shoulders, took a deep breath, and prepared myself to enter the garden.

Willow and two of her bridesmaids congregated near the temporary altar erected for the ceremony. Delicate pale pink magnolia blossoms covered the altar. I noticed the ill maid of honor was not in attendance. Had the woman's illness thrown a kink in the wedding plans?

Michelle shifted and clutched Phillip's arm. Poor kid. This entire event had to be excruciating for her. I should have talked to Phillip and asked him not to put her in such an awkward position, but it would have sounded petty coming from me. Not that he'd ever been receptive to my suggestions.

On Phillip's other side, Bitsy Harris-Dodd looked like she'd swallowed a toad—an appropriate expression for a witch. Mavis Blevins, sitting next to her, wore a similar expression.

"Odd," Greta said.

"What?"

"Your mother-in-law was out there a while ago."

I scanned the garden—no Hazel. Fortunately for me. One less person to deal with. "Probably checking with the valet to make sure he parked her broom correctly."

Greta chuckled and gave me a gentle push. "Go on with yourself."

"They all look super excited," I said, referring to Hazel's besties. "Better go rescue my kid before Hazel gets back. Wish me luck as I enter the enemy camp." I wished I hadn't been so snippy to Willow earlier today. Maybe I could slip Michelle the ring and leave before Willow saw me. If only Phillip would disappear.

I hesitated as I stepped out the door. "One foot in front of the other," I whispered.

"Good luck," Greta said behind me. "I'll set aside a coconut cake for you in the bakery tomorrow morning."

"Thanks. Tell Opie I said hi." I waved over my shoulder and headed off to get rid of Phillip's ring before it melted in my hand.

I willed Phillip to have a sudden case of diarrhea or a severe urge to pee so he'd leave. I dreaded confronting Bitsy and Mavis, but I could ignore them. Hazel would make a scene, so I needed to drop the ring off before she returned. As long as Willow continued to yap with her bridesmaids, I could slip in and out. I hoped.

On the path to the garden, the photographer from this morning came toward me, snapping his fingers. "You!" he hollered. "Go find the maid of honor. We need to get these photos done. I have one last shot I need to finish from the bride's list before the guests arrive."

I turned to see who he was barking orders at to find no one behind me. "Are you talking to me?" I asked.

"Who else would I be talking to?"

"You must have me confused for someone else. I'm here—"

"Please, lady, as a favor. I need one person who cooperates." He dropped to a bench beside the path and buried his head in his hands. "This is the first wedding I've ever shot. Doing a favor for the bride. Why is everyone so difficult? Shooting *hangry* models who live off caffeine and water and who haven't eaten in three days is so much easier.

"Mother of the groom wants it her way. The bride wants it her way, and the bridesmaids complain when I shoot their bad side. The groom, he walks around with his hands in his pockets, nodding his head. The only decent one here is the kid. Sweet girl."

"She's my daughter. Her father, my ex, is the one getting married." I held up the ring. "I'd rather be anywhere else, but I need to get his ring to her. She's not answering my text, and I can't deal with all of them."

"I have one last shot to make, and the maid of honor disappeared. For the love of Pete, save my sanity, please. If you find her for me, I'll tell your kid you're here and to meet you out front."

I stole a glance at the gazebo and saw Willow clinging to Phillip. Michelle looked uncomfortable, probably trying to ignore Willow's grip on him. Hazel's band of witches still sat at the table with bored expressions on their painted and powdered faces. The bridesmaids were knocking down mimosas and engaging in animated conversation. I'd be lucky to deliver this ring without a confrontation.

"Okay, deal," I said. "Where did she go?"

He looked at me with sad, tired eyes. "Lady, if I knew that, I wouldn't be asking. Check the bar. She might need fortification to get through the evening. Or, who knows, she might have needed to refresh her lipstick. Lord knows she left enough of it on the rim of those champagne glasses. Or check the kitchen. She might be pigging out. The way the mother of the groom chewed her out, she might be curled up under the steps in a fetal position. Take your pick."

"Okay. Okay. I'll check. In the meantime, tell my daughter to meet me in the front hall, and don't let on to the rest of the wedding party that I'm here. I'm not in the mood for drama today." His drama included.

I returned to the banquet room, and Greta was gone. The guest tables contained attractive arrangements of pale pink magnolia blossoms. An attractive woman wearing stiletto heels, a pearl choker, and a form-fitting sleeveless black dress inspected the chafing dishes on the buffet tables. I'd seen her at the spa earlier with the wedding party.

"Excuse me," I said. "Have you by any chance seen the maid of honor? She's needed in the garden for photographs."

The young woman wrinkled her nose. "I haven't seen anyone except the bakery personnel, and they're all in the kitchen."

"You're the caterer, right?" I asked. If she was, she must not sample much of her cooking. Her well-toned arms and calves made me rethink my recent absence from the gym. I sucked in my belly pooch.

"I am." She retrieved a business card from the cross-body bag she wore and extended it to me. "I recently opened a restaurant on Charter Street in the city."

SASSAFRAS AND SAGE—SASHA WITHERS, CATERER, it read.

"You look like—"

"I know. Audrey Hepburn in *Breakfast at Tiffany's*? Yes, it's part of the *shtick*." She gave a dry laugh. "If you ever need a caterer, call me. The card is also good for a discount at my restaurant. Stop by and try us."

"Will do. I better resume my search before the photographer has a nervous breakdown." I shoved the card in my purse and headed off in search of—what was the woman's name? Willow had said it at the spa, but I was so full of fiery rage, I hadn't paid attention.

I stuck my head in the bar. A lone bartender stood in front of the mirrored back bar drying glasses.

"Bar's closed." He continued wiping glasses without making eye contact. "Private party."

"No worries. The photographer is trying to gather up the wedding party," I said.

He tucked the towel into his apron. "You looking for the tipsy blonde or the old lady?"

Interesting. What would Hazel be doing with the maid of honor? "Both."

"The blonde came stumbling in a while ago asking for a glass of water." He gestured to the hallway. "Check the restroom. She didn't look so good. If she makes it through the wedding without passing out or barfing, it'll be a miracle. If you find her, you'll likely find the old lady who staggered in after her. Be careful. She isn't happy. It was like a drunken comedy act. The old lady took a swing at the blonde and missed. Almost fell flat on her face. Would have too, if she hadn't landed on a barstool."

"Are you kidding?"

The bartender made a crossing motion over his heart. "If I'm lying, I'm dying."

"Which old lady?" As if I even needed to ask.

"The groom's mother. If you ask me, she started celebrating way too early."

"You must be mistaken." Surely, he wasn't talking about Hazel. "She doesn't drink."

"Lady, I've been a bartender for twenty years. I know a drunk when I see one, and that broad was three sheets in the wind."

"Platinum hair sprayed stiff." I gestured to my hair with my hands.

"Yup, that's her all right."

"What were they arguing about?"

"Your guess is as good as mine. Neither one was coherent enough to make sense." He resumed wiping glasses.

I thanked him and continued my search. The first two ladies' rooms I checked were empty. At the third one, I pushed the door. It tended to stick, so I heaved myself against it, forcing it open. A pale blue satin shoe greeted me. I leaned in and looked around. A cloud of pale blue satin and lace billowed around the still form of . . . Kayla—that was her name.

The maid of honor lay crumpled in a heap on the floor.

CHAPTER THREE

"The last person I want to deal with on my wedding day is my ex-wife."
Phillip Cavanaugh

"Kayla?" I called.

Nothing.

I backed out of the restroom, not sure what I was seeing, and bumped into something solid.

"What are you doing here?" The voice was unmistakable.

I turned around and looked into the questioning eyes of my ex-husband.

Phillip grabbed me by the shoulders. "Isn't it enough you had a standoff with Willow at the salon this morning? Now what? You've come back to ruin the wedding too?"

I had news for him. This day was ruined long before I showed up on the scene. "Oh, spare me." I wrenched from his grasp. "And hands off, buster. Why are you even here? Shouldn't you be outside getting ready for the ceremony?"

"Everyone is frantic over Kayla. I came looking for her," Phillip said. "Someone had to take charge of this circus."

"Well, I found her. Call an ambulance." I pushed back through the door and kneeled next to her. "Kayla? Kayla, honey, can you hear me?"

No response. I checked for a pulse—weak and thready. Foamy saliva dribbled from her mouth.

Phillip leaned in over my shoulder. "My Lord, Cece! What did you do?"

I looked up in shock. "Nothing. I found her like this."

He narrowed his gaze. "And you're here because?"

"Because Michelle forgot to bring your stupid ring, you idiot!"

"Phillip, what's going—" Willow glared at me around Phillip. "What are you doing here? What's wrong with Kayla?"

I stood and shoved past Phillip and Willow. "For crying out loud, will you all quit gawking and call an ambulance?"

Phillip patted his pockets and uttered a curse word. "My phone's in the car."

"Well, I don't have mine." Willow stared down at Kayla. "What did you do?"

Two bridesmaids, one dressed in pink and the other in green, closed ranks around the bride. All three tried to get through the bathroom door at once.

I positioned myself between them and Kayla. "Stay away from her until the paramedics arrive." Since no one else was calling 9-1-1, I pulled out my phone and made the call.

"Here's your ring," I said, slapping it into Phillip's hand.

Michelle rounded the corner. "What's going on? The photographer said to meet—"

Phillip stepped in front of Michelle. "Everything's okay, honey. A lady is sick."

By now, Mavis and Bitsy, along with Geoffrey, the club manager, had joined the group.

"Where's your mother?" I asked Phillip.

Phillip looked bewildered. "I don't know."

"You don't know where she is?" I asked. "She wasn't in the garden when I got here."

Phillip shook his head. "I wasn't paying attention."

"Find her," I said.

Geoffrey herded people away from the bathroom. "Everybody back to the garden. Nothing to see here." He shot me a withering look. "Are you still here? Mr. Cavanaugh, sir. I'm so sorry."

"Don't worry, Geoff. All's good." Phillip clapped him on the shoulder. "Have you seen my mother? I've misplaced her."

Geoff shook his head. "No, sir."

"Well, if you have this under control, I need to find her." Phillip threw me an arrogant look over his shoulder.

The paramedics arrived along with a policeman I recognized as one of the newest members of the Wickford Police Department—Officer Grady. Any other time, the officer on the scene would have been my best friend and neighbor, Angie Valenti. But seeing as how Angie was seven months pregnant, her superiors pulled her from patrol and placed her on dispatch duties pending the birth of the baby.

A paramedic pulled Officer Grady aside and conferred with him.

As much as I wanted to stick around—not—I decided to make myself scarce.

"You got this, kiddo?" I asked Michelle. The witching hour rapidly approached. I needed to be as far away from this wedding as possible with an enormous glass of wine, a handful of chocolate, and an enjoyable book. "Go help Dad find your grandmother. This shindig will start soon."

"Yeah." Her lips puckered. "Is he going to go through with it?"

"Looks like it. Go on. You can do this. I'll wait up for you." I gave her a gentle push. "Don't forget to bring me home a piece of wedding cake. A gigantic piece." I had my priorities.

"Why isn't Jess here yet?"

"Good question. I hope she didn't get hung up at the hospital. That will set your father off for sure. Where's your phone? She may have tried to call," I said.

"Willow made us leave them in our cars." Michelle rolled her eyes. "She didn't want people messing with their phones during the ceremony."

"Figures." The words flew from my mouth before I could stop them.

I called Jess, but it went to voice mail. Did no one want to talk to me anymore? "Call me when you can. Don't you dare be late for your dad's wedding."

"Mom?" Michelle pressed her face against a window that overlooked the tennis court. "Is that Gran out there?"

"Where?" I looked over her shoulder.

She pointed to the path between the tennis court and the swimming pool.

"It *is* Gran!" Michelle's voice caught. "What's wrong with her?"

I watched in horror as Hazel staggered down the path toward the gazebo. The left sleeve of her designer gown hung in tatters around her wrist.

Michelle latched onto my arm. "What's going on? She looks drunk."

Considering Hazel didn't drink, the sight we were witnessing was even more disturbing. She stumbled, fell to one knee, and face-planted on the path. Maybe the bartender was right.

"Quick," I said. "Go get your dad and take him to check on her. If the paramedics have stabilized Kayla, I'll send them out to check on Hazel."

My instinct told me to get the heck out of Dodge, but not with Michelle this distraught. No matter how much I hated the thought of being here, I couldn't abandon her.

Michelle sprinted down the hall. I heard footsteps rapidly approaching behind me and turned.

"Excuse me, ma'am," Officer Grady said. "Are you the one who found the vic . . . the um . . . the maid of honor?"

"Yes." An icy sliver of dread threaded through my veins.

His radio squawked, and Angie's voice said, "A detective is en route."

"Ten-four," Grady said into the mic attached to his shoulder.

When Angie said *detective*, a mixture of feelings warred in my mind. It always brightened my day to see Alder, but they never called a detective to help with a sick case.

"A detective?" I asked, my heart sinking. I knew what the officer would say.

He cleared his throat. "I'm afraid she didn't make it."

CHAPTER FOUR

"There's been a great deal of gossip surrounding the Cavanaugh family, and poor Cece has taken the brunt of it."
Greta Oppenheimer

Officer Grady shooed me out to the garden to wait for Alder. I wandered out the door, wracked with guilt. Even though I knew I wasn't to blame for Kayla's death, it didn't stop me from imagining that everyone else would think I was. I found the body. I refused to help this morning when Willow burst into the facial room at the spa. Could I have prevented this? If I had acted instead of blowing up at Willow, would Kayla still be alive?

Greta waved me over to the table she shared with Opie and the photographer.

"Flick Donovan."

"What?" I was still kicking myself for not checking on the girl this morning at the spa.

"Remember me?" The photographer extended his hand across the table.

I shook his hand. "I do." Now that I looked at him up close, he was older than I had first thought—maybe forty—and ruggedly attractive. I could imagine him photographing a safari in the wilds of Africa, not a wedding party.

Greta fanned herself with a napkin. "I figured you'd be gone by now."

"No such luck." I envied Greta her napkin. Perspiration had popped out on my forehead, and I could feel it trickling down the nape of my neck. I wasn't sure if it was the heat, the stress, or a hot flash.

"We heard they found a body," Opie said.

I nodded. "That's exactly why I'm still here."

Greta clucked her tongue. "Oh my, any idea who it is?"

"The maid of honor," I said.

"Did you say the maid of honor?" Donovan pulled off the camera that still hung around his neck and set it on the table. "That can't be right. Kayla?"

"Yes. Kayla something." I searched my purse for something to use for a fan and came up with my checkbook.

"What happened?" He stood and scanned the garden.

"I have no idea." I knew better than to go into detail. Not that I knew any detail. I did know the police would protect the scene and treat Kayla's death as suspicious until they determined her cause of death. They also would question us. The less I speculated now, the less I would have to explain.

"Where are Willow's parents?" I asked, changing the subject. As of now, none of the guests had been admitted, but still, I would have thought her mother would be here when Willow had dressed or for the before-wedding photos. "Isn't it odd, they aren't here?"

"Her father is not at all happy with the choice of groom and is boycotting the event," Greta said. "Willow and Mrs.

Cavanaugh came in to order the cake together. I thought that was unusual, but Willow explained that her mother had died in an auto accident years ago. Apparently, Mrs. Cavanaugh stepped in and helped with the wedding planning."

Took over the wedding planning was more like it. Almost everything at this wedding screamed of Hazel, including the venue. The only thing that didn't were the pastel gowns the bridesmaids wore. With Hazel's sense of style, she would have insisted on the Pantone Color of the Year for the bridesmaids. Yes, I imagined if Hazel couldn't stop the wedding then she would commandeer the entire event. I knew from experience.

Officer Grady ushered the caterer to our table. She gave Donovan a smirk and made a show of taking a seat on the opposite side of the table. She removed her cross-body bag and placed it on her lap. Her toned arms flexed with every move.

"Are you following me?" Donovan asked. "First the spa. Now the country club."

"Screw you." She crossed her long, tanned legs.

Whoa! Where did that come from? The caterer hadn't seemed at all sassy when I talked to her earlier. Our conversation had been brief, but dang, she bit when she got riled up.

Flick Donovan reared his chair back on two legs and roared with laughter. "You did that already."

Greta nudged my foot with hers. Her eyes were fixated on the caterer's face. Greta and I watched as the drama unfolded. I fanned my face furiously with my checkbook.

"And every other woman on the planet." Sasha scooted around so she wasn't facing him. When she did, her purse flap opened, and the contents dumped onto the patio and scattered.

"She's playing hard to get," he said in a faked whisper.

Greta tapped my foot again. Greta loved drama, as did

everyone else in Wickford. I was certain this story would be repeated several times tomorrow at the bakery. Though, it would hardly top the death of the maid of honor.

Sasha bent to collect the items she'd spilled. After she retrieved everything, she continued to search. "Where's my compact?"

I looked around but saw nothing else.

"My eye drops are missing too." She tugged at the hem of her dress as she searched around and under the table. "That compact cost a fortune, and that's the third bottle of drops I've lost this weekend." She blinked. "I have to get to the store."

"We aren't going anywhere until Officer Grady is through," I said.

Sasha took a pair of sunglasses from her bag and put them on. "He needs to get on with it because I have to leave." She tapped her foot on the pavement.

I had sat at Greta and Opie's table to avoid wedding drama. It appeared I might be in for an alternative flavor of drama. Michelle and Phillip huddled with Hazel and her band of henchwomen next to Willow.

Phillip had removed his jacket and wrapped it around Hazel, patting her shoulders like she was a prized calf at the state fair. After the paramedics arrived and suggested she go to the hospital, Hazel regained her composure. She had poo-poohed the hospital idea, much to Phillip's consternation. Hazel was a tough old bird and wouldn't dare miss being in the center of the action. The only way the woman would get in that ambulance was with a sheet over her head and a tag tied to her big toe.

The two bridesmaids sat under the gazebo, chattering as if nothing out of the ordinary had occurred.

My cell rang. When I saw Jessie's number on the screen, I excused myself from the table and answered.

"Where are you?" I asked.

"In the parking lot," Jessie said. "I saw your van. What's going on? There's a cop at the door. The guests are arriving, and they won't let anyone in."

I found a bench off the beaten path and sat down. "Willow's maid of hon—" My voice broke.

"Hold on, they're bringing someone out on a stretcher." Jess's voice muffled, and I heard voices in the background. "O-m-g! What happened? Is Dad okay? Gran?"

Adrenaline coursed through my veins. I couldn't comprehend it myself. How would Jessie?

"Mom, are you there?"

I blew out a breath. "I am. Dad and Hazel are okay. Oh, Jess, you will not believe this. The maid of honor died, and I found her."

Silence.

I checked to make sure the call hadn't dropped. "Are you there?"

"What are you even doing here?" Jessie did nothing to hide the exasperation in her voice, so I explained about the ring.

"How do you always wind up in the middle of this stuff?"

"Middle of what? I brought the ring to the club. How is that being in the middle of things?"

"You know what I mean. Why didn't you send Nancy? Why would you even *want* to be here? Dad's getting married."

Not today. I gritted my teeth. "Don't start on me. I have to go."

I didn't need attitude from Jessie. That was Michelle's department. I disconnected, closed my eyes, and took a deep breath.

When I opened them, the bridesmaid in the pale pink dress pushed her chair away from the table, staggered to the edge of the patio, and tossed her cookies into a lilac bush.

CHAPTER FIVE

"As if a death on my wedding day isn't bad enough, Phillip's ex-wife has to show up."
Willow Carson

Everyone huddled around the pink-clad bridesmaid offering tissues or sips of water.

Michelle scampered to my side and whispered in my ear, "What's wrong with her?"

I put my arm around her waist and hugged her close. "I'm not sure, honey."

After pulling herself together and shaking off Phillip's hand, Hazel looked straight at me. "Why are you here?"

With all the commotion, this was the first time she'd taken notice of me. Even though she still looked a little green around the gills and her gait was unsteady, fire glinted in her eyes.

For a second, the old fear rumbled in my gut. In the past, this was where I tried to placate her. A new realization took hold. I could stand my ground. The woman who had made my life miserable for almost thirty years no longer had control over me. That had changed when I divorced Phillip.

I bequeath your miserableness to Willow.

I felt invincible, as if I had donned a cloak of power.

"All of you sit down," a voice boomed.

We all jerked our heads toward the sound, but no one returned to their chairs. The biggest man I'd ever seen stood in the doorway leading from the banquet room. He looked like a football linebacker, only bigger and bald as the day he was born. He was probably around thirty-five or forty years old. His mouth formed a straight line and looked like it had never cracked a smile, much less a roaring laugh. I couldn't see his eyes because he wore a pair of mirrored aviator sunglasses, and his chiseled jawline looked freshly shaven. I wondered if he shaved his head when he shaved his face or if he had male pattern baldness. Or both. Either way, it was an attractive look, except for the not-smiling part. A smile would increase his attractiveness a thousand-fold.

I noticed the bridesmaids, even Willow, took notice and stared in his direction, whispering among themselves. If their tongues had been hanging out laced with drool, the scene would have made a great cartoon.

"Are you all deaf?" he asked, breaking the spell. "Sit down. Now!"

Willow and the bridesmaid dressed in green led the pink-clad bridesmaid to the gazebo and helped her into a chair. The rest of us resumed our previous positions. Phillip, Michelle, and Hazel and her clique returned to the cluster of benches across the patio. I resumed my position at the table with Opie, Greta, Sasha the caterer, and Donovan the photographer.

Phillip cursed under his breath and shot me a death glare. "This is all your fault," he mouthed.

I curled my lip and sneered in answer.

"I'm Detective Zimmerman." The giant man approached the patio. "I need all of you to stay put until I have time to talk to each of you."

I swiveled my head to get a better look at him. "Where's Alder?"

Phillip shot me another glare.

I sent a glare back that would melt the paint off his precious Porsche.

Detective Zimmerman rubbed his chin. "You must be the girlfriend. Officer Valenti warned me about you."

I pushed my chair back and stood. "Where is he?"

"Detective Loverboy?" A smirk hiked one edge of his mouth. Did he have a sense of humor? "You can sit right back down. This is my case, and he has taken a personal leave of absence."

No, he did not. Personal leave, what the heck? Alder had sent me a text this morning. The one I missed when I was at the spa with Michelle. What if something had happened to his daughter, Becca? I had yet to meet her, but they were close. It would devastate him. I walked toward Zimmerman.

"Oh, Lordy, you're not going to give me trouble, are you? Because I'm already having a foul day, and I guarantee you do not want to make it worse." He pulled a notebook from his pocket. "Now. Sit. Back. Down."

I pulled out my cell to call Alder. Or Angie. Someone needed to tell me what was going on.

"Put that back in your pocket or give it to me. Your choice." Detective Zimmerman reached for my phone. "*Capisce?*"

I slid it back into my pocket and sat down. "Whatever." Now I sounded like Michelle.

"Cece, for the love of Pete, will you shut up?" Phillip said through gritted teeth.

"Yo, Pops," Zimmerman said to Phillip. "You the father of the bride?"

I almost laughed out loud but considered the circumstances and caught myself. However, his comment did my heart good. I wasn't the only one who thought Phillip looked ridiculous marrying a woman half his age.

To his credit, Phillip kept his mouth shut, but the tiny little muscle in his jaw twitched rapidly, a sure sign of his anger. I recognized his tells like the back of my hand. Zimmerman must have noticed too.

"Do not tell me you're the groom. Man, you're old enough to be her father." Zimmerman scored with a hit where it hurt —Phillip's ego.

I snickered, as did Greta and Opie. Michelle's face turned scarlet, and Hazel pulled herself ramrod straight. I almost empathized with Zimmerman. Hazel was not about to let anyone make a laughingstock of her heir apparent or the Cavanaugh name. She'd spent too much time perfecting her role as the matron of Wickford society to let a mere detective launch her from that throne. Hazel had the police chief on speed dial, and she would put the smackdown on Zimmerman's disrespect.

"You watch yourself, young man," Hazel said. "You're talking to Cavanaughs."

"I'll keep that in mind." The detective rubbed his hands together and smirked. "Who wants to go first?" He pointed to Phillip. "You're up, Pops."

Sasha thrust her arm in the air. "Excuse me. How long is this going to take?"

Zimmerman slid his glasses down the bridge of his nose and peered over at Sasha. He didn't say a word, just scowled.

Not to be deterred, she said, "I have a medical issue. I need to leave."

"Unless you're on the list for a transplant and got the call,

you can cool your heels. This will take as long as it takes."
The detective pushed his glasses back into place and turned
to Phillip. "Let's go, Daddy-O."

Sasha pursed her lips and crossed her arms in defiance.

"Don't always get your way, babe," Donovan taunted.

———

While the detective interviewed Phillip, I called Alder. His
phone went to voice mail, and I left a message. This so wasn't
like Alder. A flutter of worry sprouted in my brain. I tamped
it down. It had been less than twenty-four hours since I'd
talked to him. Yet, he hadn't mentioned a leave of absence. It
made me think whatever had caused his need for leave was
unexpected. Illness was the only thing I could bring to mind.
I said a quick prayer that his daughter was okay.

Zimmerman summoned Willow next. Phillip paced the
entire time she was with the detective. Finally, Zimmerman
motioned for me to join him. I followed him to Geoff's office,
which had been vacated for the interviews.

The detective offered me a chair then sat behind Geoff's
desk and steepled his fingers. His sunglasses rested on the top
of his shiny head, both reflecting the light coming in the
window. He stared at me for several seconds, and I stared
back. Each of us studying the other.

Finally, he put his phone on the desk and touched the
screen. "Do you mind if I record this?"

I shook my head.

"You must verbalize your approval."

"Sure, go ahead."

"How did you know the deceased?"

"I didn't."

He quirked an eyebrow. "Never met her before?"

"Nope." I settled back in my chair. I might have been

mincing words, but I hadn't been introduced to the woman; therefore, I had never met her.

"You didn't meet her this morning at Maggie's?"

"No, I *saw* her this morning, along with several other customers. Other than knowing she was Willow's maid of honor, I didn't know the woman. And I only knew she was the maid of honor because she had a sash across her chest. They all had sashes proclaiming their placement in the wedding party."

Zimmerman blew out an exasperated breath. "This is how you want to play this?"

"I'm not playing anything. I'm telling you the way it is," I said.

"Okay, you never met, but you'd seen the deceased this morning at the salon. Is that correct?"

"Yes, sir."

"I understand you assaulted the bride at the salon."

What? "I did no such thing. We argued. Good grief. What did she tell you?"

Zimmerman picked up his phone and tapped the screen several times then turned the phone to me. A picture of me throwing a towel at Willow appeared. He slid his finger across the screen, and the next photo showed the balled-up towel striking her. The next photo showed me pushing her.

"Shall I continue?" He returned the phone to record mode and placed it on the desk.

"Oh, for crying out loud." A hot flash gathered steam. I recognized the signs of a major sweat coming on. "That's hardly assault. She burst into the room where I was having a facial and would not leave. Even after the esthetician asked her to go. It's not like I threw a punch." And was I glad I didn't. I'd have to watch Willow. She was out for blood —mine.

Assault—my eye tooth. I'll show you assault.

"Then your beef was with the bride and not the deceased?"

"I told you, I didn't even know the deceased. And the bride is marrying my ex-husband, so you could say I have a beef with her," I blurted out. Why had I said that?

"Good segue. Your relationship with Daddy Moneybags is next on my list of questions."

"Daddy Moneybags?" I could barely contain myself. Phillip would have burst an artery if Zimmerman called him that to his face. How I wished I could have been a fly on the wall in that interrogation.

Zimmerman coughed. "Sorry, that was unprofessional. An observation, but unprofessional all the same."

I felt fiery, red blotches breaking out on my chest as sweat trickled down my back and landed in my waistband. "Are you through with me?"

"Not quite. Why are you here? I don't get the sense that you and your ex have *that* kind of relationship."

"I'm not sure what you're insinuating, but if it's what I think you mean, you are way out of bounds. Phillip and I have two daughters; one is in the wedding party. In that respect, we have a co-parenting relationship." I bit my tongue to keep from telling off this jerk. Nothing good would come of that. Instead, I told him about the ring, and Michelle, and the reason I'd felt inclined to show my face at this event.

"Okay, any reason someone would want to hurt the deceased?"

"How many times can I tell you I don't know her?" This guy was exasperating. And where was Alder? "Why are you even questioning people? The woman has been drunk and staggering around the entire day—even at the butt crack of dawn. She probably died of alcohol poisoning."

"Could be," he said. "But I can't rule out foul play. And in my experience, the person with the most to gain is usually the perpetrator."

The pressure I'd been under since I walked into the office with Detective Zimmerman dissipated. "I had nothing to gain, so that lets me off the hook."

He laced and unlaced his fingers, popping his knuckles. The sound sent a chill through me. Phillip was a knuckle-popper, and I detested the habit.

"But you have something to gain by the wedding being postponed, don't you?" *Pop! Pop! Pop!* His eyes bored into mine.

I shivered. "No. Phillip is my ex for a reason. It doesn't matter to me if he gets married."

"Didn't hurt your ego a little that his bride is . . ." He stopped and let his eyes survey me. "Probably half your age?"

This guy had a knack for instilling comfort then jerking you right back into panic mode.

"Yes, Detective. After almost thirty years of marriage, it devastated me. It hurt. But then I found out our entire marriage had been a joke to him. He'd cheated more than once. Many times. I have nothing to gain by this wedding being postponed."

"I understand you've been influential in solving several of my colleague's cases."

I sat up a little straighter at the mention of Alder. Had he been talking about me at the station? "Not really." No need to throw him under the bus. But if this guy figured I was helpful, that might benefit me. At least get me off the suspect list.

Zimmerman cleared his throat. "What about your ex's mother? Is the bride looking for a sugar daddy? Would it concern Mrs. Cavanaugh that her future daughter-in-law might be a gold digger?"

Bingo. Hazel called me a gold digger frequently. I remembered all the ways Hazel tried to disrupt my wedding with

Phillip. Would she resort to murder? "That idea crossed my mind. But his mother is more of a master manipulator. She would never soil her hands."

"Would she soil someone else's hands?"

My opinion interests him.

"No, Hazel is a one-woman show. She does her own dirty work, but if she would go after anyone, it would be Willow. But not killing her. Hazel is all about making life miserable for her victims."

"What about your ex? Any reason he'd have it in for the maid of honor?"

"No, he's a jerk and a cheater, but he's not a killer."

"Think your ex might have been doing a little *boomchika-wowwow* on the side, and it got back to his bride?" Zimmerman tapped his temple. "Maybe she had a score to settle with her bestie?"

"Cheating is second nature with Phillip. But you're on your own with Willow. I know nothing about her except she's not above sleeping around." I felt emboldened by him seeking my advice. "Are you convinced this is a homicide? The thought of food poisoning crossed my mind, but death from food poisoning isn't common in the US. It happens so don't rule it out—especially since three women have exhibited similar symptoms. Though, only the maid of honor died. Maybe she had a medical condition that exacerbated it."

Cece, for cripe's sake, shut your mouth.

"You are a wealth of information. Who were the other women?"

I told him about Hazel and her stumbling parade in the garden. She might not be a murderer, but she would kill me now for sure. "Also, the bridesmaid dressed in pink. I don't know her name. She got sick right before you arrived."

Zimmerman poked at his phone then pocketed it. "I think I have enough from you. Go get your kid and take her home. I'm assuming she lives with you and not the ex. She's seen enough for one day."

Gladly.

I pulled the door open and had taken a step when Zimmerman said, "Ms. Cavanaugh."

"Yes," I said, turning to face him.

He squinted one eye and pointed his finger at me. "I am not Case Alder. I will not tolerate you obfuscating one of my cases. *Capisce?*"

Obfuscating? It took me a minute to figure that one out. "I have no reason to complicate your case." Like the idiot I was, I saluted him. *Who does that?*

If I were being chased by a band of rabid wolves, I wouldn't have moved quicker. I went to get Michelle, but she opted to stay with Phillip and Hazel.

"I'll make sure she gets home okay," Phillip said.

I gave my daughter a worried look, but she smiled and said, "It's okay. I want to stay."

I didn't need to be told twice.

CHAPTER SIX

"Cece grumbles and fusses at me a lot, but we're getting to be friends."
Nancy Lustbader

At home, I found my assistant, Nancy, in my kitchen, eating lasagna. The lasagna I saved for my dinner. The last piece of the batch my housekeeper, Beatrice, brought me.

"How's your dinner?" I asked, not holding back the snark in my tone.

"Mmm, good," she replied.

"There's garlic toast too," I said.

"Nope, already ate it." She continued to shovel my pasta into her mouth.

After Phillip left me, I'd gone to work at this little hole-in-the-wall cleaning service. Nancy was the receptionist. She didn't like me, and I didn't like her. Long story short, the boss fired me. He shut down his business, sold everything, and moved to Florida, putting Nancy out of a job and a place to live since she lived in a duplex he owned.

She'd shown up on my porch with her luggage and a sob story. My only excuse for letting her move into the apartment over my garage and giving her a job was I had *sucker* written on my forehead in big, bold letters.

In retrospect, it worked out for both of us, and we tolerated one another.

Sometimes.

My business was growing, and I needed the help, and the garage apartment *had* been vacant. Nancy came with annoying habits, many annoying habits, but who didn't? I kind of enjoyed her quirkiness; it seemed to keep me grounded. I'd never admit it to her. We had settled into a work routine, and as long as she continued to be a reliable worker, we'd be fine. I had to work around her annoyances at home. Like her eating my lasagna and garlic toast and making herself at home in my home, which was outside the boundaries of her apartment.

"Don't forget, we're cleaning Maggie's Salon and Day Spa tomorrow and Monday," I said.

"I've got one condo to finish. You want me to push that out?" Nancy asked. "Grant won't care."

One project that had been keeping me afloat since Phillip left was Hunter Springs, a multi-use development on the edge of town. Grant Hunter, a friend, and now Nancy's occasional date, had hired my company to clean new condos before they went on the real estate market. It didn't make me a lot of money, but it provided steady work. Or would until Hunter finished the condos. That part of the development was nearing completion, so that had me worried. Because we had an inside track with the boss, I felt confident when he started the single-family home phase of the development, he'd keep us on. Unless his and Nancy's relationship took a turn for the worse.

"No, do what you need to do. You can meet me at Maggie's when you finish."

I opened the fridge and scanned the bleak contents. Looking forward to Beatrice's fabulous lasagna had kept me going the last couple of hours. Now I had to find something else. I glanced at the milk carton to make sure it hadn't expired and decided on cereal. There was a definite advantage to single life. I could eat cereal or popcorn or whatever for dinner and not get complaints. With senior year activities and a part-time job at the recreation center, Michelle rarely arrived home in time for dinner.

Between bites of cereal, I sent Alder a text.

Me: You there?

I waited. When he didn't text back, I called his cell phone and got voice mail. "Hey, I'm worried. I guess you heard there was an incident at the club, and no, it did not involve me. Well sorta, but not really. Detective Zimmerman said you had taken a personal leave. Is Becca okay? Are you okay? Call me."

Nancy took her plate to the sink and rinsed it. "What's going on?"

"I'm not sure." I explained about the maid of honor and the new detective saying that Alder had taken personal leave.

"That's not like Alder. He's always at your beck and call." Nancy giggled. "Have you talked to Angie? I saw her pull in her driveway about thirty minutes ago."

"Not yet, but I'm going over there." My best friend, Angie, the cop-turned-dispatcher, and her husband, Dave, lived next door. Angie and I had been friends forever, and I couldn't ask for better neighbors.

As I headed out the sliding door, I said, "Don't eat that piece of cheesecake I saved."

Nancy gulped. "Oops. Too late. I had it for breakfast."

Angie sat at her kitchen table cradling her seven-month-pregnant belly. "Please tell me it gets better. My back is killing me. I have to pee all the time, and I can't remember the last time I've seen my toes."

"So, home pedicures are out, right?" I remembered those days all too well. Michelle was seventeen, but it seemed like yesterday. Angie was about to become a first-time mom at forty-nine, and to say she was freaking out was a colossal understatement.

"The next two months will be an experience." I poured myself a glass of tea and joined her. "I could go into detail, but I'll let it be a surprise. You get a baby, dirty diapers, colic, and sore boobs in the deal."

Angie grimaced.

"You want me to go on?"

She held up her hand. "I get it. I get it. Don't rub it in."

"Any idea why Alder's taken a leave of absence?"

"I was going to ask you. Must be something big if you don't know. The chief has been tight-lipped. All kinds of rumors running rampant at the station. The biggest being that you two eloped. Apparently, that's not it."

I choked and spewed tea. "Are you serious? No way. How does anyone even know about us?"

"You're kidding, right? Alder being off the market is big news. Every single woman at the station has crushed on him." Angie pulled herself from the chair and threw a paper towel my way.

I swiped at the tea on the table. "Well, Detective Zimmerman knows Alder and I are an item." I narrowed my eyes. "Are you responsible for that?"

This time Angie spewed tea. "For your own good, my friend."

"You outed me to save me from myself?"

"Leo Zimmerman is not someone to trifle with. The only reason I told him about you and Alder was to protect you. Zimmerman respects Alder. I figured it would lessen the blow of you being there if he knew you and Alder were together. But you've got to play it straight with Zimmerman. He came from the city and won't give you the leeway that Alder does."

"How did you even know I was there?"

"You gave your name when you called 9-1-1. When I got the referral from Central Dispatch, I realized it was Phillip's wedding." Angie laughed. "I guess the better question is, why were you there?"

I massaged my temples, hoping to preempt a burgeoning headache. "If I had known how today would turn out, I would have left the ring on Michelle's nightstand."

The door from the garage opened, and Dave walked in, wiping his hands on a golf towel. He bent and kissed Angie on the cheek. "Sorry, I'm late. Stopped off for a drink after we finished."

"Your dinner's in the oven. I couldn't wait any longer. I didn't get lunch today." Angie pushed her chair away from the table.

"I'll get it. Stay put. And what have I told you about skipping meals?"

I nodded in agreement.

"Right," Angie said. "We had a busy day, and the other dispatcher called in sick."

"I better let you two catch up on your day." I hugged Angie.

"Remember what I said about Zimmerman," Angie said. "He's not Alder."

I laughed. "He said the same thing. If you get any news about Alder, call me. I'm worried about him." With the possibility of another murder, it wasn't like Alder to let someone else work a case.

"He's fine, I'm sure. The rumor mill hasn't gotten fully engaged, but when it does, I'll let you know."

I walked between the hedge separating our backyards, pondering my next move. I decided to call Alder again, and if that didn't work, I'd drive to his house.

———

Michelle sat in the kitchen chatting with Nancy, derailing my plan. Phillip had dropped her off while I was visiting Angie.

"How's your grandmother?" I asked. Hazel and I had a tenuous relationship, but my girls loved her, and she would be a part of my life as long as she drew breath. Hazel overindulged them, but they were her only grandchildren, so I had always kept my mouth shut about her grandparenting style.

"Not good," Michelle said.

"Well, it figures. She could have gone to the hospital." I worked hard to keep my opinion to myself, but sometimes when Hazel did something stupid, like refusing medical attention when something had happened to her, I couldn't help myself.

"No, she feels fine. Jess went home with her and is spending the night to make sure she's okay. That detective blasted Gran with questions and accusations." Michelle wrinkled her nose. "He accused her of sabotaging the wedding."

I agreed with the detective, but I bit my tongue. While I would never put it past Hazel, I didn't think she would physically harm anyone. Hazel chose words as her weapons. She had an arsenal and a knack for using them to cut deep and wide.

"Did Hazel say what happened or where she disappeared to?" I asked.

In the years I'd known Hazel, I'd never seen her take a drink. This wedding might have been the tipping point. She'd gotten me out of the picture. Now she had to contend with Willow. That would not sit well with Hazel. She only cared about preserving the Cavanaugh name.

Michelle shrugged. "She said she didn't remember. One minute she was getting a refill on her drink, then the next thing she remembered was when Dad came to get her."

Nancy pulled three bottles of water from the fridge and slid them across the table to us. "Sounds like she blacked out to me. Is she an alcoholic?"

"No," Michelle and I both said.

"That happened to my last boyfriend on payday. He'd get drunk, pass out, and lose four or five hours." Nancy giggled. "Lost a few jobs too. They thought he was sleeping, and he had passed out cold."

"Gran's not like that. I'm going to go call Jessie and check on Gran." She shot Nancy a sour look as she left the room.

Nancy raised her hands in the air. "Sorry. Don't get your panties in a twist, kid. I was only trying to be helpful."

I tried Alder's phone several more times and decided to drive to his house to check on him. Most of the time he returned my calls promptly.

Alder taking personal leave at the spur of the moment scared the bejeebers out of me. His ex-wife, Joyce, had kept their daughter a secret from him until she was six years old. He carried around a lot of guilt for not being there when Becca was a baby, and he'd spent the next two decades making it up to her. He didn't bear the responsibility for his ex-wife's actions, but he continued to blame himself. I had not yet met Becca, but I'd seen her from a distance a few times.

For reasons I cannot explain, I asked Nancy to come along. All right, I can explain. I had one vehicle, my work van —hot pink with green lettering. Or two, if I counted Michelle's bumblebee yellow Mustang. Nancy drove a black Jeep—much less conspicuous. I wanted to be inconspicuous. I trusted Alder; I truly did. He'd never given me one minute of worry. Well, there was that time I saw him at the gym working out with a younger woman. The woman turned out to be his daughter, Becca. Though, at the time I wasn't divorced, and Alder and I weren't a thing.

Maybe I'd let the last couple of murder cases I'd gotten involved in go to my head. Or I enjoyed snooping. Either way, if there was nothing to worry about, I didn't want Alder thinking I didn't trust him, and I sure didn't want him finding out I had snooped on him.

Nancy made one pass down his street. Alder lived in an older part of town. The houses in this section were among the first homes built in Wickford. Once upon a time, it had been the elite section of town inhabited by the mayor, banker, doctor, and anyone who was someone. The area had fallen into disrepair as families moved on. Twenty years ago, people began moving in and restoring the aging homes. Alder's was a one-level bungalow with a wrap-around porch. The color was buttery, pale yellow with lots of white ginger-bread. A much different style of home than the one he planned to build.

He had purchased land out in the country, away from civi-lization, where he planned to build his retirement home. He and I had made the trip several times. The seclusion and soli-tude made for an inspiring place to hike, picnic, or enjoy the company of one another—which we did often.

His city-issued car sat in the driveway, but his pickup wasn't in its normal spot at the curb. Instead, a shiny red Mazda Miata occupied the space. I breathed a sigh of relief. The car belonged to Becca. I remembered Alder griping about her going into debt for the car when she had a perfectly fine vehicle—paid for.

"They're probably having a father-daughter weekend," I said, knowing full well Alder wouldn't take a leave of absence to go on a weekend outing. Vacation days or personal time, but not a full-fledged leave. "Let's go."

It bothered me he hadn't confided in me, but he had sent a vague text, and we'd been playing phone tag. An awful thought crossed my mind. What if he wanted to break up with me? That could be the reason he wasn't leaving messages.

I scoffed at the idea. It wasn't like this was high school and we were going steady.

"Tell yourself whatever lets you sleep at night," Nancy said.

I stuck out my tongue. "Don't be a downer." Yet, a nagging thought settled in my core, dragging me into a pit of worry.

"Or she could be house-sitting while he's having a wild fling with a hoochie from the police department," Nancy quipped.

I slugged her arm. "Not funny. Let's go. He'll call me when he gets a chance. He may have taken her out to his property."

We reached the end of the block, and Nancy turned left.

"Isn't that his truck?" she asked, pointing to a pickup traveling toward us.

It passed before I could see the occupants. At the next stop sign, Nancy pulled a U-turn.

"No," I said. "Let's get home. He'll call me. If they've been out to the property hiking or fishing, the last thing they need is us pulling up."

Nancy pressed her foot to the gas pedal. "There were three people in that truck. I got a good look. Alder and two women."

"I don't care. Maybe Becca brought a friend. Turn around and let's go home."

Instead, Nancy made a right onto Alder's street. "One little peek won't hurt. That's why you came over here, isn't it? Don't you want to know who's there?"

"Yes." I waved my hand in the air. "No. I mean, yes. Of course, I want to know. But I've changed my mind. I trust Alder. We both know what it's like to have a spouse who cheats. Besides, we aren't married."

Nancy roared with laughter. "Liar, liar. Your pants will go up in flames. You're dying to find out who was with him. So, let's find out." She pulled her car to the curb four houses away from his.

"And how stupid would I look if it's his sister?"

"Does he even have a sister?" Nancy asked.

He had turned his truck around when he parked, and it now faced us. I prayed he didn't recognize Nancy's Jeep. To make sure he didn't see me, I slid down in the seat, so I barely could see over the dash.

"Yes, he does, and this was a terrible idea," I said.

A tap on the passenger window sent a chill of fear through me. I looked up into the wrinkled face of a sweet grandmotherly type. "You have car trouble?" she yelled through the glass.

I opened my window a smidge. "No, we're fine."

She held a leash attached to—a rat. The rodent wore a tiny sweater and harness. The woman squinted to get a better look inside the Jeep.

"You sure? My neighbor just got home. I'm sure he'd be

glad to help. He's a police officer." She raised her hand and waved to Alder.

"No!" I screamed. "We're good." I pointed to Nancy. "She wanted to make a phone call. Can't drive and talk on a cell phone. It's dangerous."

"Yeah, that's it." Nancy rummaged around in her purse and pulled out her phone. "Gotta call our pizza order in, so it's ready when we get there."

I glanced at Alder, hoping he hadn't seen the woman. He had climbed from his truck and gone around to the passenger side where he opened the door. The first woman out of the truck was Becca. The second woman, older than Becca, stepped out next dressed in an elegant, flowing caftan with her head wrapped in a matching turban.

Alder placed his arm around the woman's shoulder, and she leaned into him. The three of them walked up the sidewalk.

The older woman standing beside Nancy's Jeep cleared her throat. "You sure you don't need assistance? Detective Alder is always willing to help."

"We're good." I wasn't. Tears welled up in my eyes, and I wanted to puke.

"Suit yourself." She bent over, picked up the rat, and tucked it into the pocket of her housedress.

I stared into the little beady, black eyes and shivered.

Nancy leaned over me and stared out my window. "Is that a rat?"

She took the words I'd wanted to say right from my mouth.

The old woman stuck her hand into her pocket and stroked the rodent. "It's a hairless dog, you ninny."

"Looks like a giant rat to me," Nancy said, even louder this time.

I had to agree. Not that I'd ever seen one in real life. At

least not one in the wild, much less one on a leash or in a woman's pocket.

"If you're finished insulting Lulubell, I have to go. I promised his daughter I'd bring over a pot of my homemade soup for her mother." She waved in Alder's direction and hobbled off down the street toward his house.

Nancy whistled a shrill, ear-splitting whistle. "Becca's mother? As in Alder's ex-wife? No wonder you haven't heard from him. Mama's back in the house."

CHAPTER SEVEN

"I tell Cece whatever she wants to hear and then do what I want. It worked for thirty years."
Phillip Cavanaugh

It's just a friendly visit. I repeated those words to myself as I unlocked the door to Maggie's Salon and Day Spa the next morning. Just a friendly visit from the ex-wife—the ex-wife who cheated on him. Lack of sleep made me crabby, so it was for the best that Nancy wasn't here yet. I had tossed and turned all night, wondering what Joyce's visit meant and why Alder hadn't told me.

I locked the door behind me and put my supplies on the counter. Before I could pull my phone from my pocket to check for messages, I heard tapping on the door.

If I avoided eye contact, maybe they'd go away.

The tapping grew more insistent.

"It's Sunday. Maggie's is closed!" I yelled.

"Cece, I see you in there. Open the door." My ex-husband stood at the door, *tap tap tapping* like a woodpecker drilling for bugs. He wore golf attire I had purchased—Ralph Lauren stone-colored shorts with a navy Polo shirt.

I blew out a breath and unlocked the door. "What do you want, and how did you find me?"

"The entire town knows you're here." He threw a glance at my hot pink van parked at the curb. "It's hard to be inconspicuous when you're driving a neon billboard."

"True." And that was why I did it—and to irk his mother, who saw it as an insult to the precious Cavanaugh name. "You didn't answer the first part of my question. What do you want?"

"To talk about yesterday."

"You need my permission to reschedule the wedding?" I picked up my dust rag and spray bottle and started wiping the furniture in the waiting room. Time was precious. My patience sank to an all-time low, and my crabbiness was at an all-time high.

"Funny." He followed behind me.

I wiped the couches, chairs, and end tables—stopping only to restack a pile of magazines.

"Stand still a minute. I need to talk to you."

I rolled my eyes, trotted to the shampoo area, and wiped the chairs. "You want to talk now? You didn't want to talk the whole time you were boinking Willow. Our talking days are over. Unless it has to do with Michelle or Jessie, we have nothing else to say."

"Get over yourself," he said. "The universe does not revolve around Cece Cavanaugh."

"Doesn't revolve around you either, buster," I fired back.

"Get a grip, will you? And you wonder where Michelle gets her drama queen tendencies."

"Your mother! I see a pattern, and it doesn't come from my side of the family."

"Right," he said. "Like your mother isn't a spectacle in and of herself."

"You need to leave. I don't have time for this today. Or any day." I stopped cleaning and planted my hands on my hips. "Wait, does this have to do with my argument with Willow? The one where she accused me of assaulting her? Complete with photos? If that's the case, get out. I did not assault her. And if she said I did, she's a liar. I threw a towel at her. That's it."

I threw my dust rag at him and hit his shoulder. "There. Do you feel assaulted?"

"You shoved her too." Phillip brushed his shoulder then picked up the rag and handed it to me.

"To get her out of the room. She wouldn't take a hint," I said. "And it wasn't a shove. My word against hers."

Phillip pulled out a newspaper he'd tucked under his arm. "This tells a different story." He thrust the Wickford "About Town" column under my nose.

There on page five, in black and white, was a photo of me with both hands on Willow's chest. "That looks worse than it was. It was a nudge. She burst into the room where Michelle and I were having facials and refused to leave. What was I supposed to do?"

Phillip folded the paper and stuck it back under his arm.

I opened my mouth, but he cut me off. "Stop it. You're acting like a lunatic. I want to talk about Kayla."

My mouth dropped open. "The dead woman. Why? Did Willow kill her? Speaking of Willow, have you told Michelle she's pregnant?"

Phillip's eyes narrowed. "You have lost your mind. Willow isn't pregnant."

I laughed. "Right, and I'm the Virgin Mary."

"Hey, if you're not getting any from the cop, I can step in. We have experience in that area." He winked. "We used to be great in the love department. Waddya say? A stroll down memory lane."

"Oh, grow up. What is wrong with you? If it weren't for a murder, you'd be married. Wait, that never stopped you before."

"It was worth a shot. Admit it. You gave it a thought, didn't you?"

I shook my head. "You're despicable. And with Willow pregnant."

Phillip groaned. "Where did you get that idea?"

I wagged my finger. "Virgin mimosas. That's how. The caterer served virgin mimosas at Willow's spa day yesterday."

Phillip laughed. "Wow, that's a stretch, even for you. Kayla doesn't drink."

"Yeah, right. Like I believe that." I moved up and down the aisle of sinks, wiping each one. "You're still a disgrace."

"Willow is not pregnant." Phillip patted a chair. "Sit down?"

"No way."

"This is serious. I need to talk to you."

I wondered if Hazel still felt ill after whatever had happened to her yesterday. Was he trying to squirm out of telling the girls by making me do it? No, the old biddy would never admit if she were still sick.

I sat. "This better be good. And you need to make it snappy because I'm burning daylight."

"Mother would kill me if she found out I was talking to you, but I don't know what else to do." Phillip shifted from one foot to the other. "Lord, I can't even believe I'm asking you this."

I snapped my fingers. "Snappy, remember? Don't beat around the bush. What's going on?"

He raked his hands through his hair, making the spikes even spikier. If that was possible. "Okay, so here's the deal. I haven't figured out how you helped solve those last couple of murders, but you need—criminently, listen to me. I'm the nutcase."

"You want me to snoop around and find out what happened to Willow's maid of honor? Ha! No way. I mean, I'm sorry the poor girl died, but it's none of my business. I can't get involved." Alder might not be working the case, but he'd still find out about it. It was bad enough I'd found the girl. I didn't need more involvement. "Besides, they haven't even released her cause of death. I suspect she drank too much and died of alcohol poisoning." I stood and wiped another sink. "Count me out."

"Did you not listen to me? Kayla doesn't drink."

"Kayla was so hungover yesterday at the spa, she made a spectacle of herself," I said.

"Look who's talking."

I hiked my lip in a sneer.

"Willow is convinced someone killed her," Phillip said.

"We know what an *Einstein* Willow is."

Phillip held up his hand. "Don't. I will not enter into a debate with you about Willow. My concern is Mother."

"Concern about her? Pray tell why."

"Mother may have interfered with the wedding."

I feigned shock. "Hazel? No way." It wouldn't be the first time. How many times had I told Phillip that Hazel was trying to sabotage our wedding and, after that, our marriage? My words falling on deaf ears every single time. I wondered if she'd tried to buy Willow off or what she'd used as a threat.

"Mother won't admit it. I thought she and Willow had all the details ironed out. Then the day of the wedding we have a different caterer and photographer. The florist changed up the flower order. Mother is furious with Willow, and Willow is furious with her. I'm stuck in the middle and don't know who to believe."

"Oh, cry me a river. That's nothing new for you." Like he didn't expect Hazel to interfere. Interference was her middle name. The magnolias tipped me off. They were Hazel's favorite flower. "I met the caterer and photographer yesterday."

"Not the ones Mother hired. Willow rounded them up at the last minute. I'm not sure if there was a mix-up or they canceled or what. The photographer is a guy she met on a modeling job. The caterer models part-time."

I don't know what shocked me more, that Willow was a model or the fact that anyone would cancel on a Cavanaugh function at the last minute. That reeked of interference— Hazel's interference.

"What about Greta and Opie?" I asked. "They're booked months in advance. There's no way they could bake and decorate a cake at the last minute."

"Greta called me with some nonsense about Mother wanting to cancel the cake order. I asked Willow if she and Mother were changing something and she said no. So, I told Greta to keep the order as it was. They're the only ones who came through. And Geoff at the club. If those two had bailed on us, we'd have been sunk."

I'd like to sink him. "So, what if Hazel sabotaged the wedding? I don't see a connection. You think she'd kill the maid of honor to stop the wedding? That's a stretch—even for Hazel."

"It's not just about Mother being a suspect. Do you realize how this will affect our name? Willow could be a suspect. That idiot Detective Zimmerman practically accused me. And you, well, you found the girl."

Boy, he had nerve. "No, a thousand times no. Any friend of Willow's is not a friend of mine. You're just mad because he called you Daddy Moneybags. And the Cavanaugh name, puh-leeze. Your mother has an unhealthy relationship with your family name."

The only one stressing over the Cavanaugh name was Hazel. She probably *would* kill to protect it. For two months after I'd bought the hot pink van with Cavanaugh Cleaning spelled out in lime green, Hazel had blown up my cell phone with text messages threatening to get an injunction to keep me from using *her* name.

"It's not just Mother. What about the girls? If our name gets dragged through the mud, it will affect them. You know how sensitive Michelle is. And what about your business? Will people hire you if your family is being investigated for murder?"

Ugh, he had a point. I had to stop following every instinct to shut him out and think instead about my girls and my only source of income. Darn if my efforts to make Hazel angry weren't biting me in the butt now. "If I do this, and I'm not saying I will, what's in it for me?"

Phillip sighed. "What do you want?"

I tapped my chin, considering his proposal. "Get your mother to back off of me and my business—"

"Done."

"Not so fast. Pay off the balance of what I owe on the van."

"How much?"

I held up ten fingers.

He pulled his checkbook from his pocket and wiggled it. "Done."

"And . . ." I drew out the word for dramatic effect. "When you reschedule your wedding, let Michelle off the hook. Don't make her stand up with you as your best girl. Do you know how humiliating that is for a seventeen-year-old?"

"But—"

"No buts. Phillip, she loves you and would eat a cockroach

if you asked her to, but don't ask her to do this. Let her sit with her sister and Hazel. Don't make her stand up there in front of the entire town of Wickford while you marry a woman half your age."

The vein in Phillip's temple throbbed. "If it bothers her so much, why didn't she tell me?"

"Cockroach," I said. "She'll do whatever you ask. She won't like it, but she'll do it."

"You'll check and see what you can find out about this girl?" he asked.

"I will." This was an awful idea, but the woman's death intrigued me no matter how much I didn't actually want to be involved. If Kayla's death was ruled a homicide, who wanted her dead? What was the motive? How had they killed her? Besides, it was the perfect activity to distract me from the thoughts I'd been having about Alder and his ex-wife. And I'd be lying if I said it didn't excite me to do this to spite him for leaving me in the dark, even if he didn't know about it.

Phillip extended his hand. "Then we've got a deal."

I bypassed that hand and reached for his checkbook.

He snatched it back. "Not so quick. You make this go away, keep the Cavanaugh name out of the newspaper, and you get the check. We'll call it my little insurance policy."

I scoffed. "More like blackmail."

"That's one way to put it," he said. "It's a sliding scale. The longer it takes, the less the check will be. Now, how about a little fun?"

"Get real. Go play golf and leave me alone."

CHAPTER EIGHT

"Cece will bounce back from whatever life throws at her. She's a wonderful person with a powerful will."
Greta Oppenheimer

I'd made a deal with the devil, but if it got my van paid off and my daughter off the hook, score. Phillip would pay hell getting Hazel to ease off of me, but two out of three wasn't bad. I could manage Hazel.

Before he left, Phillip gave me the names and lowdown on Willow's bridesmaids. Felicity Gaines, the pink bridesmaid, tended bar at Lamber's Bar in the city. During the day, she picked up modeling jobs with an agency called Glow Girl. Felicity had gotten sick on the day of the wedding.

Gracelynn Jackson, the green bridesmaid, waited tables at Barney's Rise and Shine Café in the city too. She also modeled for Glow Girl. And surprise, surprise, Kayla, the dead maid of honor, and Willow both worked for Glow Girl.

I shoved the note with the information into my purse. The thought of doing anything to ease Hazel's concern set my teeth on edge. The old bat deserved whatever was coming to her, but I had to admit I got a thrill thinking about digging into this case. Who would have guessed I had a penchant for snooping? I had been a reporter for my high school newspaper way back in the day—a job thrust upon me by the journalism teacher. The thought of interviewing people had made me queasy. Once I graduated and earned my nursing degree, the introverted Cece burst from her shell. Working around patients in a hospital setting forced me to interact. Marrying Phillip and having to host social gatherings for his clients completed the transition from introvert to extrovert. Now chatting up people and being social were second nature to me.

Oppenheimer's Bakery occupied a spot on historic Main Street, one block over from Maggie's. Greta promised me a coconut cake. I figured now was an excellent time for a break, a slice of that cake, and conversation.

The entire block leading to Oppenheimer's held the fragrant aroma of yeast and cinnamony goodness—making my quick stroll extra delicious. As I entered, the little bell over the door announced my arrival.

Greta balanced a long tray of cream-filled donuts as she unloaded them into the display case.

"Oh, those look yummy," I said. Cream-filled was my favorite.

Greta placed the tray on the back counter and rubbed her hands on the towel tucked into her apron. "Opie just boxed up your cake. Want me to add a donut?"

I patted my hips. "As much as I love donuts, cake is enough. You have time to share a slice?"

"Sure. The rush has come and gone." Greta untied her apron and slung it over a stool. "Opie, watch the counter. Cece and I are going to the patio for coffee and cake."

We settled outside with two generous slices of cake and

coffee, and she said, "Terrible thing about that woman yesterday. I can't imagine what's come over Wickford these days."

I took a bite of cake and nodded. With Greta, it was best to let her talk. If I asked too many questions, she'd clam up.

"Shame about the wedding getting canceled." She put her hand over her mouth and winked. "Oops. Maybe not, heh?"

I turned her question into a question. "How does that work? I mean, you had the cake there and set up. You can't save it for when they reschedule."

Greta laughed and rubbed her middle. "It does not go to waste, or rather it goes to my waist. Since it's perishable, the couple will lose their money. They are welcome to the cake. Most times, they don't want it."

"If you ever get leftovers, you can always call me," I said, taking another big bite.

A smile crossed Greta's face, followed by a frown. "Sometimes they argue for their money back. But not Mr. Cavanaugh. He is very generous. His mother is a different story. You know"—Greta leaned in—"she did not want me to make the cake."

"Really?" This time I leaned in, careful not to upset my coffee, which I drank only to be polite. Tea was more to my liking, but they didn't serve it at the bakery. At Oppenheimer's, plain old coffee was the beverage of choice.

"Truth. She came into the bakery just last week and told me they made other arrangements, and my services were no longer necessary."

"But you were there. With a cake," I said.

"Uh-huh, sure was. Mr. Cavanaugh signed my contract, not his mother." Greta stopped for a bite of cake and moaned afterward. "That Opie makes a fine cake, if I say so myself. Where was I? Oh, when she left the shop, I called Mr. Cavanaugh to find out what the devil was going on."

"And?"

"He told me she must have gotten confused. They had no other arrangements and were looking forward to serving our cake. His exact words were 'I can't imagine serving my guests anything other than an Oppenheimer cake.'"

Opie opened the door and shouted, "Woman, you best get back in here. We're getting a line out the front door, and I got cookies needing to come out of the oven."

Greta finished her cake and drained her cup. "Men. What would he do without me? Let's box the rest of this for you. Michelle loves my cake, so don't gobble it down before she gets a slice."

———

On my way back to the spa, I called Phillip to find out which caterer and florist Hazel contracted for the wedding. I wanted to meet with them to see what their story was. Willow's bridesmaids were on my list. I had no desire to talk to Willow, so I would avoid her at all costs. If I needed any information from her, I'd make Phillip my go-between. I didn't relish the thought of talking to him again, but it was better than dealing with the home-wrecker.

At noon, I stopped for a break and noticed Nancy standing at the front door.

"I thought you'd never see me," she said when I let her in. "I've been knocking and texting you for fifteen minutes."

I checked my phone and found several missed messages from her and a call and a text from Alder. My stomach clenched. Was this the dreaded call? The one where he told me his ex-wife was back in town. The one where he let me down easy so he could get back with her.

"Hey, are you okay?" Nancy asked.

"Sorry. Must've muted my phone. I missed a call from Alder too."

"Dun. Dun. Dun," Nancy said in an ominous tone, peering over my shoulder. "Wonder what he wanted."

I turned my phone away from her prying eyes. "I'll find out. Grab a rag. I've finished the reception area and I'm still working on the hair salon part. You can head back to the spa. Willow's crew partied there most of the day. They had lunch catered in too. Food's all gone, thank goodness, but they left the decorations, used napkins, and plastic cutlery on the tables. We need to clear them."

"Yuck, they left that stuff overnight. That's nasty." Nancy waved her hand in front of her nose.

"Quit being dramatic. It doesn't stink. It's just leftover paper and plastic products."

"Okay," Nancy said.

"I'll return Alder's call then sweep and mop the front section. When I'm done, I'll help you while the floor dries."

Nancy grabbed a handful of trash bags and headed to the back.

I stared at my phone, wondering if I should even listen to his message. What was the point? The last ones had been vague, which meant he was being evasive. But if Becca was ill, it made sense that Joyce would be back in the picture, but Becca looked healthy when Nancy and I saw her. *Not all illnesses are visible*, I told myself.

There was only one way to find out. *Rip the bandage off, Cece.* I selected the voice mail icon and listened.

"Call me when you get a chance" was what he'd said. Ditto for the text message.

I punched in his number with shaky fingers. His phone went straight to voice mail. He didn't even have it turned on.

I took a deep breath and tried to keep the panic from my voice. "Got your message. What's up? Nancy and I are working at Maggie's Salon and Day Spa. If you get a chance, stop by. I'm worried. Hope everything is okay."

I disconnected, feeling a bit off-balance in my relationship with him. I hoped he had a suitable explanation for whatever was going on with his ex-wife, but it still left me unsettled on the off chance she might be up to something. We'd never met, and I didn't know how she felt about what had happened in their past. All I had to go on was what Alder told me. It was the unknown that upset me.

I pocketed my phone, setting the volume on high in case he called back.

After I swept and mopped the reception area, I joined Nancy. She had removed all the tacky wedding decorations and filled several trash bags.

"You're quick," I said.

Nancy answered by sweeping her arm along a table, gathering plastic forks and spoons, cups, and the paper table covering as she did, and pushing them into a trash bag she'd taped to the end of the table. "Nothing to it." She unhooked the bag, tied it, and placed it next to the door with the others.

"Looks like you have a system worked out." I opened the back door and held it with my foot while grabbing the ties of the bags. "I'll take these out and then sweep. How about you break down those tables and lean them against the wall? I'm not sure where Maggie stores them or if they belong to the caterer, so they can deal with them."

The outside trash bins were almost full. I shoved in all the bags except two and barely got the lids closed. I'd have to haul off these two and anything else that needed disposal. Wickford had a strict policy that all trash awaiting pickup must be in containers. They refused to collect straggler bags and loose garbage.

Nancy was struggling with the tables when I came back inside. I gave her a hand then returned to sweeping while she wiped the surfaces.

"You ever been to a club named Lamber's?" I asked. Nancy had a past I was afraid to question. When I first met her, I suspected she worked for one of those dial-a-porn places. I'd overheard a couple of phone conversations that made me blush. She'd also taught me some wicked good stuff about surveillance techniques. Not about how to dress to follow someone since she tended toward rhinestones and sequins and flashy outfits, but she had the basics of spying down to an art. It made me wonder what she'd done in the past and how she'd wound up as a receptionist at our former place of employment—Bonafide CSC.

Nancy pulled out her phone and tapped the screen. After a few seconds, she said, "Yeah, I've been there once. How come?"

"I was thinking about going tomorrow night and wondered if you want to tag along?" I raked the broom under a massage bed and a plastic bottle shot out. I swept it into the dustpan, and as I emptied it into the trash, I saw a bottle of eye drops. The caterer complained of losing multiple bottles of eye drops. These must have been hers. Too bad. They were too nasty to retrieve.

"Ha! You don't club. What's up? Spill it."

I told her about my deal with Phillip and the information he'd shared. "The way I see it, the bridesmaids and Willow are definitely suspects. But I don't have a good motive for any of them. The only person who had a vested interest in stopping this wedding is Hazel."

Nancy rubbed her hands together. "Count me in. It said on their website that Mondays, ladies drink for half-price. That's us." She paused. "What's in it for me, besides you buying me drinks?"

I shouldn't have shared the part of my plan about getting Phillip to pay off my van. Nancy had been working for me since the previous June. I had considered giving her a raise but held off to make sure my finances could support it. With Phillip paying off my van, that would free up extra cash. Nancy had turned into a competent assistant and had taken on the Hunter Springs project by herself. She saw Hunter often, and I stayed out of the way while their relationship blossomed.

When I'd first met Grant, he'd shown an interest in me—an interest I did not reciprocate. He was an exceptional guy, and we would always be friends, but we didn't share a romantic spark. Last Thanksgiving, he'd told me he didn't think we had chemistry, and he'd like to go out with Nancy. They'd been dating since then.

I still helped Nancy at Hunter Springs occasionally, but with her out there, I'd been able to turn my attention to marketing my business and doing other projects I acquired. If my company kept growing, I might even have to hire another person. That was down the road. But for now, Nancy deserved additional compensation.

"A raise," I said.

Nancy quirked a brow. "What are we waiting for? Can I borrow your brown leather boots?"

"Let's not get crazy." I tied another bag of trash and headed to my van.

"You told me you'd make it up to me the last time you almost got me killed!" Nancy yelled as I slammed the door.

She was right. I had felt so guilty about almost getting her killed, I promised she could wear the boots. I never dreamed as flaky as she was that she'd remember, much less call me out on it.

I peeked back inside. "If I let you wear the boots to the club, then we're even," I said.

Nancy pumped her fist. "Yes! I love those boots."

I did too.

CHAPTER NINE

"Ms. Cavanaugh will not deter my investigation, or we will have words. I won't let an untrained housewife get in my way."
Detective Zimmerman

Nancy offered to finish up at the spa Monday morning, allowing me time to make a trip to Barney's Rise and Shine. Barney's only served breakfast and lunch, so I took a chance that Gracelynn, Willow's green-clad bridesmaid, would be working. As I backed out of my driveway, I saw a navy-blue sedan pulled to the curb at the corner of my street.

I smiled when I saw Alder's unmarked police car and slowed when I came up beside it. Why he hadn't pulled into my driveway puzzled me. My left eye twitched. Something was not right. The car looked similar, but it wasn't Alder's. He prided himself on keeping his department-issued vehicle immaculate. This car sported an ugly scratch on the side and a ding in the fender.

My smile faded when I saw Detective Zimmerman sitting

behind the wheel. He gave a two-finger wave when I passed by him. I reasoned that if he wanted to talk to me, he'd have come to my house instead of staking out my neighborhood. Still, his presence left me so flustered I forgot to turn on my signal and ran the stop sign.

All the way out of town, I kept expecting him to follow me, pull me over, and give me a ticket. Did detectives even write traffic tickets?

Was he staking me out? Why would he even consider me stakeout worthy?

My hands shook as I signaled and crept onto the highway entrance ramp. I kept watching in my rearview mirror, preparing to abort my mission if I saw Zimmerman's blue car. No way I'd let him catch me talking to one of Willow's bridesmaids.

When I reached Barney's Rise and Shine, I convinced myself that Zimmerman had not followed me, but stress had my stomach tied into so many knots, I doubted I'd be able to eat. To make sure he didn't follow me, I sat in the parking lot for a full fifteen minutes then pulled out and drove several blocks before circling back and parking. There was still no sign of his unmarked police car.

Barney's had open seating. Plenty of open seating. Gracelynn, a tall redhead, stood near a cluster of booths in the back tending to the lone customer in the café. I wandered over and claimed a nearby booth. I was fiddling with the menu when she arrived with her order pad.

She placed a glass of water on the table. "Welcome to Barney's Rise and Shine. What can I get you?"

"A hot tea and an order of toast," I said from behind the menu.

She scribbled my order without making eye contact. "Is that it? We have cinnamon rolls fresh out of the oven."

"I'm good." I closed the menu.

She squinted. "I recognize you."

"Hi." I slid the menu behind the napkin holder.

"What are you doing here?"

"Getting breakfast," I said.

"Right." She tapped her pen on the order pad. "You live in Wickford, don't you?"

"I do."

"You drove into the city for tea and toast. You're Phillip Cavanaugh's ex-wife. I'm not buying it."

The only other customer in the café stood at the register paying his check.

"You have a minute to talk?" I asked.

"Why?" She glanced around like she would beg off because of customers.

"Nothing bad. I promise." I explained my deal with Phillip. Not all of it in case she snitched to Willow. I didn't have Phillip's check yet, so I didn't want the deal to go sour before I got the cash in my hot little hands.

"I talked to that detective," she said. "There's nothing more to tell."

"Something might jog your memory."

"Are you sure Willow is okay with you doing this? You are Phillip's ex-wife," she said.

I nodded. "He came to me and asked for my help. With the Cavanaugh name being associated with the murder, he's worried about appearances. It will help Willow. Probably you too."

"What do you mean, me too?"

"We were all there when Kayla died."

"Wait, you think I had something to do with Kayla's death?" Her voice quivered.

"I'm just looking at all sides to see who had motive," I said.

"I didn't have a motive to kill one of my best friends. And

I will not tell you anything that might make one of my friends look guilty."

"I'm just trying to get to know more about everyone," I said.

"I don't like this one bit."

"Think about it. If you're not guilty, you have nothing to lose. And the upside is the sooner this is cleared up, the sooner Willow and Phillip can get on with their wedding plans."

She sighed. "Let me think about it while I get your tea and turn in your order."

I waited and waited. When an older woman with a sag in her shoulders brought the tea and toast, I realized Gracelynn wasn't coming back.

"What happened to the other server?" I asked.

The woman shook her head. "Beats me. Said she remembered an appointment," she said in a disgusted tone. "That's not like Gracelynn at all. She's the one server I can count on. Competent help is impossible to find these days. I thanked my lucky stars when I found her. If she's turned into a flake, I'm sunk."

I nodded in commiseration. "I know what you mean. My assistant is a flake too. But she's a reliable flake."

She laughed then slid into the booth. "Do you mind?"

I hesitated, knowing I needed to get back home, but said, "Why not?" Maybe she could give me some insight into Gracelynn.

She reached her hand across the table. "I'm Vivian. Viv to my friends."

"I'm Cece," I said and extended my hand to shake hers. "Nice to meet you."

"Gracelynn isn't so bad. A friend of hers died over the weekend. That might explain her behavior. I should have insisted she take time off, but she's the best help I have. I can't rely on the others to make their own shifts, much less pick up an extra one."

I lifted the tea bag from my cup and set it aside. "That's too bad. Was the death sudden?"

Viv looked around the empty restaurant then whispered, "Gracelynn said the girl may have been murdered."

"Oh my. That's horrible."

"The worst part is Gracelynn was there when it happened. It happened at a wedding. A muckety-muck big shot out in Wickford was getting married. The girl who died was the maid of honor." Viv rubbed her hands, massaging arthritic knuckles.

"Whoa! Do they have any suspects?" I asked.

Viv shook her head. "She didn't say. She said the police questioned the entire wedding party, including the muckety-muck's ex-wife."

My stomach lurched. "She doesn't think the ex-wife had anything to do with it, does she?"

Viv smirked. "Beats me, but it looks suspicious, right? I mean, why would the ex-wife be there?"

I thought for a moment. "I'm sure she had a reason."
"Sure."

"Is it possible Gracelynn had anything to do with it?"

"Oh, heavens no." She chuckled. "That girl doesn't have it in her. She's got a tender heart, that one. No ma'am, she could never in a million years hurt someone. She had a mouse problem in her condo a few months back, and I gave her several of those spring-loaded traps. She refused them and bought a humane contraption that doesn't whack 'em dead. Then she let the critters loose in the park. But who knows? Guess anyone can fool you. I never figured she'd leave me high and dry today."

Two utility workers walked in the front door and waved to Viv.

She waved back. "Hey guys, have a seat, and I'll get you a couple coffees." She levered herself from the booth.

"Yeah, I need to get going. Thanks." I finished my toast and brushed crumbs from my hands.

I didn't know what was up with Gracelynn. Not for one hot minute did I think she remembered an appointment. I intended to find out. She might not hurt a mouse, but that didn't make her innocent in my book. Not by a longshot.

———

On the drive back to Wickford, I stopped by Main Street Florist, the only one in Wickford, and one of the two florists Hazel called when she needed floral arrangements.

The owner wasn't in, which bode well for me. If she had been, I would have made an excuse that I was browsing for flowers, then left. Instead, a young woman stood behind the counter.

I walked around looking at the various arrangements, reminiscing back to the time when I'd been able to have fresh flowers delivered any time I wanted. Now, the only flowers I had were ones I cut from my garden or when Alder brought a bouquet.

The thought of him made me wince. What was going on? It wasn't like him to be out of touch, but to be fair, he had left messages. We just hadn't connected. I wanted to go to his house, but my heart couldn't take it if his ex-wife was still there. I glanced at my phone, checking for missed messages, and came up empty. Whatever was going on, I had to trust him. *Trust* being the operative word.

During my marriage, Phillip had shaken my trust to the core with his cheating. Not with one woman, as I had learned when he walked out on me, but with many women throughout our thirty years of marriage. Trusting again was something I'd been working on. I didn't need to go through another upheaval. I sighed and slipped my phone into my pocket. *It'll work out. Have faith.*

Angie always bragged about what a catch Alder was, and she had an uncanny ability to sniff out a louse. She'd warned me for years about Phillip—even before he and I had married. Turned out her intuition was solid. She claimed she hadn't known he was cheating, and I believed her. She had never liked him on principle.

A refrigerated case on the side wall held an abundance of gerbera daisies in spring colors of pink, green, and blue. A hand-lettered sign announced they were on sale for half-price.

"Can I help you?" a young woman, whom I'd never met, asked.

"You work here?"

"It's temporary. My aunt owns the store." She smiled. "I'm staying with her for a few weeks."

"Ah, I wondered why you didn't look familiar," I said. "Gorgeous daisies."

She opened the case and pulled out a handful. "I can give you a good price."

"That's an awful lot of them."

"Yeah." She shrugged. "We had a last-minute order change."

"That's odd. Can they do that?" I pressed.

"A week before the wedding, a woman came in and changed the order from daisies to magnolia blossoms. I learned the hard way we're not supposed to cancel if we've placed the order with our supplier."

My ears perked at the mention of magnolia blossoms, and my conversation with Greta about the bakery cancellation filtered back into my thoughts. The colors of the daisies matched the dresses Willow's bridal party wore. "Were you paid for the daisies? How does that even work?"

"No. We're stuck with these. I'm lucky my aunt didn't take it out of my pay." She leaned in close. "Between you and me, I can make you a better offer if you take all of them."

A few might brighten up my kitchen, but then they'd remind me of Willow and Phillip. "Not my taste," I said. Nor were Willow and Phillip. "Any idea who changed the order?" I asked.

"Oh, sure. I worked that day. An older woman. I'll never forget. When my aunt found out, she blew a gasket. But the woman was so forceful. Not the kind who takes no for an answer." The girl made a slashing motion across her throat. "Turned out she was my aunt's friend, so my aunt forgave me and said it was okay. But I can't give out any information. My aunt would fire me for sure. I can't afford another mistake."

"No worries." I knew who changed the order, and it wasn't Willow. "On second thought, I'll take three bouquets of those daisies."

"Are you sure? That's fantastic. It'll help get me out of trouble with my aunt."

"Can you have them delivered?" I asked.

She nodded, wrote up the order, and handed me the invoice. "Sure thing. Where shall I send them?"

I gave her cash and Hazel's address.

"You want to pick out a card? We have a nice selection," the girl asked as she punched the sale into the cash register.

"No, I want to surprise her." I chuckled at my brilliant idea.

My work here was complete. I wished I could see Hazel's face when the flowers arrived. I imagined her eyes darkening when she tried to figure out who sent them. She wouldn't have a clue I had. She'd probably come all unglued on Willow.

I didn't plan on it, but since my drive home took me past Alder's neighborhood, I figured one little peek wouldn't hurt. Not turn onto his street—just take a peek from the corner.

I didn't know what I expected to see when I stopped at the corner of his street, but it wasn't him and his ex-wife sitting on the front porch drinking coffee. Tears stung my eyes, and all the encouraging words I'd prepared for myself dissolved in salty streams down my face. At the next cross street, I pulled into a parking lot and called Angie, blubbering incoherent words about Alder, his ex-wife, and chocolate.

———

Angie met me at her front door with a box of tissue, a frosty glass of iced tea, and her secret stash of chocolate.

"Don't tell Dave about the candy. He's been a stickler for me watching my sugar intake with this pregnancy."

My tears had dried by the time I sat down at Angie's table, but they started again when she bent down and hugged me. "There's a simple explanation for Alder's ex-wife being in town. You need to call him. He's always been straight with you."

"I've tried calling. It goes to voice mail. I've tried texting." I hiccupped and took a sip of tea.

"And he's not returning your calls?" she asked.

I nodded. "He does. We keep missing one another. That's why I drove by his neighborhood."

"How do you even know it's his ex-wife? That was so long ago. Long before he moved to Wickford."

I explained about Nancy and me driving past the night before and meeting his neighbor.

"You're getting to be quite the snoop, aren't you?" Angie retrieved the tea pitcher and refreshed our glasses. "You need to stop jumping to conclusions. I'll admit it doesn't look good, but Alder is a straight-up guy. He will not lead you on. I've known him for years. If he's dated in the past, he's never talked about it at work, and he talks about you all the time.

He's always been open and aboveboard. He would not do that if he wanted to reconnect with his ex-wife. She doesn't even live in the area, does she?"

I sniffled and wiped my nose. "She lives in Europe. Belgium, I think."

"See, there's your explanation." Angie smiled. "She's probably here for something to do with their daughter."

"You're probably right. I'm making an enormous deal over nothing." I squared my shoulders. "What's wrong with me? I need to stop whining." I had promised myself I wouldn't let another man do to me what Phillip had done. My feelings for Alder were stronger than I cared to admit. We ate dinner together two or three times a week, and we talked on the phone almost daily, but neither of us had uttered the L-word. Alder was on the verge a while back, but I'd put the kibosh on it. If anyone was to blame for us not advancing in our relationship, it was me.

"In other news, the suspicious death at Phillip's wedding is now a homicide investigation." Angie sat up a little straighter. "They're waiting for the tox screen to come back."

I set my glass down. "They think she was poisoned?"

"I didn't say that," Angie said.

"But they're looking for something if they requested a tox screen." I added that bit of information to the other things I'd learned.

The wheels in my head started turning. This news did not bode well for Hazel, given what I'd learned about her sabotaging the wedding. I needed to get on with my investigation if I wanted that check from Phillip. If Hazel got arrested for Kayla's murder, whether or not she was guilty, it would be a disaster. If the Cavanaugh name spiraled down the tubes, Phillip would never pay off my van, and I wouldn't be able to give Nancy the raise I had all but promised her.

"Hey, I have a hypothetical question," I said.

Angie leaned in. "Let's hear it."

"Do detectives stake out houses of people who aren't suspects?"

"Was Zimmerman parked outside your house?"

"No!"

"Okay, what's going on? What have you done?"

"Jeez! Forget it. It was a hypothetical question. Nothing is going on. I have to get back to work," I said. "Nancy's been at it alone all morning."

"That's it?" Angie's eyes narrowed. "You don't have a comment about another murder in Wickford."

"Nope, none of my business." I scooted my chair back and stood. "Sounds like a job for Detective Zimmerman."

"I'm not buying it. I wouldn't be your best friend if I didn't repeat my warning about Zimmerman. He is not Alder. He won't think twice about taking you down, and Alder cannot protect you. And, hypothetically, if he was parked outside your house, it may not mean you're a suspect, but he's watching you, so be careful."

I wagged my hand. "Pish posh, you worry too much. I have work to do." Like talking to the caterer, the photographer, the bridesmaids, and, eek, maybe even Hazel. It would irk the tar out of me to do it, but I wasn't letting Hazel or even Willow stand between me and a paid-off van. This girl had her priorities.

....

CHAPTER TEN

....

"When Cece asked me if I wanted to go clubbing, it surprised me. She should cut loose once in a while."
Nancy Lustbader

Nancy and I finished up in time to grab a quick bite to eat, clean up, and head to the city for a night of clubbing—also known as snooping.

She wore skin-tight, giraffe-print leggings, a gauzy white gypsy-inspired top, and my brown Saint Laurent over-the-knee leather boots. I cringed when I'd handed them to her, but I had promised. At least I would be there to protect them.

I parked the car, and we walked in the front door of Lamber's Bar.

"I can't believe you're wearing that," Nancy said, referring to my dress jeans, royal blue blouse, and sensible pumps. "You might at least dress flashier. Next time I'll take you shopping in my closet."

Like I'd let that happen. "We're not here to party, remember? The sooner I talk to this woman and get the information I need, the better."

Nancy struck a pose and flounced into the club, calling over her shoulder, "You talk. I'll get a drink and do some dancing. It's been ages since I've been to a club."

She strutted off to the dance floor where a multitude of people gyrated to the music. It had been years, more like decades, since I'd been in a nightclub. My social events tended more toward balls at the country club, weddings, and garden parties. Those days were behind me since the divorce. I tapped my foot to the music. Then I told myself one dance wouldn't hurt.

I pushed into the crowd and started swaying to the music. I couldn't tell who was partnered up with whom and figured no one else would watch me as I danced solo. The beat was satisfying. I let myself cut loose and mimicked the other dancers' moves.

I felt a tap on my shoulder and turned.

A burly guy with a mohawk reached for my hand. "You got moves, Mama. Wanna dance?"

"Uh, no thanks. I was just leaving." I gulped and backed away. My shirt caught on the back of a chair, but I kept going, expecting it to slide over easily. Two buttons popped off, revealing my bra. The guy kept moving toward me, leering like a hungry coyote. Where was Nancy when I needed her? I held my blouse together and slunk off to the restroom, hoping the guy wouldn't follow me. Before I pushed into the bathroom, I took a quick look behind me to make sure. He'd already found someone else and was busting a move on the dance floor.

I blinked away the glare of the bathroom light, wondering how I'd talked myself into this. Nancy had known what to expect, but silly me had no clue. How did people do this? It was like a zoo out there, and the people were animals. When I looked into the mirror, my hair stood out in all directions. I patted it down as much as possible. I rescued my blouse and my dignity with two safety pins I found in my wallet and went in search of the bar. What did one order at a club? Would chardonnay sound dumb? A waitress passed by carrying a tray full of martini glasses filled with electric blue drinks topped with cherries and slices of pineapple.

People swarmed the bar. I stood on my tiptoes, trying to get a glimpse of the bartender. If Felicity Gaines, the pink bridesmaid, wasn't working tonight, Nancy and I would have to come back. There wasn't one bartender, but three. All three females. Two had their backs to me and the third one, who was facing me, was not Felicity. The second one turned to deliver a drink to an inebriated man. I couldn't tell if she was Felicity, so I edged closer to the bar, willing a stool to vacate.

"What can I get you?"

I looked up into her face. Not Felicity.

I pointed over my shoulder. "The blue drink in the martini glass. I just saw a tray of them."

She laughed. "Aquamarine martini. That's my favorite. It's the house special."

The woman with her back to me grabbed her purse. "I'm going out back for fresh air. Will you cover for me?"

"You okay?" my bartender asked.

The other woman turned sideways. "I'm fine. Just need air."

"Go on, Felicity. I got you, girl," my bartender said.

My ears perked. My elation crashed when she exited the back door. She hadn't appeared to recognize me, but with my earlier experience with Gracelynn, I wasn't going to let her get away. Gracelynn may have called to warn her.

I grabbed my purse and headed toward the door.

"Wait," my bartender called. "I've got your drink. You haven't paid yet."

I pulled a ten from my purse, praying it was enough, and threw it on the counter. "I'll be right back. Save it for me."

Outside, I searched for Felicity, hoping she hadn't tried to ditch me. She was the bridesmaid who had gotten sick while we were waiting for the detective.

The night was black as ink. I could make out boxes stacked along a cinder-block wall, but nothing else. Sobbing noises came from the other side of the wall. I activated the flashlight on my cell phone to light my way, hoping I didn't spook her.

She was sitting on an overturned box, crying into her apron. I clicked off my flashlight, pulled a box up, and sat next to her.

"Hey, are you okay?"

She startled and screamed.

I held up my hands, hoping she wouldn't take off. "Sorry I scared you. I'm here with a friend and clubs aren't my thing. I needed to get away from the racket," I said. "When I saw the exit door, I figured I could duck out for a few minutes. That's when I heard you crying."

She sniffled.

I pulled a tissue from my purse and handed it to her. She still hadn't connected the dots, so I continued. "Are you okay?"

Her shoulders lifted then settled. "One of my best friends died Saturday."

Her words struck a nerve. I thought of Angie. Would I be holding it together if anything ever happened to her? We had known each other since childhood and were more like sisters than friends. We shared all of our secrets. My kids even joked that she was like a second mom to them. Losing her was unimaginable.

I patted Felicity's back and let her cry. Her pain seared my heart. "I'm so sorry. That's so recent. No wonder you're having a rough time. Aren't you able to take time off?"

"No, the bills don't stop just because you lose a friend. If I don't work, I don't get paid. And the guy who owns this place would fire me. I've taken off too much time as it is."

"That stinks," I said. "How long have you known your friend?"

"We met in college," she sobbed. "Our entire group met in college. We were all like sisters."

"How horrible," I said.

She explained about the wedding and how Kayla had died before the ceremony.

"That's terrible. Do they know what happened?" I asked in a soothing tone.

"She was sick all day—not herself."

"Too much bachelorette party?" I asked. I remembered what the country club bartender said about her staggering around.

"No, she doesn't drink. I'm the one who had too much to drink the night before. I even switched to non-alcoholic drinks the day of the wedding."

That triggered my curiosity. I was convinced Kayla had died from alcohol poisoning. But she wasn't drinking alcohol the night before or the day of the wedding. Hazel didn't drink, and now I knew Felicity drank the night before but switched off the day of the wedding.

"What about Gracelynn? What are her drinking habits?" *Oops.*

"Gracelynn drinks like a fish, but she can hold her al—" Felicity stopped and moved in closer. "How did you know her name?"

"Um, you mentioned it when you told me about being sorority sisters."

"No, I didn't. And I didn't tell you we were in a sorority. I told you we met in college," she said, her voice rising an octave.

I backpedaled to keep the conversation going. "I assumed you were sorority sisters. And I'm certain you mentioned her name."

"Who are you?" She opened her flashlight app and shined it on my face. "I know you. I mean, I don't know you, but I saw you at the wedding and at the spa. You're Phillip's ex-wife." She jumped to her feet. "I don't know what you're up to, but we're done." She stomped to the door, and I followed.

"Wait," I said. "It's not what you think. Please give me a few minutes to explain."

She stopped and faced me. "Why should I? You're not being honest with me. Why should I believe you now?"

"Look, I have a best friend. If someone did this to her, I would want answers, regardless of where they came from. Come on. Sit back down and let me explain to you. I'm trying to help—really I am."

She walked back to the area where we'd been sitting and sat. "This better be good."

"Phillip asked me to look into Kayla's death. He's worried about Willow. With the Cavanaugh name being in the news so much, he's also worried about his mother and our daughters."

"Willow knows you're doing this?" she asked.

I nodded. Willow probably didn't have a clue Phillip talked to me, but I hoped to get all the information I needed from Felicity before she verified my story.

With alcohol poisoning off the table, I needed to ramp up my game and figure out how Kayla died. I didn't have time to wait for tox screen results. Every day this investigation continued, the dollar signs for my van disappeared.

"What can you tell me about Kayla? Who she was. I know

she modeled. And that you all had been friends since college. Did the other girls have anything against Kayla?" I asked.

She thought for a moment. "I'm not snitching on anyone, if that's what you're after."

I shook my head. "Were you all best friends, or were some of you more friends with one person than the others? How did your group work?"

"It's hard to say. The dynamics changed up—a lot. There was a bit of jealousy in our group. Everyone warned Willow about messing around with Phillip, but the truth is we envied Willow. He had money." She gulped. "Sorry. That must have hurt."

I shrugged.

"When she told us she was engaged, and she wanted us to be in the wedding—let's just say there was a bunch of arm-twisting. None of us wanted to do it. We assumed she was rushing into it with Phillip. And he's so old. Sorry. He's a lot older than her."

"But you did," I prodded. "Was she closer to Kayla than to you and Gracelynn?"

"Not really. Willow and Kayla roomed together in college, and Gracelynn and I did. Willow is the first in our group to get married. Well, I guess she's not married yet. Kayla may have felt more obligated to Willow than the rest of us."

"Because they were roommates?" I asked.

"Yeah. Willow and Gracelynn were competing for a prestigious modeling job." Felicity snorted. "Kayla was too, but the chances of her getting it were slim. It didn't stop her though."

"What modeling job?" I asked.

"It's an exclusive deal, modeling for a top designer. It's a once-in-a-lifetime opportunity—a career maker." Felicity frowned. "I was eliminated early on."

"You were competing against one another for this job?"

"Yeah, in the beginning. Now it's between Willow and Gracelynn," Felicity said. "One of them will get the exclusive."

"Sounds like it." I now had another avenue to explore.

"There was a man issue too," Felicity said, changing the subject. "Gracelynn was seeing someone. When she broke it off, Kayla swooped in. That didn't go over well with Gracelynn, who bad-mouthed her to Willow." Felicity scooted a box over, slipped off her shoes, and lifted her feet to rest on the box. "They both thought Kayla had taken advantage of the situation by encouraging Gracelynn to break up with the guy. I've never seen Gracelynn so angry. The wedding plans were already rolling, and with all the grief Phillip's mother was giving Willow, she was just too overwhelmed to change the wedding party."

"Do you know who the man was?" I asked.

"No clue. Gracelynn and Kayla were all hush-hush about him," Felicity said. "And Willow wasn't talking. They purposely left me out of the loop."

A door slammed, and I heard Nancy's voice. "Cece, are you out here?"

Mild cursing followed a crashing noise. "Ack, I think I broke something."

You better not have broken my boots.

"Oww."

"What's going on?" Felicity asked.

"She's with me." I hit my flashlight app. "Hang on, Nancy."

I found my way around the wall and saw Nancy lying in a pile of crumpled boxes.

"My ankle. Ow!" Nancy cried.

Felicity joined me, and we helped Nancy to her feet.

"Are you okay?" Felicity asked.

Before Nancy answered, I dove in. "How did you find me?"

"I asked a bartender. You kind of stand out in this place. And thanks for your concern," Nancy said to me. "And no, I'm not okay. My ankle is killing me."

I will kill you.

"Can I help you get her to your car?" Felicity asked.

"That would be great." I slung one of Nancy's arms around my neck. She went limp and slid to the ground. "Oh, good grief. Help us. We can't drag you to the car. Though, I'd like to."

"Is she drunk?" Felicity asked.

I sighed. "No telling."

We both bent over and pulled Nancy up.

"Nancy," I said. "Put one of your arms around her neck and the other around mine and let us help you. Put some weight on the good ankle because we can't carry you or we'll both get hurt." I slid my arm around her waist.

"Ow, it hurts too bad," Nancy cried. "Take the boot off."

"No," I said. "If you broke your ankle, you need the stability the boot gives it."

"Should I go get some ice?" Felicity asked.

"No," Nancy said. "But a drink might help."

"One too many drinks got you into this mess," I said.

"Is my lipstick smeared?" Nancy patted her lips. "I need a mirror."

"You don't even have lipstick on. You probably left it on the rim of a glass," I said.

We had taken about three steps when Nancy slid down to a sitting position; her legs splayed awkwardly. She couldn't possibly be comfortable, but perhaps she was too numb to notice.

"Nancy, come on." I tugged her arm and was rewarded

with her slumping against my leg and wrapping an arm around it with a death grip.

"Cece, you're *sooo* good to me." Nancy's words came out slurred.

"How many drinks did you have?" I pulled Nancy off my leg and sat her upright, standing behind her so I could get a better grip under her arms. "You weren't alone that long."

Nancy giggled. "Yummy gummies."

"What?" I patted down Nancy's hair, which looked like she'd been dragged through a briar patch.

Felicity groaned. "She's been eating spiked gummies. I saw a couple of girls passing them around earlier. They soak them overnight then sneak them in, in plastic bags."

"That sounds dangerous," I said. Who even knew that was a thing?

"Yummy gummies," Nancy said again and fell over onto the pavement.

"Why don't you go get your car and pull it around?" Felicity said. "I'll wait here with her."

"Nooo," Nancy wailed. "Don't leave me alone."

"I'm not leaving you. I'm getting the car."

"Nooo, take me with you."

The back door of the club opened. "Felicity, are you out here?" a man's voice boomed through the night air.

"Crap, that's my boss. I have to go. Sorry."

"Can we continue this conversation tomorrow?" I asked.

"I don't know. Let me get back to you. I don't think I can help."

I hurried and scribbled my number on a scrap of paper and handed it to her. "Call me, please. I am trying to help." *I really am trying to pay off my van.*

"You want me to call someone for you?" Felicity had already started to retreat.

"No, I got this," I said, even though I didn't.

I pulled Nancy to a sitting position. "Why wouldn't you let me go get the car?" I asked after Felicity had gone.

"What if she's the killer? You'd leave me alone with her. She might whack me right here in the alley," Nancy whined.

"*I* will whack you right here in the alley and dump your body in the trash bin. Sit here while I get the car." I stalked off, leaving Nancy yelling curse words at my back.

CHAPTER ELEVEN

"I normally would never gamble, but Nancy makes it fun."
Beatrice Giovannetti

The next morning, Nancy sat in my great room nursing a sprained ankle. Beatrice, my housekeeper, had arrived and stood in the doorway talking to her. I'd let Nancy sleep on the sofa in my office so she didn't have to walk up the stairs to the garage apartment.

"You got enough ice?" I asked.

She pursed her lips and nodded. "Yeah, Beatrice made me an ice pack. I'm sorry about your boots."

My boots had not escaped injury. Nancy had scuffed both toes and gouged chunks out of the leather. Lesson learned.

"No worries." I made two cups of tea and joined her.

"No thanks." Nancy lifted a to-go cup from Café du Soleil, one of my favorite hangouts. "Beatrice was a doll. She stopped and got me a coffee on her way here. I can't drink that tea you make. Not enough caffeine to keep my engine running."

Grrr! I frowned at Nancy. "Beatrice isn't on your payroll, so leave her alone."

"Technically, she's not on yours, either," Nancy shot back.

Beatrice laughed. "Oh, I wasn't doing her errands. I lost a bet and owed her a coffee."

Nancy tilted her cup toward me. "Yeah, thanks for helping me win the bet."

"What bet?" These two teaming up with one another did not bode well for me.

"She bet me you'd leave this investigation alone, and I bet her you'd get right smack in the middle of it." Nancy took a long sip of coffee then held her cup high in the air. "Score."

"You two are incorrigible." I took the cup of tea I'd made for Nancy to the sink.

"Can I talk to you?" Beatrice asked.

I spun around and leaned against the counter. "Sure. What's up?"

"With Mr. Cavanaugh getting married . . ." Her words trailed off and tears sprang to her eyes.

"Hey, what's the matter?" I put my arms around her. In all the months that Beatrice had worked for me, I'd never once seen her get emotional.

She sobbed against my shoulder. "The agency is reassigning me."

I pulled away and held her at arm's length. "How come?"

Tears continued to slide down her face.

"It's Hazel, isn't it?" When Phillip and I first separated, Hazel had gone to impressive lengths to spy on me, hoping to find a spicy tidbit to help Phillip in the divorce. One of her tricks was to hire Beatrice to tend my house, claiming a housekeeper was for Michelle's benefit since we lived in squalor—not. At first, I had been resistant, but Beatrice and I had bonded and turned the tables on Hazel, with Beatrice feeding only glowing reports about me and my activities. Not that I had terrible stuff to report, but Beatrice always made me sound more like Mother Teresa than I deserved.

"Mrs. Cavanaugh called the agency and told them she didn't need my services here." She pulled a tissue from her apron pocket and dabbed her eyes.

I knew Hazel would pull the plug someday. I assumed it would be after Michelle left for college. Beatrice had become like a part of our family. The thought of losing her hurt, but the truth was I couldn't afford to pay her wages. Unless . . .

"I have an idea," I said. "Trust me. I'll get this figured out. You aren't going anywhere."

Beatrice's lower lip quivered. "Are you sure? You're struggling to make your business work. I don't want to add a burden to your budget. I'd work for free if I could, but I'm barely making ends meet."

"Don't you worry. You don't have to work for free. In fact, I may even work out a raise for you. Now dry your eyes. It will be fine." I hugged her again, hoping my mouth hadn't made a promise I wouldn't be able to keep. If my plan worked, I'd get Phillip to add Beatrice's salary to our deal. "You're part of the family."

She took one last swipe at her eyes and stood. "Then I'll get back to work and earn my keep."

"You more than earn your keep. Leave this to me. You've had my back all these months—now it's my turn to have yours."

"Then shoo and let me get my work done." She gave me a gentle push. "The detective called yesterday. Said he would stop by this morning." Beatrice took the cup I'd put in the sink and placed it in the dishwasher. "I got in a rush to get home yesterday and forgot to leave you a note."

I looked at my snagged yoga pants and my three-sizes-too-big T-shirt. "Eek! I have to change."

Beatrice nodded and disappeared into the pantry.

"I'd say. If Alder sees you like that, he'll run the other way." Nancy stood in the doorway, pain etched on her face. "Dang, that hurts."

"You take it easy today. Is there anything happening at Hunter Springs that I need to take care of?" I asked.

"Nope. I've got it covered this week. Next week will be a different story. What happened with that girl at the club?" Nancy asked.

"I would have filled you in last night, but you had a few too many yummy gummies. Willow, Gracelynn, and Kayla were competing for a big modeling job, and Gracelynn and Kayla were squabbling over a man."

"Man trouble? Did she say who the man was?" Nancy asked.

"No."

"It wasn't your ex, was it?" Nancy chuckled. "That would be something."

"That's a thought. I wouldn't put it past Phillip to string along those girls. It must be an ego thing with him and a money thing for them. What is it with old guys and their egos?" I rolled my eyes. Was it possible Phillip was dallying with Willow's friends? That sure would give Willow a motive. Gracelynn too. If Kayla had threatened to out Phillip to Willow, it could also give him a motive. My list of suspects kept growing. I wanted to place the blame on Hazel, but I knew better. Besides, that would put an end to my deal with Phillip.

"Big bucks makes all kinds of old look better," Nancy said.

"Are you speaking from experience?" I hoped not. Grant Hunter had a few years on Nancy, and he fit the big-bucks description. If Nancy ever did anything to hurt him, she'd be answering to me. Even though Grant and I had never developed a romantic relationship, we still had a strong friendship.

Nancy grinned. "I'll never tell."

"There's one way to find out about Phillip." I picked up my cell and called him.

When he answered, I jumped in with my big mouth. "Are you cheating on Willow?"

Phillip sputtered, and I imagined him spitting coffee on his desk. "Are you off your meds again?"

"Funny. Were you fooling around with the girl who died?"

"Your imagination is working overtime."

I could imagine the vein throbbing at his temple right next to the slightest hint of gray hair. "Not like it would be the first time you fooled around."

"If you want your van paid off, focus your attention on the important stuff. What I do and who I do it with is no longer your business."

"You never thought it was my business when we were married either."

My retort fell on deaf ears. He disconnected.

The doorbell rang.

Crap! I ran up the stairs, calling over my shoulder, "Beatrice, will you get that? Tell him I'll be down in a second."

———

I changed, brushed my teeth, and went to face Alder. Now I would get answers to why his ex-wife was in Wickford. Part of me felt relief; the other part felt panic.

The downstairs was quiet as I made my way to the kitchen. Normally, Alder would be chatting up Beatrice, and she'd be flirting with him. Since we'd been dating, he'd been at the house more than usual, and he and Beatrice had formed a fast friendship. He'd often bring her a bakery item from Oppenheimer's or a small bouquet. She'd spoil him and have a casserole ready for him to take home and freeze.

The stools at the breakfast bar were empty, which piqued my curiosity. Beatrice came out of the laundry carrying a basket of clean clothes.

"Where's Alder?" I asked.

Beatrice looked confused. "Oh, you thought I meant Detective Alder. No, this is a different detective. He's in the living room. Didn't you see him when you came down?"

My stomach lurched. Detective Zimmerman, complete with his reflective sunglasses, was in my living room. What could he want?

Zimmerman stood by the fireplace holding a photo of me and Phillip and the girls. "How can I help you, Detective?"

"Still got photos of the ex. Commendable. My ex has probably already burned the photos with me or taken scissors to them." He placed the photo back on the mantel.

I understood why. "I'm sure you didn't stop by to admire my family photos. What can I do for you?"

"You're right. Let's have a brief chat over coffee." Zimmerman gestured to the couch. "Why don't you have a seat? Perhaps the sweet woman who let me in can wrestle us up a cup of java."

"Not! The sweet woman works for me, and I don't drink coffee." I stood my ground even though he had made himself at home. If he sat, I'd never get rid of him. "I was leaving. Can we make this quick?"

"First, I'm astonished Alder lets you get away without having coffee. He's a caffeine addict." Zimmerman snickered. "Now that wasn't very professional. Sorry."

He settled onto the sofa and patted the cushion. "Have a seat and get comfortable. You might have to be late. I have a few more questions."

I sighed and sat in the chair opposite him. He could

forget about Beatrice bringing refreshments. He could get his caffeine fix after he left, which I hoped would be soon.

He pulled a notebook from his pocket. "Tell me more about your ex."

"What?"

Zimmerman removed the cap from his pen and made a note. "For starters, how did he become your ex?"

"Divorce," I said, crossing my arms.

He looked over the top of his sunglasses. "That's standard. What led to the divorce? You cheat? He cheat? Or just irreconcilable differences?"

"I don't understand how this applies to your case," I said, letting the exasperation in my tone come through loud and clear.

He laughed. "Might be very relevant. Cheaters usually continue to cheat."

"Are you speaking from experience?"

I thought I saw a slight grimace, but he continued, "Do you think your ex was sleeping around on his bride-to-be?"

I put my hand to my mouth and feigned shock. "Why, Detective, that never occurred to me and doesn't concern me."

"So, he cheated?" He made another note in his book. "Excellent information. How about you? Were you and Alder a thing before your divorce?"

Alder would fry him for prying. "That is none of your business. But no, we were not a thing." We might not even be a thing now.

"Rumor has it you've helped Alder on his investigations. I heard you even got a commendation from the mayor for helping solve a case." Zimmerman flashed a smile.

With those glasses on, I couldn't tell if his smile reached his eyes. Was he fishing to discredit Alder?

"No," I said. "Alder's an outstanding detective. He doesn't need any help. I mean, my help. Not your help."

"Aww, don't be modest. I know you played an enormous part in solving the homicide at the school last year."

I puffed out my chest and sat straighter. "Well, I was at the school on a job, and people tend to confide in me."

"You must be a fantastic listener. That's the first thing they teach us in detective school." He sat back and rubbed his palms on his thighs.

Detective school, really? Who does he think he's talking to? "I'm sure you're very good at your job."

He stood up quickly, and I jumped.

"You're right, Ms. Cavanaugh. I am good at my job. I can smell a con job a mile away." He stared at me. At least, his reflective glasses stared at me. Who knew what his eyes were doing?

"I . . . I . . ."

"Ms. Cavanaugh, I can tell you one thing. Alder has the patience of a saint. I do not. There is no room in my investigation for a nosy woman." Zimmerman pulled off his glasses. This time his eyes bored into mine, and they were not smiling. "Do you understand where I'm going with this."

I nodded, wishing he'd put those glasses back on. If he wasn't so imposing, he'd be a handsome man, but his stare turned my spine into jelly.

"Just so we're clear, articulate the words for me."

Now he was just being a jerk and talking down to me. "I read you loud and clear, Detective. There's no need to be demeaning."

He continued to stare.

"Now you're being rude," I said. "Are we finished?"

"Not until you say the words. I want your assurance that you will not stick your nose into my investigation." Zimmerman slid his glasses on.

"No worries, Detective." On general principle, I would not repeat his words. This guy was not standing between me and a paid-off van. Even if he was intimidating. Every day the investigation lingered, the check for my van got smaller, but a paid-off van meant nothing if I were in jail. I'd have to rely on Nancy to continue the business without me. That was a scary thought.

I stood and walked to the door. "I'll see you out."

Zimmerman followed me. When he stepped over the threshold, he turned. "I will keep an eye on you, so do not disappoint me. I do not want to put you in jail, but I'm not above making your life miserable."

CHAPTER TWELVE

"Drama—who needs it? If I had known shooting Willow's wedding would cause so much drama, I would have said no."
Flick Donovan

After Zimmerman left, Felicity called and asked if I would meet her. She said she had an appointment in the neighboring town and could talk—around noon. I jotted down the address and told her I'd see her there.

At noon, I pulled up to the curb and parked outside the address Felicity had given me. She must have been waiting right inside because she immediately came out and hopped in my van.

"Hey," she said. "You got time to grab a bite? My lunch break is an hour. We can eat and chat. There's a yummy organic place down the street that just opened."

"Sure. Point me in the right direction." I hoped she had some useful information.

Three blocks later, Felicity motioned to an empty spot at

the curb in front of a cute brick building with a green-and-white-striped awning with outside seating on the sidewalk.

"Let's go inside," she said. "It gets noisy out here with the traffic, and I can't take the exhaust fumes."

Felicity pulled open the door. "The food here is exceptional." She weaved between tables and found us a spot in the back corner.

I slid into the booth. "Are you doing okay?" I didn't know what Felicity's support system was like, but I knew she was hurting. I didn't want to rush too quickly with my questions.

"It's hard. I've never lost a friend before." She unfurled her napkin and placed it in her lap. "It's like a piece of me disappeared. I didn't get to say goodbye."

"Have you been able to talk to the other girls? That might help."

"Not really. A text message here or there," she said.

"I know, for myself, I'd need that support. Being around your friends and talking about Kayla and your memories might be what you need to work through your grief. It might help the other girls too."

"You're right. I'll think about setting something up for us," she said.

"How long have you been modeling?" I asked, hoping to put her at ease.

"Since I was twelve. My mother was one of *those* mothers. She started me out in pageants when I was a toddler."

Felicity's pinched expression made me laugh. "I'm guessing you didn't enjoy the pageants," I said.

"Absolutely not."

"How is modeling different?" I asked.

"It wasn't when I was a kid, but I do it now because it's my choice."

I frowned. "Michelle, my youngest, has always been fascinated with modeling."

"You sound like you don't want to encourage her," she said.

"No offense, but I never saw it as a viable option."

"You should come out to a photo shoot and see what it's all about before you dismiss it entirely. Next time we have one close, I'll call you," Felicity said. "You might be surprised."

"Thanks. I'll think about it." It might be a good idea for me to see exactly what they did. Though, Michelle never stuck with anything too long, so I didn't think it was something to be concerned with. She still had high school graduation and college to get through.

"Were you aware Phillip's mother pulled some shenanigans with the wedding planning?"

Her sudden statement caught me off guard. "What do you mean?" I decided to play dumb. There were a few gaps I hoped she'd fill from Willow's perspective.

"She totally railroaded Willow's wedding. From the venue right down to the wedding flowers."

I thought about that for a moment. "Are you telling me Hazel and Willow didn't plan the wedding together?"

Felicity laughed. "Sure. That's what Mrs. Cavanaugh called it. It was more like she rode herd on Willow and browbeat her into all the decisions."

"I can't believe Hazel hired Sassafras and Sage. She has a caterer she always uses."

"No, Willow did that, and the photographer too."

"I don't understand."

Felicity sighed. "There was some snafu. Willow never shared the details, but I'd bet Phillip's mother was involved."

"So, Willow hired Sassafras and Sage and the photographer?" I asked. That didn't make any sense.

"She was lucky Sasha had an opening."

"What do you know about the flower order?" I asked.

Felicity nodded. "Willow blew up when the florist arrived with magnolia blossoms. She ordered gerbera daisies to match our dresses. I guess Mrs. Cavanaugh did that to spite her."

"Hazel is tough," I said.

Felicity pulled out two menus from behind the napkin holder and handed one to me. "I keep forgetting she was your mother-in-law too." A blush settled on her cheeks. "This must be horrible for you."

I waved a hand dismissively. "I'm over it. And Hazel is a handful. A little part of me feels sorry for Willow." In more ways than one. Not only would she get Hazel for a mother-in-law, but she would also get a man twice her age. Phillip took care of himself with exercise and fairly healthy eating habits, but his type A personality led to high blood pressure, and his father's side of the family had a history of diabetes. He didn't routinely smoke, but he indulged in the occasional cigar after he played golf. In the not-too-distant future, Willow would be taking care of an old man. If they lasted long enough.

"Did they reschedule the wedding?" I asked.

"Not yet. They're waiting for everything to blow over. Besides, trying to re-book their venue will be a nightmare this late."

A waitress brought us chilled water in a decanter and took our orders. I ordered a salad for me and one to take home for Nancy. When I pulled out my phone to send her a text, I saw a missed call with no voice mail from Alder.

Why were Alder and I suddenly not connecting? It was as if the universe was conspiring to keep us apart. A part of me felt good that he was still calling and texting, but another part of me worried why he wasn't leaving messages. It wasn't like him to be so evasive. I thought about excusing myself to return his call, but Felicity was being so open, I didn't want to derail our conversation.

"You called the caterer by her first name. Are you acquainted with her?" I poured water into both of our glasses.

"We all go way back," she said.

I doubted that since none of them looked over twenty-five or twenty-six. "Did she go to college with you?"

Felicity giggled. "Not that far back. She and Gracelynn met on a photo shoot. Gracelynn invited her to hang with us, and the rest is history. She'd been part of our group until they had a falling out. Out of respect for our friendship with Gracelynn, we've kind of been avoiding Sasha."

"Until Willow needed her to cater the wedding," I said.

"Yeah, it seemed wrong, but Sasha had recently opened her restaurant and needed the work. Willow patched things up with her. Honestly, we acted a bit like mean girls, but Sasha didn't act like it bothered her."

I bet. I added Sasha to my suspect list, which continued to grow instead of shrink.

"What was the falling out about between Sasha and Gracelynn?" I asked.

"You didn't hear this from me, okay?" Felicity leaned closer.

I drew a line across my mouth, indicating my lips were zipped.

"Gracelynn has a bit of a jealous streak. Sasha fit in with our group, and it irked Gracelynn how well we all got along with Sasha."

"But—"

"I know. Gracelynn brought her into the group. When Sasha started getting the better modeling jobs, that sent Gracelynn over the edge. She lost one particularly coveted job to Sasha, and that was the end of the friendship. Shortly after that, Sasha got fired from Glow Girl."

"What happened?"

Felicity shrugged. "I don't know, but I heard Kayla might be involved."

I still had Gracelynn as my number one because of the man problem. Phillip was my number two, because he may have been the man. Initially, I wouldn't have pegged him as a murderer, but I hadn't pegged him as a cheater either. So, he stayed on my list, if for no other reason than spite. Willow, Sasha, and Felicity stayed on my radar too. I truly didn't believe Hazel had it in her to murder someone. Not physically, anyway. She mutilated her victims with words and threats. Hazel's weapon of choice was her tongue. If she were a killer, she would have bumped me off a long time ago.

Our server set our lunches in front of us and said, "Enjoy. If we can get you anything else, let me know."

Felicity had ordered a small plate of plain greens and picked at them with her fork.

"I'm curious," I said. "The day of the wedding, Kayla got sick and died. Later Hazel fell ill, then you showed symptoms of illness." I leaned across the table so my words would not drift to the adjacent tables. "Do you suppose it was something you ate? Sasha catered the brunch at the spa. Did she cater the rehearsal dinner too?"

"Yes, both events. But if food caused it, would others have gotten sick? And your former mother-in-law didn't attend the spa brunch."

Good questions. We ate in silence while I pondered her questions.

"Was there any food or hors d'oeuvres out for the wedding party before the wedding started?"

"No," Felicity said. "And that set Phillip's mother off. Honestly, that woman is a tyrant. Willow has her hands full."

"What can you tell me about the photographer?" I asked.

Felicity jabbed at a leaf of lettuce. "Flick? He's a creeper."

"Really? Why would Willow ask him to photograph her wedding?" I asked.

"Now there's the question." She dipped a forkful of lettuce into a small container of salad dressing. "I suppose she was desperate. Flick's a brilliant photographer if you can put up with his grabbiness. I guess she figured Phillip would deck him if he got out of line at the wedding."

"If he's such a creep, why does your modeling agency keep using him? Surely, there are complaints." Flick Donovan moved higher up my suspect list. If he was grabby with these women, no telling what he'd do if one of them turned him down or, worse, reported him.

"He's the best photographer in the area. All the agencies compete for him, so we don't get a choice. Glow Girl calls the shots, and if we want to work, we go to the photographer they use."

"Any chance you can get Gracelynn to talk to me? I stopped by the café where she works, and she ducked out the back door." I forked in one last bite of salad and chased it with a swig of tea.

"She's an odd one. Call her. It probably wasn't a good idea to surprise her." Felicity scribbled down a number on a scrap of paper and handed it to me. "Here's her cell. But don't be shocked if she won't talk to you. She's not a talker, and she's loyal to Willow—when she's not mad at her. With you being Phillip's ex-wife, she probably thought talking to you would be disloyal to Willow. Try her and see. If you don't have any luck, I'll see what I can do."

———

My investigation wandered all over the place. Too many suspects and no concrete clues. Nancy was still lounging in my great room when I returned home.

"How's the ankle?" I asked, placing the takeout container on the end table.

In answer, she wiggled her foot. "It's feeling better. Thanks for lunch. I'm starving."

I went to my office, formerly Phillip's den, and called Alder. Instead of him picking up, I got voice mail. "Alder, what's going on? This isn't like you. I'm worried."

Next, I called Gracelynn. When she answered, I jumped in. "Please don't hang up."

"Who is this?"

"It's Cece Cavanaugh. I just had lunch with Felicity, and she gave me your number."

"She told you to call me? I don't believe you. What do you want?"

"Just to talk. I promise. Phillip knows I'm doing this. He asked me to help. I won't take a lot of time. Please." I laid it on thick, hoping she'd reconsider.

"Not while I'm working," she said.

"You name the place. I'm in Wickford, but I can drive into the city."

"Meet me in the Barney's parking lot. I'll be there at six."

Driving into the city during rush hour made my stomach churn.

Wickford's only traffic problem occurred when someone, usually old man Giffey, Wickford's only taxi driver, went on a bender and knocked down a stop sign at one of the intersections around the town square.

I waited twenty minutes for Gracelynn to show up. When I went inside, Viv handed me a note.

I'm sorry. I can't do this to Willow. It doesn't feel right. I'm going to talk to her and, if she's okay with it, then I'll talk to you.

Crap! I called Phillip to let him know he needed to tell Willow what he'd asked me to do or else Gracelynn would never talk to me. Then, I sent Gracelynn a text and never heard back. Since I was in the city anyway, I drove over to Sassafras and Sage, hoping to have a chat with Sasha. As I drove down Charter Street, I passed a photography studio and saw the photographer from the wedding standing at a door laden with cameras.

He'd said Phillip and Willow's wedding was the first one he'd shot. The sign over the door said F. D. Photography.

I parked at the curb and raced up the sidewalk. "Excuse me," I said.

He turned around. "Sorry, I'm closed."

"I'm Cece Cavanaugh from the wedding the other day. We shared a table, remember?"

He looked at me with bored eyes. "How could I possibly forget?"

"Do you have a minute?"

"Lady, I've put in a full day here. Haven't eaten since breakfast and I'm running on empty." He juggled the cameras and finished locking the door. "You can call tomorrow if you want to make an appointment."

I had him within my grasp. I couldn't afford to let him go. "How about I buy you dinner?" My budget was hardly in the range where I could afford to be buying people dinner. It wasn't like I could write it off as a business expense, but I had the coupon from Sassafras and Sage that Sasha had given me.

He took in a deep breath then exhaled. "Your treat?"

I nodded. "If I get to pick the place."

"I never turn down a free meal. What's your pleasure?"

———

When we were seated in Sassafras and Sage, I leaned in. "I didn't realize the other day that you knew the wedding party."

"What of it?" he asked.

We'd ordered, and the server had brought our drinks. I

knew he had a soured relationship with Sasha. She'd made that clear Saturday when we were sequestered in the garden at the club. It occurred to me that he might be involved with the other women. He could be the man Kayla and Gracelynn fought about. All along I'd thought it was Phillip.

Now that I had Flick Donovan here, what could I ask without spooking him? This was where my lack of experience as an investigator put me in a precarious situation.

"It was lucky for Willow you had an opening to shoot the wedding," I ventured.

"Didn't turn out so lucky, if you ask me." He stabbed a piece of steak and jabbed it in his mouth.

"True. At the wedding, you said Willow's was the first wedding you had ever shot. What type of photography do you do?"

He finished chewing, took a swig of beer, and said, "Clothing."

"Clothing?"

"Yeah, high-end clothing. Advertising."

"Ah, so you're photographing models wearing the clothing?"

He laughed. "That's usually the way it works. A dress displayed on a hanger doesn't have a lot of appeal. Would you give a dress a second glance if you saw it in a magazine without a model wearing it? It's my job to make the pieces as attractive as possible."

"Do you have any ads I'd recognize?"

"If you've ever looked at a fashion magazine, you've seen my ads. Only the big names. You won't see my ads on a park bench or the side of a bus. I shoot only top-notch models. It's in my contract. They have to meet a certain criterion to model these designers."

Willow is a top-notch model? "Makes sense to me. Is that how you know Willow and her wedding party?"

He narrowed his eyes. "Yeah, they've all modeled for me. Why?"

"No reason. I wondered why you accepted a job as a wedding photographer."

"Nothing but a favor for Willow." Donovan paused. "The detective already talked to me. He warned me about you."

"I'm not doing this for myself. I'm doing this for the family. He has no authority to stop me from asking questions." I crossed my fingers and hoped that was true. "A favor, if you will."

"Sounds shady to me."

This guy was tough, but I was tougher. At least I hoped I was. "Look, I know you must like Willow if you're willing to photograph her wedding. All I'm trying to do is clear my family and hers with it. Assuming you have nothing to hide, what does it hurt to help?"

He raised both hands in a surrendering motion. "Okay, but if this comes back to bite me, I'll rat you out to the cops. Her photographer canceled last minute, and she begged. You've seen her. She's gorgeous. How could I tell her no? Besides, I wanted to use the wedding photos in my portfolio. Not that I want to shoot weddings, but shooting bridal gowns for top designers is big money."

"From what I've been told, the photographer didn't cancel," I said.

"Umm, didn't matter. Willow asked. I obliged. Friends do that." He pushed his plate away. Elbows on the table, he rested his face in his hands and gave me the once-over. "Why you are so interested in what I do?"

"No reason, really. It's just intriguing. When I was younger, I had given some thought to modeling." *Not.*

He laughed out loud, a belly laugh that captured the attention of nearby tables. When he settled down, he said,

"Have you seen the women who model for me? They live on carrot sticks and celery."

Now he'd hurt my feelings. "You don't have to be so blunt."

"Sorry. You seem like a pleasant lady, very attractive, but believe me, modeling is not your jam. First, you aren't tall enough. Even if you'd been thin enough back in your day, you don't have the height or bone structure to pull off fashion modeling."

Now it was my turn to be blunt. "Do you ever date your models?"

He had just taken a slug of beer and choked. After a round of coughing, he said, "What? Why would you ask that?"

"Oh, come on. The gals in Willow's wedding are gorgeous. You mean to tell me you've never been tempted? If I remember correctly from the wedding, you and Sasha had a thing."

"Yeah, we might have. My personal life is none of your business," Donovan said.

"Has she ever modeled for you?" I asked.

"Yes. Sasha and I had a thing. She wanted commitment, and I didn't. Unfortunately, she became bitter about it. She reported me to Glow Girl, the modeling agency I shoot for. It got ugly. I'm in the middle of negotiating a new contract with them, and she's made it very difficult."

"Were you ever involved with any of the other women?" I asked.

His face turned scarlet. "How is this helping? I think we need to wrap this up."

I had hit a nerve. He had a track record.

Sasha walked in the front door of the restaurant laden with packages. She stopped and glanced around the room. When she saw Flick and me, she trotted right to our table.

"Get out!" she yelled, lashing out at him. "You are not welcome here."

She turned to me. "It can't be a coincidence you were at the wedding—now you're here with Flick."

The diners at the nearby tables had stopped eating and were staring at us.

Flick gathered his camera gear and stood. "Don't get all twisty, darlin'. I'm leaving." He threw two twenties on the table, bent and kissed Sasha on the cheek, and left before she realized what had happened.

"Hey, wait. I told you'd I'd pay." I grabbed the bills and held them up, but he was already out the door.

I left the money on the table for our server, slid from the booth, and headed for the door. When I reached for the door handle, I felt a hand on my shoulder.

"Wait!" Sasha said. "What's this all about? Tell me what's going on. Why were you in here with Flick?"

I turned. "I had some questions about Saturday."

"What kind of questions?"

"About Kayla's death. Phillip asked me to look into what happened to her. Maybe you can help since you were there and knew her. Can we talk?"

"Are you with the police department?" she asked.

"No, I'm doing this on my own at the request of the family."

Sasha glanced around the restaurant. Her outburst at Flick had garnered the attention of diners. She motioned to a small hallway. "Let's go back to my office."

I followed.

She sat down behind a perfectly cleared desk, and I marveled at her tidiness. My desk looked like a tornado-ravaged cornfield.

"Thanks for taking the time to talk to me." I settled in a chair across from her desk.

"It's not like you gave me much choice. I needed you out of my dining room, and I wanted an explanation for why you and Flick were here. This was the obvious choice."

"I know this is strange—"

"Strange does not explain why you were here with Flick Donovan." Sasha pushed up the sleeves of her cardigan and leaned forward. "He's pond scum."

"Phillip, and by extension Willow, asked me to look into what happened to Kayla. I've got some theories, but they are slowly being proven incorrect, so I'm struggling."

"I don't understand. Are you a private investigator? How do you fit into this, other than being Phillip's ex-wife? Honestly, when I learned you were Phillip's ex, I was curious why you were even at the wedding." She laughed. "It's not like Willow is a big fan of yours."

I rolled my eyes. "That goes double for me. But that's not why I'm here. I have a knack for investigation. Phillip doesn't want the family name associated with this investigation, and frankly, neither do I. I have two daughters and a business to worry about. As a business owner, you have to appreciate that."

"How can I help?"

"Obviously there are some bad feelings between you and Donovan," I said.

"Yeah, no hiding that. He's a commitment-phobe."

"Was that all there was to it?" I asked.

Sasha crossed her arms and leaned back in her chair. "I'm jealous of my own friends. What can I say? He took Grace-lynn out a couple of times after we broke up, and I hated it. I couldn't stand to see him fawning over her. I hated it so much that when the opportunity came along for the restaurant, I hopped on it. It belonged to my aunt. When she died, she left it to me. I continued at Glow Girl until I was sure I could support myself, then I left. Flick kept coming around trying to get back with me, but I told him we were done unless he could commit. I wanted more than a boyfriend. I wanted a future."

"You left Glow Girl of your own accord?" I asked.

"Sure. They were very understanding and said if the restaurant didn't succeed, I'd be welcome to come back. I enjoyed working there. I just needed to put some distance between me and Flick. This restaurant was the perfect opportunity."

I thought about what Felicity had said. "You didn't get fired from Glow Girl?"

She laughed. "Felicity or Gracelynn must have spread that rumor. Felicity dated him a while ago and has never gotten past their breakup. Jealousy is a horrible trait. And it runs rampant at Glow Girl."

"Did your breakup with Flick have anything to do with Kayla or Gracelynn?"

"I told you my issue with Flick was commitment." Tears welled in Sasha's eyes and she swiped them away. "Do you think he had something to do with Kayla's death?"

"That's what I'm trying to piece together. I first assumed that Kayla died from alcohol poisoning."

"No." Sasha wagged her finger. "She's not a drinker."

"Several people saw her staggering at the spa and at the club, including the club bartender. You were serving drinks. Any chance she was getting the drinks mixed up?"

"Absolutely not. I served all the drinks at the spa." Sasha's cell phone vibrated, and she stole a glance. "How much longer?"

"I'll hurry. What about at the club? You were in the banquet room when I saw you. Did you have any helpers outside where the drinks were?"

"No, but I marked the decanters to eliminate mix-ups." She glanced at her phone again and sighed.

"Something killed Kayla. Felicity and my former mother-in-law became violently ill the day of the wedding, presumably from the same thing."

Sasha stiffened and pushed her chair back. "Are you accusing me of something?"

"Oh my gosh, no. I wanted your help to determine what might have happened. I have a medical background—former nurse. I don't know for certain, but I believe Kayla was poisoned, as were the two others." I weighed my next words. "I'm trying to determine where the poison was introduced. The only place they all have in common was the day of the wedding. But that doesn't mean it wasn't given to Kayla and Felicity earlier. And the common places were the rehearsal, the spa day, and the country club. You catered all three places."

"So, you *are* accusing me?" Sasha's voice grew shrill. "I could never hurt Kayla."

"No, calm down. We're talking common points of entry. Let's put that aside for a minute and concentrate on Kayla and Felicity. I'm assuming you don't know Hazel, my former mother-in-law."

"I just met her Saturday, and I hope to never deal with her again. She constantly made snide remarks about everything. She didn't like that I hadn't served iced tea. She wanted appetizers for the wedding party. Who does that? What bride wants to eat while she's having photos taken?

"There is something odd. It may not even be connected. A few months back, right after I opened the restaurant, Felicity and Gracelynn convinced me to let Flick use the restaurant for a photo shoot. He liked the rustic, earthy vibe and thought it would go great for a Victorian line of lingerie he was shooting. We were still on speaking terms back then. I wasn't modeling, but he convinced me to let him shoot a couple of poses of me. We were all here: Felicity, Willow,

Kayla, and Gracelynn. There was a huge dust-up between Kayla and Felicity."

"Interesting. What was it about?" I asked.

"Flick. Everything was always about Flick. He caused so much tension between everyone." Sasha sighed. "That's why he wasn't at the rehearsal dinner. He told Willow he had another commitment, but I had told him to stay away. That's why I was so surprised to see him here. He knows how I feel, yet he still came. He's incorrigible."

Her phone chimed again, and she glanced at the screen. "Can you excuse me a minute? I need to take care of something."

"Sure. Want me to wait here?" I asked.

She nodded and left.

While I waited, I called Alder again. Like always lately, I got his voice mail.

"Hey, it's Cece. We need to talk." I disconnected. Instead of spiraling down a hole of suspicion and resentment, I reviewed what I'd learned so far. The one person I kept coming back to was Flick Donovan. He seemed to be at the center of all the conflict with these women. Perhaps he had killed Kayla and attempted to kill Felicity, with Hazel being collateral damage. What better way to get rid of people than to have them all in the same place? Then Sasha would look like the guilty party if, in fact, her catering was what had poisoned everyone. If Sasha had reported Flick to Glow Girl, he could be setting her up to take the fall for Kayla. That would be a heck of a way to even the score.

Sasha returned, carrying a small device, a frown on her face. "I have to cut you short. I'm sorry, but I have to deal with this." She held the device aloft. "I had a leak in the restroom's ceiling, and my contractor found this."

"What is it?" I asked.

She collapsed in her chair. "It's a camera. Someone

planted a camera in my restroom. Someone has been spying on my customers, invading their privacy."

"That's creepy," I said.

"I need to make a call to find out what my liability is and how I can figure out who put it there." Her face puckered. "This is just too much. First Kayla. Now this."

"It's possible it was there before you bought the restaurant. Is it functional?"

"What is certain is it wasn't here when I bought the restaurant. Someone has hidden it since I've been here. I had all the ductwork cleaned when I moved in, and it wasn't there then. Can you excuse me? I really need to take care of this."

I stood. "Sure. If you think of anything else that might help, I would appreciate it if you'd call me."

She was already tapping a number into her phone and my words went unheard.

CHAPTER THIRTEEN

"My ex-wife is never satisfied. If you give Cece a hundred dollars, she wants two."
Phillip Cavanaugh

I had yet to figure out where Hazel came from when Michelle and I had seen her staggering up the sidewalk at the club. Now that I no longer had a membership, I didn't have access to the grounds, and Geoff wouldn't let me in unescorted.

I sat in my van in the Highland Park Country Club parking lot, tapping the steering wheel, waiting for Phillip to show. The only way I could access the club was to be the guest of a member, and those people were Phillip's friends and business associates. Their wives, my former friends, were the ones who had abandoned me after Phillip left. I would not ask one of them. Angie and Dave had never opted for country club life, so asking them wasn't an option.

I either had to get into the club after-hours or get someone to go with me. Two years ago, the club had experienced a series of break-ins and had increased security. I had been on the security committee at the time. We'd hired a firm to patrol the grounds after-hours. There was no way I wanted to tangle with those guys. Each guard was armed and made rounds with a trained attack dog.

I might have learned nothing about initiating an investigation and what trouble to avoid, but sheer logic told me that, at forty-nine, I was no match for a German shepherd trained to sniff out intruders. The alternative was Phillip. He was the one who asked me to snoop, so he'd be the one to get me access. The thought set my nerves on edge. I had no desire to be around him, but having the van free and clear and being able to keep Beatrice employed made the decision easier.

I had almost given up when he wheeled his Porsche in and parked next to me.

"I swear," he said as he exited his car, "that van gives me a headache. Couldn't you have chosen a more refined color scheme?"

"Yes, I could have, but I love it just the way it is," I lied. Truth was, I didn't care for the hot pink with lime green lettering, but I loved that it irritated him and his mother. The colors were vibrant, and the van stood out—a brilliant advertising strategy. And I loved seeing the Cavanaugh name in brilliant lime green. It brought a smile to my face.

"Before we do this, I want to add something to the deal," I said.

Phillip growled. "I don't think so. You're already pushing your limit."

I turned around and took a step toward my van. "I'm done. Figure this out yourself. Zimmerman's on to me. The longer I'm involved, the more I put myself at risk."

When he didn't respond, I continued walking. "I'm leaving."

"Fine. Okay." Phillip caught up to me. "What do you want?"

"Beatrice," I said.

"You already have Beatrice."

"Your mother cut off funding. The agency called Beatrice and told her this was her last week."

"I'll talk to Mother," Phillip said.

"No, I don't want her involved. You call the agency and extend Beatrice's time."

"You're killing me."

I rolled my eyes. "Do it for Michelle."

Phillip laughed. "For Michelle? That's a stretch."

"Since I've gone back to work, the house gets lonely. Beatrice being there gives me peace of mind knowing Michelle isn't coming home to an empty house." I laid it on thick. Michelle and Beatrice got along great, and it put me at ease not having to worry about what my teenager was doing when I wasn't home. It wasn't a lie.

"She's seventeen. She doesn't need a babysitter," Phillip said.

"She's been in trouble before." I recited Michelle's shoplifting incident. "It's one less worry. Okay?"

Phillip raised his hands in surrender. "Okay."

I went for broke. "Hire her outright. Bypass the agency and give her a raise."

"Now you're pressing your luck. I'm not made of money."

"This isn't for me. This is for Michelle."

Phillip smirked. "I'll do it until fall when Michelle goes to school. Then you're on your own. How much housekeeping can one person need?"

"Fine," I said. It wasn't fine. I'd have to find a way to extend Beatrice longer. If not for me, for her. That was what I told myself. It was nice having her in the house. It was so big and so empty, and I dreaded Michelle leaving for college.

Sure, Nancy would still be there, but Beatrice lent a comforting feeling to my home, and I'd grown used to her presence.

"Why are we here?" Phillip asked as he pulled open the main door and walked through it ahead of me. Nothing new there.

"Where was Hazel when she disappeared at the wedding? And why did she leave?" I would put my head together with Beatrice to conjure an annual contract and at least get Phillip to commit to a year. That would give me a year to work out how to keep her employed.

"Disappear?" Phillip snickered. "That sounds devious. You're letting your imagination run wild."

I made a slicing motion across my throat. "Knock it off and help me figure this out. Hazel was nowhere to be found when Kayla showed up dead in the restroom. No one knew where Hazel was or what she was doing."

He sighed. "You sound like the police now. Detective Zimmerman is convinced Mother had something to do with Kayla's death. If you want me to stick to the agreement, you'd better get this squared away."

"I'm trying, but you've got to give me something to go on. The bartender saw Hazel with Kayla. That makes her the last person to see Kayla alive." I picked up my pace, trying to keep up with him. "If Hazel is innocent, we need to prove it."

"She went to the bathroom. Alone. Kayla left before Mother. It was purely a coincidence if they were in the bar together."

"The bartender said they were arguing and that your mother threw a punch at Kayla."

"Ha! That's funny," Phillip said.

Phillip was the master of denial where his mother was concerned. Hazel could have killed me at the dinner table in front of my entire family, and Phillip would have had an excuse for her.

"Where did your mother go? How did her dress get ripped? Why did the bartender say she was drunk? Something happened, and she's not telling the truth." The words spilled out and felt good. For thirty years, I'd wanted to give Phillip a piece of my mind about his mother, but she'd held such a grip over him and our marriage that I didn't dare. Divorce had liberated my tongue.

"You're accusing her of lying?" Phillip waved at the receptionist as we walked toward the dining room. She raised an eyebrow but said nothing.

I didn't answer.

I steered around him and headed out the door to the garden. I stopped and looked around, concentrating on the scene before me. "You were sitting over there," I said, pointing to a bench near the gazebo. "At what point did Hazel leave?"

Phillip glanced around and shrugged. "I told you, I don't know."

We walked to the spot where Hazel face-planted after staggering up the walk. "I've never been beyond the tennis courts. Have you?" I kept walking in the direction where Hazel had emerged.

"What's the point of this?" Phillip trudged beside me.

"Don't be a jerk. Let me do this my way. Okay?"

"You're right. Sorry."

The walkway meandered past the tennis courts, swerved back to the left, and headed to the other end of the club. I watched for signs of security cameras but didn't see any. "Will you ask Geoff if any of this area is under camera surveillance?"

Phillip scoffed. "Are you serious?"

I shot him my death stare. The one I'd used when the kids were little that offered instant death to anyone who defied my mom authority.

"Okay. Okay."

We continued down the twisting walkway. Large bushes grew along either side, providing a screen for anyone who ventured this way. The walkway ended abruptly at a small patio next to a door. The area contained a small outdoor table, four chairs, and a bench. Probably a smoking spot for the employees. From here, looking back the way we'd come, nothing was visible but foliage.

"Where does this go?" I twisted the door handle, but it didn't budge. I spotted a security camera fastened to the side of the building.

Phillip backed away and looked up, taking in the surroundings. "We're at the far end of the club. By the bathroom where you found Kayla."

I nodded.

"I suspect this door is in that hallway. Only one way to find out." Phillip took off at a rapid clip back to where we'd been, and I followed. He didn't stop until we were back inside, standing by a door in the hallway where the restroom was. "This door should open onto that patio." He hesitated.

"Why are you waiting? Open it." I pushed the handle, but he placed his hand over mine.

"Stop."

"Why?" I brushed his hand away. "I want to see if we're right."

"What if we are?" Phillip blocked the way. His eyes met mine, and I saw his anxiety. "Let's just leave. What does any of this prove?"

"Wait," I said, realization striking me. "I'm trying to prove your mother is innocent. Are you worried she might be guilty?"

Phillip sank to the floor and put his head in his hands. "Maybe. She's been off-the-hinges crazy since Willow and I announced the wedding."

Finally, he realized the measures Hazel would take to put a wrench in his plans. When she'd tried to sabotage our wedding all those years ago, he'd laughed. Made it sound like I was overreacting.

I cuffed him on the shoulder. "Get real. This is nothing new. Your mother has been manipulative her whole life."

I glanced around, stalling to let my thoughts fall into place. "If the bartender saw Hazel come through the bar, then she was in the building. How did she make it to the sidewalk where you found her if she didn't exit this door? No one saw her come back through, and I didn't pass her in the hall. And to get here, she had to walk right past the bathroom where I found Kayla."

Phillip stood, and his demeanor changed. The worry that had etched his face turned into anger. The vein in his temple twitched.

"Enough. I didn't ask you to help so you could accuse my mother of murder."

"Whoa! I'm not accusing her. I made an observation. I have to look at all sides of this and not leave anything out."

I pushed the emergency release bar on the door and stepped out, missing the fact that the walkway was several inches below the door's threshold. The difference in elevation brought me to my knees, and as I fell, I saw Detective Zimmerman.

"Not the exit I was expecting," Detective Zimmerman said. He rushed over and helped me to my feet.

Phillip stood in the doorway, his mouth hanging open.

"Where did you come from?" I demanded.

"I was in the parking lot two cars from where you parked. I figured when your ex pulled in, I needed to stick around." Zimmerman's smug expression made me want to punch him.

I limped to the bench and sat. "Aren't you special?"

"Now what, pray tell, brings you here?" Zimmerman looked at Phillip. "A little rendezvous of the exes?"

Phillip snorted.

Warmth trickled down my leg. I had ripped my capris and had a gash at my knee.

"Do you have a tissue?" Zimmerman asked.

I searched my purse and found a small packet and pressed a tissue to my knee.

"Let me look." The detective peeled away the tissue and examined the wound. "Superficial. Probably doesn't need stitches."

I jerked my leg away. "It's an abrasion. I'm fine." I gathered my wits despite my throbbing knee. "Let's go," I said to Phillip.

Phillip turned and started through the door.

"Not so fast, Daddy Moneybags. My instinct tells me you two were up to something, so give me the lowdown." Zimmerman stood his ground.

What did I have to lose? I explained my theory to him. Regardless of how I felt about Hazel, she didn't deserve to be a suspect for something she clearly didn't do. "Have you checked the surveillance camera for footage?"

A hint of a smile formed on the detective's face. He should practice smiling more often. "That's not the way this works. You don't get to ask questions, and I don't share what I've learned."

If that's the way you want to play this. I crossed my arms. "Then I have no more information to share."

"Works for me," the detective said. "Now I suggest you go home and leave the detecting to the professional."

"Hmmph!" I skirted past Phillip and entered the club.

"Don't make me tell you again, Ms. Cavanaugh," Zimmerman warned.

"Call Geoff when you get back to your office," I said when Phillip and I were at our cars. "Ask him if he has a copy of the security video."

CHAPTER FOURTEEN

"One of Cecelia's biggest flaws, among the many others, is sticking her nose in other people's business."
Hazel Cavanaugh

As much as I hated the idea, I had to talk to Hazel. Phillip gave in to her whims too easily, and he wouldn't ask her the hard questions. Hazel already despised me, so I had nothing to lose.

Phillip headed back to the office, and I headed to the Cavanaugh family home, Marymount. Pretentious or not, the Cavanaugh estate had its own name.

Marymount sat on the edge of Wickford on 125 acres of prime grape-growing property. I thought it ironic considering she didn't drink. Between the vineyards and the winery, Hazel had no money worries.

I still had a house key but opted to ring the bell. Ingrid, the housekeeper, answered the door with a shocked expression.

"Is Mrs. Cavanaugh expecting you?" she asked.

I shrugged. "No. Tell her I talked to Phillip, and it's important. She'll want to hear what I have to say."

She led me to the front sitting room and left to find the mistress of the house. Or was it matron? Either sounded better than old windbag.

Hazel had redecorated since the last time I'd been here. She binged every five or six years and changed up the entire house. This time she'd chosen a French provincial theme. I had to admit it was beautiful, and a tinge of jealousy coursed through my veins. I struggled every day to pay bills and keep my business afloat. She could redecorate four thousand square feet on a whim.

"What do you want?" Hazel's icy tone startled me.

I shook it off and remembered how much better I'd feel when the van payments were gone. "Nice to see you too."

A shadow of concern crossed her face. "Is everything okay with the girls?"

"They're fine." I leaped in feet first, putting the fake pleasantries aside. "We need to talk about Saturday. Phillip asked me to find out what happened at the club."

"By what occurred, I assume you mean the untimely death of that young woman." Hazel had assumed her battle stance —the one I was all too familiar with—both hands planted on her hips, feet slightly apart, and her face drawn into a stern mask. I wondered how Willow kept from cracking under Hazel's intimidating scowl.

I had several sarcastic replies, but under the circumstances, I took the high road. "Yes."

Ingrid appeared with a tray of hot tea and scones. My mouth watered. Hazel's cook made the best scones ever, and her homemade peach preserves were to die for. Back when I'd been a reluctant visitor, those treats were the only highlight of my visits.

Hazel waved a dismissive arm. "We won't be needing that."

My mouth turned into cotton. *Crap!*

Ingrid's cheeks turned bright pink. She mumbled an apology and left.

"What does Phillip want you to do?"

I eyed the sofa. "Can we sit down?"

Hazel sighed. "If we must." She sat in one of two antique wingback chairs.

I perched on the edge of the sofa, my insides quivering like a bad gelatin dessert.

"Spit it out. I don't have all day." She glanced at the Bulgari wristwatch Phillip and I had given her for her seventieth birthday.

I took a deep breath. "The bartender saw you follow Kayla to the bathroom. 'Staggered in after' was his exact wording."

Hazel bristled. "I—"

I held my hand up. "I know. I know. You don't drink, but what happened that day? Why did the bartender say you were drunk? I saw you when you fell on the walkway, right before Phillip came to get you. You were staggering. You ripped your dress. Several people claim to have heard you arguing with Willow and again with Kayla."

She glared. "I do not owe you or anyone else an explanation."

I laced my fingers across my forehead and massaged my temples with my thumbs. "Look, as hard as it is to imagine—even for me—I'm trying to help. Not for your sake, but for Jessie and Michelle. So, drop the self-righteousness and help me."

"Oh, all right. What do I have to lose?" Hazel leaned back and seemed to relax. Then she tensed. "I swear on all that is holy, if this gets back to the club, I will destroy you."

Bitsy and Mavis were the only two people Hazel had to worry about spreading rumors. Those biddies, including Hazel, had the waggiest tongues in town. Her only saving grace was if either of her friends squealed, she had enough dirt to take them out. I couldn't stand being in the same room with either of them, so me spilling the goods would not happen.

I waved my hand in the air. "You have bigger things to worry about. I'm the least of them." I enjoyed having something to hold over her head. Something, if juicy enough, I could hold over her head for the future.

"What is it you want?" Hazel asked.

"That's easy. What happened between the time you left the patio and the time Phillip found you?"

Her expression didn't change. She simply said, "I went inside."

I laughed. "You will need to expound on that. Why did you leave in the first place?"

"If I recall, I felt light-headed. I needed a change of scenery. This entire wedding had me on edge. Willow can be so . . ." Hazel snapped her head in my direction. "I don't see any purpose to this."

"Did you and Willow argue?" I pressed.

Hazel nodded. "She's persistent, that one."

"Did you cancel the caterer, photographer, and change the florist order to sabotage the wedding?" Knowing who Hazel canceled would make my job easier. I could scratch talking to her caterer off my list.

Hazel gave a wicked laugh. "That's what Willow would have you think? No, I did not. I canceled the caterer and the photographer because that little trollop snuck behind my back and hired her friends. I had to go into protection mode to save the Cavanaugh reputation. I use those services all the time, and I didn't want Willow ruining my reputation."

"Willow was responsible for that?"

"She came to me two weeks before the wedding and told me she had made other plans. I then had to call my caterer and photographer or else my reputation would have been hanging out on a limb. She ordered those cheap-looking daisies instead of the magnolia blossoms we had agreed on."

"But she had the magnolia blossoms at the wedding. You changed them back, didn't you?" I wanted her to admit it.

"Yes. I couldn't let her disgrace our name any more than she already had. Magnolias are elegant. Those daisies were low-class. I demanded the florist order the magnolias. And you know what Willow had the nerve to do?" Hazel asked.

"I can't imagine." I had a sneaking hunch where she was going with this.

"She had those flowers delivered to me—three giant bouquets." Hazel's penciled-on eyebrows rose to an indignant arch. "I had Ingrid toss them in the garbage, and I called Lillian, my friend who owns the florist, and told her if she ever wanted Cavanaugh business again, she had better think twice about doing business with Willow."

I opened my mouth in an *O* and feigned shock. Willow was getting even with Hazel without even knowing it.

Hazel continued, "Willow brought in her own caterer to do the buffet. We had agreed on a sit-down dinner, not a cafeteria line. After I had gone through all the trouble to arrange this ill-conceived event, she had the nerve to go behind my back."

I remembered my conversation with Phillip. The one where he told me Greta had called him when Hazel tried to cancel the bakery order.

"What happened with Oppenheimer's Bakery? Why didn't Willow's caterer have a cake?" Something wasn't right. Phillip suspected Hazel was the mastermind behind the cancellations, and here she was telling me it was Willow.

Hazel hadn't told Phillip, which was interesting because it would have been a perfect wedge to shove between him and Willow. Willow must have really hurt her pride.

"That was the piece Willow didn't have covered. We had hired Oppenheimer's in the beginning, and Willow couldn't cancel because her caterer doesn't do wedding cake."

"Greta said you called her, but she took it to Phillip who overrode you," I said.

Hazel laughed. "I wanted to give the little gold digger a taste of her own medicine. Figured I'd leave her hanging without a cake. But Greta had other plans. I must talk to her about that. I may never give her another order again for going behind my back to Phillip."

I was no longer the gold digger in the family. Unless Phillip had told her about our deal.

This whole cancellation thing was so convoluted, but something Hazel would do to get even for Willow changing providers.

"How come you left Phillip in the dark about this cancellation business?" I asked.

"Are you serious?" Hazel's pinched expression added to the disdain in her voice. "Phillip's in *lust*. You should know that better than me. My comments about that girl go in one ear and are quickly muffled by his lack of common sense. The man cannot be reasoned with."

Finding it hard to drum up any sympathy, I simply nodded.

Hazel continued to rail against Willow. I held up my hand to redirect attention.

"What?"

"Can we get back to what we were discussing? I'm sure you have better things to occupy your time." And I wanted to get out of here before I smacked her.

"Get on with it," she said.

"What do you remember about going back inside the club? The bartender said he saw the two of you arguing."

Hazel smirked. "Who didn't I argue with? First Phillip, for the absurdness of this entire event. Willow failed to have appetizers for the family and wedding party while we suffered through the dreadful photo-taking. Which, if you ask me, was ludicrous. You'd have assumed those women were on a photo shoot for a bridal magazine. I have never witnessed so much carrying on. It was disgraceful. Poor Michelle was not included. They let her sit on the side like some poor stepsister. On top of all that, Willow barked orders like she was the Queen of Wickford."

I laughed. We both knew who held that title. "What about Kayla?"

"Who?"

"The maid of honor," I said.

"No, we didn't argue per se. I went to the bar for a glass of water to take something for my headache. She ambushed me and told me to ease off Willow. I merely told her I had not been the one to start anything. Willow had an agenda." Hazel leaned forward. "If Phillip planned to go through with that marriage, I needed to set the record straight with that girl. I'll not have her upstaging me with my son or anyone else."

Right. "The bartender said you came in right behind Kayla. He said you took a swing at her."

Hazel narrowed her gaze. "I most certainly did not." She paused for a minute. "I've never struck anyone in my life. Why would I start now?"

"Uh, because you were angry," I said.

"I think I would remember hitting someone. I suspect I lost my balance and reached out for assistance. Yes, I'm sure that's what happened. Perhaps the bartender needs to have his eyes examined."

Yeah, perhaps you need to have your head examined. "When Kayla left, where did you go?"

"It's all fuzzy. I remember taking the aspirin, but that's where my memory doesn't seem to be working."

"Hazel, it's important to find out how you came to be on that walkway. You were nowhere around when I found Kayla, but the bartender saw you arguing with her."

Hazel bristled. "I was not arguing with her. Discussing. We had a discussion."

"Whatever. Phillip found you facedown on the walkway, coming from a different direction. You looked like you'd been in a drunken brawl. Did you fall?"

"I don't remember." Hazel snipped her words.

I raised the leg of my capris and showed her my knee. "I have a theory I want to run by you."

"Really, Cecelia. We've talked enough. I do not understand why you are even involved," Hazel said.

"Listen to me. There's a door past the restroom. I exited that door today. There's an enormous drop-off, which I didn't expect. I fell and scraped my knee. Is it possible you used that door?" I asked.

"It's possible."

"It would make sense considering where Phillip found you," I pressed.

"You're giving me a headache. We're done. Ingrid," Hazel said in a commanding voice.

She must have been standing outside the room because she appeared almost instantly. "Yes, ma'am?" she asked in a soft voice.

"Please show Cece to the door. We're through." Hazel stood and left the room, leaving me with my mouth agape.

"I can find my way out." I got to my feet and trudged to the door. Then I halted. "Wait. Go get her. I have another question."

The housekeeper narrowed her eyes. "You need to leave."

"No!" I insisted. I knew my way around the house and didn't need her help to find Hazel. When she zigged to cut me off, I zagged and sped around her. This time of day, Hazel took tea in her garden.

I stormed through the house, peering into rooms as I raced down the hallway on the off chance she hadn't gone to the patio.

She had.

"There you are," I said, stepping out the door.

Hazel gave me a death glare. "I told you I was done."

"I have one more question. After that, I'll leave you alone."

The housekeeper roared through the door, almost knocking me over. "Mrs. Cavanaugh, ma'am, I'm so sorry."

"Leave us alone, Ingrid," Hazel said with resignation in her voice.

She motioned for me to sit down in a lounge chair. "What is with you, Cecelia? You need to leave well enough alone."

"I can't," I said. *I have a paid-off van on the line, you witch.* "I initially concluded Kayla died of alcohol poisoning, but Phillip said she didn't drink."

"Yes, that's why they served virgin mimosas." Her bored tone indicated I needed to get to the point or risk an unwanted departure.

It hit me in an instant. "O-m-g! I've been thinking all along she died of alcohol poisoning, but that's not it."

"You're repeating yourself," Hazel said.

"There was a frothy substance around her mouth. She was poisoned but not by alcohol."

Hazel leaned forward. "Interesting."

"Kayla had been acting like she'd had too much to drink. You also had an episode where you appeared to be drunk—"

"I was not intoxicated."

I held up my hand. "I know. But you remember that other bridesmaid got sick while we were waiting in the garden for the detective to show up." All the pieces were falling into place.

"Yes."

"Somehow you all ingested the same poison. That's the common link. Did the caterer serve any hors d'oeuvres to the wedding party before the wedding started?"

"No."

"No?" I asked.

"No. No food of any sort," Hazel said.

"That blows my theory," I said. "Willow had a buffet set up at the spa."

"At the spa? Who does that? What is wrong with her?" Hazel blew out a breath. "I'll never be able to show my face in there again."

"Calm down. That's not the point. I'm trying to pin down what all of you had in common. You weren't at the spa, so it had to be the day of the wedding or at rehearsal dinner."

"Well, you narrowed it down even more. I didn't attend the rehearsal. Do you even know what you're doing, Cecelia, because I'm losing patience with you."

I shrugged, beginning to think this was a losing battle, and I was wasting my time. Michelle, Beatrice, and my van were the only things keeping me going. I needed a fresh angle.

"Okay, Kayla got sick first, and whatever it was affected her worse. You were the next one to get ill, next the brides-maid. As far as we know, it affected no one else." I leaned back in the lounger and closed my eyes, trying to piece it all together. "You and Felicity recovered. Did Kayla ingest more or what?"

I sat there with my eyes closed. I heard a bird twittering in the distance and Hazel's foot tapping on the patio. I concentrated on letting the sounds fall away, waiting for silence to fill my mind.

"Excuse me, ma'am. May I refresh your drink?" The housekeeper interrupted the stillness.

My eyes fluttered open. "The drinks."

Hazel and Ingrid stared at me.

"Shall I bring another glass?" Ingrid asked.

"No." I waved her off. "It had to be the drinks. Only it makes little sense."

"Go on. We're fine." Hazel shooed her off. "What are you talking about?"

I sat up and twisted around in my chair to face Hazel. "The poison was in the mimosas. Willow's caterer served mimosas at the spa the morning of the wedding, and she served them before the wedding at the club. Did you drink anything before you got sick?"

Hazel's eyes widened. "Yes. Several virgin mimosas. It was warm out, and that caterer Willow hired didn't even have the decency to have water or iced tea out for us. Who doesn't offer their guests a selection?"

"Hmm."

"Why didn't the other girl or I die?" Hazel shivered.

"If I had to guess, I'd say she served them at the rehearsal dinner too. You already said you weren't at the dinner, and you weren't at the spa. Maybe Felicity didn't drink any until the morning of the wedding."

"Willow tried to poison all of us? Killed her maid of honor?"

I saw a glint of hope in Hazel's eyes, and it was my pleasure to douse her dream. If I was right, Willow wouldn't be spending any time in the Big House. I couldn't help myself for what I said next. "I can see where she might have it in for you, but why would she want to kill her best friend or make the other one sick?"

Hazel sneered. "Who did it then?"

I tapped my forehead with my index finger. "That's what I intend to find out. It either has something to do with modeling or with that photographer. All those girls are connected by their modeling careers and that photographer. And there's always Phillip."

"What are you implying?" Hazel pointed a finger at me. "You are not accusing my son, are you?"

I wasn't, but I loved messing with her. "Could be. Was he screwing around with the maid of honor?"

"Get out. Now!" Hazel screamed.

"Gladly," I said. "Oh, by the way, do you think Willow is pregnant?"

CHAPTER FIFTEEN

"Wickford is getting a lot of unsavory characters. I'll be keeping a report of the bad eggs."
Velma Quigley

I drove back to the house to pick up Nancy, pleased with myself for frustrating Hazel. My only concern was Phillip. I had texted him immediately after I left to tell him what had happened. I hadn't thought out my accusation, and I didn't need Hazel messing up my deal with Phillip. Lucky for me, he laughed it off, because it could have gone so wrong.

Nancy sat on my front porch. When I pulled into the drive, she beat a hasty path to the van.

"What's up?"

"Are you up for another surveillance mission?" I asked.

Nancy rubbed her hands together deviously. "Are we going to cruise past Alder's house again?"

"Only if you drive."

After switching vehicles, we headed toward Alder's neighborhood.

"You sure you're up for this?" Nancy flicked the visor down to block the sun.

"It's now or never. He's texted me many times and left several messages. We haven't been able to connect. I'm dying to know what's going on and why we keep missing one another," I said.

We were silent on the way over. Me, thinking about what I would do when we arrived. Nancy, who knew what she was thinking?

Nancy barreled onto Alder's street, driving several miles over the posted speed limit.

I grabbed the door handle to keep from sliding out of the seat. "Jeez, slow down."

Nancy slammed the brakes. The Jeep came to a halt in front of Alder's neighbor's house.

"Good grief." I slunk down. "Don't stop here for cripe's sake."

Nancy jammed the gas pedal, and the Jeep lurched forward. "Make your mind up."

At the end of the block, Nancy stopped. "Well?"

"Well, what?" I sat up straight.

"You wanna go back again?"

"Yes. Drive normal this time. I didn't see anything because I was hunkered down in the seat."

A light tap on the window scared the tar out of me. It was the old woman with the rat dog.

"You ordering pizza again?" she asked through the glass.

"No." I rolled the window down. "Just passing through."

"Looks like you're casing the neighborhood." She picked the dog up and shoved it into her pocket. "Just so's you know, I have one of them doorbells that will take your picture if you go messing around. You better steer clear of my house or else."

Nancy laughed. "Or else what? Your rat gonna bite me and give me rabies?"

The old woman sneered at Nancy and pulled a flip phone from her pocket. She punched in a number and waited.

I rolled my eyes at Nancy. "Come on. Let's go."

"No, wait. If she's calling her geriatric husband, this could be fun," Nancy said.

"We got us a minor problem in the neighborhood." She paused. "Hi, Detective Alder, it's me, Velm—"

"Nancy, get out of here. Now!" I screamed.

Nancy hit the gas and off we went, me clinging to the door handle, and Nancy screaming at the top of her lungs. She didn't even slow down until we hit Main Street.

"He answered her call," I said. "He answered the rat lady's phone call. Every time I call him, it goes to voice mail. He is definitely avoiding me."

"Probably," Nancy said. "But that was kind of fun. You wanna go back?"

———

I did not want to go back. I wanted to know why Alder wasn't answering my phone calls. The last time down his street, while Nancy was flying at breakneck speed, I saw his truck parked in the driveway and his police vehicle parked at the curb. Unless she'd parked in the garage, Becca's car was not there.

"Any sign of the ex-wife?" Nancy asked.

I took several deep breaths, willing my heart to stop racing. "Who could tell? I was too worried about being seen."

"Meh! So what? You want to find out what's going on, right?"

Nancy turned into my driveway and parked next to a car I didn't recognize.

"Yes." I peered into the car and it was empty.

"If you can't get him to answer the phone, you need to march right up to his front door and give him what for." Nancy cackled. "I'll be right behind you."

"Yeah, egging me on all the way. What if Joyce is there or Becca? How awkward would that be?" I slammed the car door and headed up the walk.

"At least you'll know if he'll answer the door. May not be the answer you want." Nancy caught up to me. "What answer do you want?"

Before I could ponder the question, I stepped onto my porch and saw Willow standing beside one of the twin rocking chairs.

She held her hand up and took a step back. "Before you get mad, hear me out."

The last person I wanted to deal with today, or any day, was Willow.

I launched into her. "How dare you tell everyone I assaulted you at the spa. That's not true. You were the one stalking me while I was with *my* daughter, and by the way, her name is Michelle. Not Shelly."

"I'm sorry. I'm sorry. The whole thing sort of spiraled out of control. Can we talk?" Willow pleaded.

Nancy leaned in closer, chomping on a wad of bubblegum. "This should be interesting. Old versus new."

I gave her the stink eye. "Don't you have something to do?"

Nancy blew a bubble and let it pop. "Nah, I don't think so."

"Sure, you do. Go work on our schedule."

"What sched—"

I narrowed my gaze and set my mouth in a firm line.

"Oh, that schedule. Okay, I'll get to work on it, boss."

Nancy clipped her words, and I instantly regretted my attitude.

After Nancy trudged into the house and let the door slam, I turned to Willow. "Does Phillip know you're here?"

She shook her head. "No. What does that matter?"

"Just curious." I thought about Phillip coming on to me at the spa and briefly felt sorry for her. It passed. She knew what she was getting into, and if she didn't, she'd soon find out. Phillip wouldn't stop cheating; of that, I was sure.

Tears sprang to her eyes. "He told me he asked you to look into Kayla's death. My friends told me you've been asking questions."

I nodded toward the rockers. "You're here. You might as well sit down."

"I can't believe she's gone." She blinked rapidly but didn't hide the tears that were beginning to form. "Have you found anything?"

I struggled with what information to tell her. "Not much. I'm still talking to people. I have a question for you."

Willow hiked an eyebrow. "Yeah?"

"What do you know about the caterer and the photographer you hired?"

She winced and looked away. "Why?"

"Humor me, okay?"

"Sasha and I have done modeling jobs before. She recently left the agency. That's when she opened her restaurant and catering business."

"Did she quit or was she let go?"

"She quit. Why?" Willow asked.

"Just curious. All of you worked for the same agency. Modeling?"

"Yes, how does this relate to Kayla's death?"

"I don't know, yet. How about the photographer?" My left

eye twitched from being nice. I wanted to gut-punch her, not act like her best bud.

"Flick?" She paused. "He's the best photographer around. If you need to add photos to your portfolio, you hire him. All the quality ad companies use him too."

"He ever date any of the models?"

A blush spread across her cheeks.

"I'll take that as a yes. Who did he date?"

She frowned. "I wouldn't call it dating. Well, maybe with Felicity."

"She's the bartender, right?"

Willow nodded. "They were in a relationship for over a year. He moved on to Sasha, but that didn't last long, and it didn't stop him from hitting on other girls."

Sounded like Phillip. Only he had been married for almost thirty years and continued to embark on affair after affair. A part of me wanted to pity Willow. I was sure Phillip would not stop his catting around after they got married. The other part of me hoped she got to experience being cheated on and lied to.

"Did Kayla ever have a thing going on with him?"

"I know he went with Gracelynn after Sasha broke up with him. I don't recall Kayla ever mentioning it. Doesn't mean she didn't, though."

"How long since he and Felicity split up?" I asked.

She thought for a moment. "Six months. He acted all broken up about it, but he returned to his old ways. It was almost a running joke about who Flick would be with next."

"So Sasha came after Felicity?" I wished I had a notebook to write all this down. Keeping these names straight was killing me, but I didn't want to interrupt and take a chance she'd stop talking.

"Yeah. Sasha, I think, and then Gracelynn. Or maybe he didn't go out with Gracelynn. I don't remember."

With all the dumping going on, I was sure there was a motive in there. But sounded to me like Flick would have been the victim. Though, Sasha looked like an excellent target if all the dumpees were blaming her rather than Flick. Any of these women, including Felicity, could have been doing a slow burn waiting for the right time to strike, and what better place than at a wedding where they were all present.

I tamped down my feelings for Willow, who sat on my porch talking about infidelity. It hadn't mattered to her that Phillip had been married with a family. She just set her sights on him and mowed down everyone in her path. Not that I was bitter.

But in hindsight, it took two. Willow wasn't the only one to blame for destroying my marriage. And if truth be told, I was happier now than when Phillip and I were together. I just hadn't known it.

"Cece?"

I looked up, realizing I had gotten lost in my thoughts. "Sorry, where was I?" I willed myself to get through this. If I did, I vowed never to cross paths with Willow again. I thought about Alder and his ex-wife. A different situation. They split long before I entered the picture, but did my presence inhibit them from getting back together? Apparently not. The smart thing to do would be to step away before I got hurt. But I feared it was too late. My heart felt heavy with fear, anxiety, and sadness.

"We were talking about Flick," she said.

"There's one oddity that puzzles me." I paused and turned to face her. "Kayla got sick and died. Hazel appeared to be drunk and had a tumble in the garden. When we were all seated, awaiting the detective, Felicity got sick. How do you account for half of your wedding party and Hazel getting sick? What did they have in common? And why didn't you or Gracelynn get sick? Why didn't Phillip? Why didn't Michelle? There has to be a common thread." I speculated about the food, and why I'd ruled that out. "The drinks are the only place a poison could have been introduced."

"Poison?" Willow gasped. "You think someone poisoned our drinks? That's ridiculous."

"It's the only thing that makes sense." I remembered my suspicion about Willow's "delicate condition" and Phillip's denial and shuddered. "Are you pregnant?"

"What? Not that it's any of your business, but why would you ask that?"

"It is my business. Anything that concerns my daughters is my business. If you and Phillip bring a child into this world, it will affect Jessie and Michelle. Mostly Michelle. She's the baby of the family and it will crush her. And Phillip is old enough to be a grandfather."

Willow stood up. "You self-righteous busybody. I am not pregnant, so you can spare me your theatrics. But, if Phillip and I have a child, we will not be consulting you."

"Whatever. Sit down and let's figure this out."

She hadn't convinced me she wasn't pregnant. And she didn't sit down. Instead, she slung her purse over her shoulder and trotted to her car.

My shoulders slumped. As much as I didn't want to, I needed to make this right. *No groveling*, I told myself.

"Wait, I'm sorry." I gagged on the words.

Willow stopped at her car. "You're a mean woman, Cece Cavanaugh."

That almost made me laugh, but I swallowed back my chuckle. If anyone had a right to be mean, it was me. "We can agree to disagree. We will never see eye to eye, but what's done is done. The important thing is to figure out who killed Kayla and why."

She leaned against her car and crossed her arms. "Okay, you're right. For the record, I am not pregnant."

"Irrelevant," I said. "Let's concentrate on this."

"Where do we go from here?"

I thought for a minute. "I still keep coming around to why all of you didn't get sick. Just because Hazel didn't attend the rehearsal or spa day doesn't mean what happened to Kayla didn't start there. Maybe Kayla ingested more than anyone. I'm thinking the mimosas, but that makes little sense if you didn't get sick."

Willow shrugged. "I served mimosas at the rehearsal, the spa, and we had them during the time we were getting ready for the wedding. But I never drank one. Gracelynn and Felicity wouldn't pass on alcohol. They love their booze. Kayla drank the non-alcoholic version. And come to think of it, Phillip's mother helped herself to several the day of the wedding. She complained because there was no iced tea or other beverages. I hate that she's so hard to please. No matter what I—"

"Don't even," I cut in. "Let's go with the theory that someone poisoned the virgin mimosas. Whoever poisoned them knew Kayla would drink the non-alcoholic version. Who was at the rehearsal?"

"The entire wedding party. Everyone except Hazel and Michelle. Oh, Flick wasn't there either. He had something else and couldn't make it," Willow said. "Sasha closed down Sassafras and Sage so we could have the entire place."

"Why wasn't Flick at rehearsal?" I asked.

"He had another job."

"It looks like the same people were at the spa except for Hazel. Michelle was there, but not in the massage rooms." I cringed. "Maggie sent us two drinks from your buffet—a non-alcoholic one for Michelle and a regular one for me." My heart seized and I felt sick. "My daughter could have been poisoned." I bent from the waist and took several deep breaths.

Willow patted my back. "Hey, are you okay?"

"No. No, I am not." I held my thumb and forefinger close together. "If someone tampered with those drinks, Michelle was this close to being poisoned."

"Wow!" Willow exclaimed. "Just wow."

"What did you drink?" I asked.

"I had a couple regular mimosas during rehearsal, but nothing the day of the wedding. My stomach was in knots, especially at the club. Hazel was in my face the minute she walked in. Then I saw the magnolias instead of the daisies. I couldn't drink or I might have gotten up the courage to smash her face in."

I knew the feeling. "I suppose Phillip coerced the bartender into making him a bourbon and branch? He'd never drink a mimosa."

Willow thought on that for a moment. "I guess so."

I knew more about Phillip than she'd ever know.

"One last question. Were any of your friends jealous of you?" I asked.

"That's a silly question. There was a lot of jealousy where Flick was concerned, but no, they were excited that I'd finally . . . well, you know."

I knew. "I think jealousy is the root of Kayla's murder."

"Who would do something like this?"

I took a deep breath. "Exactly. Which one of your friends is a killer?"

CHAPTER SIXTEEN

"Who would I expect to find when I'm getting ready to question a suspect? Cece Cavanaugh is like the proverbial bad penny."
Detective Zimmerman

I handed Nancy the list I'd made the night before. We had made the drive into the city to restock our supplies. "If you think of anything else, get it." I pulled up to the front door of the supply house. "I'll pick you up in an hour."

"Aren't you coming?" Nancy asked.

"I'm going to Sassafras and Sage to talk to Sasha. The more I think about her, she might be the guilty party. She served the drinks and could have poisoned everyone. She was at every function. If I could believe what Willow told me, Sasha, Gracelynn, and Felicity all had motives."

Nancy's jaw worked on a huge wad of gum. "Do tell."

"Sasha had a fling with the photographer, Flick Donovan, that ended when he wouldn't commit, and he moved on to Gracelynn."

"Oh, sounds like a motive to me." Nancy rubbed her hands together. "This reminds me of one of those mystery movies. He sounds like a prime-time jerk. Were these women friends?"

I nodded. "Why kill Kayla and not Donovan?"

"Exactly! Fire up this van. You aren't doing this without me. I wanna go," Nancy whined. "We can come back after we talk to the caterer."

"We?"

Nancy nodded like a bobblehead doll.

Against my better judgment, I took her with me. The restaurant was dark, and the front door was locked when we arrived. It was half past nine, and the sign indicated they opened at six. I didn't detect any movement through the front window.

"Let's go around back," I said, turning toward the alley.

Nancy followed.

A side alley separated Sassafras and Sage from its neighbor on the left. We headed into the alley and came out in a parking lot behind the building. A small hybrid car sat next to the Sassafras and Sage catering truck.

On this side of the building, two doors led inside. I peered into the window of one door and saw a narrow hallway with a staircase leading to the second floor. All these store-fronts had apartments above them.

"Does she live up there?" Nancy pointed to a window above us. "The window's open."

I shrugged. "Beats me. Could be a renter."

Back in the early days, it wasn't unusual for the shop-keeper to live above the store, but in more recent times, the shopkeepers lived in the suburbs and rented out the apart-ments to singles or college students who attended the local university.

The other door led to the restaurant. I cupped my hands

around my eyes and pressed my face to the glass. This was definitely the kitchen of Sassafras and Sage, complete with a gleaming stainless-steel prep table and a multi-burner stove.

Nancy gasped behind me.

"What's wr—" I turned to see Detective Zimmerman parking his car next to the hybrid.

"We have company," Nancy whispered.

My first instinct was to run, but we had done nothing wrong. It wasn't illegal to look in a window. Was it considered being a peeping Tom? I wasn't looking into a residence, just a restaurant kitchen.

Nancy pressed her face against the window and let out a shriek.

I kept my eye on Zimmerman as he approached. "What's the matter?"

"Cece," she whispered. "There's a body in there with a knife sticking in its back."

"What did you say?" I broke eye contact with Zimmerman and looked in the window. A body in a white chef's coat lay facedown on the floor. Several excuses for why we were here ran through my mind, but I knew none of them would pass muster with Zimmerman.

"Morning, ladies." The detective joined us at the door. "Customers enter through the front of the restaurant. Or are you here for a handout?"

I gulped and stepped away. "Uh, no. We worried why Sasha hadn't opened the restaurant and came around back to check."

"A little far from home for breakfast, aren't you?" Zimmerman asked.

"I could say that to you." I laughed a bit too loud.

Nancy jabbed me in the side. "Ou-yay ow-knay there's an ody-bay in there?"

"What's this about a body?" Zimmerman asked.

He eased Nancy aside and peered through the window.

"Crap," he muttered. He pulled a cell phone from his pocket and placed a call. "Send an ambulance and an officer to Sassafras and Sage on Charter Street."

Zimmerman pulled a glove from his pocket and tried the door. "What did you touch?"

Nancy shook her head like it was on a spring. "Nothing. I swear."

Zimmerman stared me down. "What about you?"

I nodded. "I tried the front door, and it was locked. We came around here and looked in the window. We didn't touch the door handle."

Zimmerman scoffed. "Didn't I tell you to stay out of my investigation?"

"We came to talk to Sasha—"

Nancy interrupted, "About catering an event."

"Yes." I remembered the card Sasha had given me, pulled it from my purse, and shoved it in the detective's face. "I wanted to hire her for—"

"A baby shower for Angie Valenti," Nancy interrupted again.

My mouth dropped open. "Yeah, a baby shower for Angie. You know her."

"Sure, you were." Zimmerman winked.

"Who is it?" I asked. "Who's in there?"

"Now that's the question, isn't it?" Zimmerman's demeanor turned serious. "You two go sit in your van and do not leave until I talk to you."

I cringed. "You saw my van?"

"Lady, I'd have had to be blind not to see that monstrosity sitting at the curb."

Nancy and I trudged to my van as sirens wailed toward us.

———

After extensive questioning, the police let us go. I put my van in drive and pulled away from the curb.

"Wonder what'll happen to the restaurant?" Nancy mused.

It turned out the body was Sasha, and Zimmerman promised we hadn't seen the last of him.

"Beats me." My theory that Sasha had murdered Kayla came to an abrupt halt when Zimmerman said there was now another homicide connected to his case. Since Sasha's murder happened outside his jurisdiction, he wouldn't be working the case, but he'd be involved, which meant he'd still be hanging around bugging me.

For the moment, Sasha's murder occupied him, which gave me a bit of time to do some additional reconnaissance without him being on my tail.

I made two consecutive right turns.

"Where are we going?" Nancy asked when I didn't turn toward the supply house.

"To visit a certain photographer," I said.

"Whee!" Nancy slapped the dashboard. "Let's boogie."

I drove several blocks, turned right, then turned left back onto Charter Street, making sure we'd come out past Sassafras and Sage and before the photography studio.

"We don't have a lot of time," I said. "Zimmerman will be all over Donovan, but we can at least talk while Zimmerman is busy. Once he's done at the crime scene, all bets are off."

We passed the studio, and I swung a U-turn several blocks away from Flick Donovan's photography studio and parked at the curb. I didn't need eagle-eye Zimmerman seeing my van in the neighborhood.

My last encounter with Donovan had ended with him walking out on me.

Someone had propped open the main entrance door, and Nancy and I walked in. We had two options, a door on the right or a flight of stairs leading into a darkened hallway. Presumably to an apartment.

I looked at Nancy. "Waddya think? Stairs or door?"

"I ain't going up those stairs. Not as dark as it is. I don't even see a light switch down here." Nancy felt around on the wall.

"Excellent point. The door it is." A sign next to the door read PRIVATE STUDIO—PLEASE KNOCK.

I knocked, and the door swung open, revealing an open room with various lighting fixtures and spotlights suspended from the ceiling, a series of cloth backdrops that lined the exposed brick walls, and a multitude of tripods and cameras.

"Hello," I called out. "Anyone here?"

No answer.

After our encounter at Sassafras and Sage, I moved cautiously, extra alert for stray dead bodies. The gigantic window facing the street provided plenty of light. When I stopped, Nancy bumped into me.

"Umpf."

"Do you have to be on my heels?" I asked.

"Sorry."

"Let's look around. No telling what we might find." I knew it was a bold move, but it was an opportunity I couldn't pass up. I walked around the perimeter of the room, taking in the space where Donovan photographed his models.

Nancy finally took off in a direction of her own. When I heard footsteps running down the stairs, I froze.

"Nancy." I held a finger to my lips. "Shh."

Nancy nodded.

A mammoth hot flash took hold and drenched me in a river of sweat. I moved behind a ceiling-to-floor backdrop and motioned for Nancy to do the same. She slid behind a pearly gray textured screen, her feet and legs sticking out below.

The footsteps stopped at the base of the stairs. I peeked around the backdrop and saw a shadow moving underneath the door. I heard the lock click into place.

After what seemed like forever, the shadow moved and the front door of the building slammed shut. Outside, an engine revved to life.

"Stay put," I said to Nancy. "Let's make sure they're gone."

When the rush of blood in my temples subsided, I stepped from behind my backdrop. "Come on out."

"Whoa, that was close," Nancy said.

She had donned a pink feather boa and a top hat. Normally, I would have giggled at her antics, but now was not the time.

"Seriously? What is wrong with you?" I yanked the boa from around her neck. "Come on. We have work to do."

"What are we looking for?" Nancy threw the hat across the room and landed a perfect shot on the coat rack.

"I don't know. Looking for evidence to tie Donovan to the murder. I mean murders." I found a desk buried under a pile of portfolios. "Will you keep an eye out the window? We don't want to be surprised again."

"If someone comes, what are we gonna do?" Nancy stood at the front window.

"First, girlfriend, you need to be less conspicuous. Anyone coming down the street will see you." I searched the room for an escape route, and in the back corner, I spotted a door. I cracked it open a bit and saw a parking area much like the one behind Sassafras and Sage. "If anyone comes, head for this door."

Nancy nodded. She retreated a few steps and looked around the window frame.

"That's better, but step to the side." I slid open the middle desk drawer and rummaged around. It contained notepads, ink pens—general office supplies along with a few random items I didn't recognize but assumed were necessary for a professional photographer. Nothing that looked ominous.

I continued searching. In the top left drawer, I found a small packet of tissues, sunglasses, a bottle of eye drops, memory cards, and various cables. Nothing sinister.

I finished searching the drawers, and finding nothing, I opened a portfolio and flipped through the pages. No one in this group of photos looked familiar. I set it aside and opened another. This one was all bikini shots. All the photos showed Willow with way more exposed skin than I wanted to see.

Nancy whistled.

"Is everything okay?" I opened another portfolio.

"Yeah, just nervous," Nancy admitted.

"You're making me nervous. Be quiet." The next portfolio contained shots of evening wear—fancy dresses. Sasha, Felicity, and Kayla all appeared in various shots. Tucked in the back, I found several torn photos. I laid them out like a giant jigsaw and began piecing them together.

I assembled all the photos and stepped back. There were photos of all the women in Willow's wedding party, including photos of Sasha and several of Willow. These were not ordinary modeling photos. None of the women appeared to be posed. It was like someone took the photos when the women were not aware. Like photos a creeper takes with a hidden camera.

Was Donovan spying on the models? Why were the torn photos in one portfolio? Were these the photos from the hidden camera at Sassafras and Sage?

"Cece!" Nancy shouted. "I think he's here. A guy just got out of a car, and he's carrying a camera."

"Come on, let's go." I gathered the pieces of one of Willow's photos, put them into my pocket, and shoved the rest back into the portfolio. When I heard the door in the foyer squeak open, I ran for the back door. "Come on."

The door slammed behind me, and I scampered down the steps. A large roll-off trash bin sat in the corner. I ran behind it.

"Whew, another close call." I turned to give Nancy a high five, but she wasn't there. I glanced over the top of the bin, expecting to see her hoofing it across the parking lot. No sign of her. Had she misunderstood and made a break for the van?

I gauged the distance between the bin and the alley and made my escape. When I got to the front of the building, I ran down the street to where we'd parked the van. There was no sign of Nancy in the van or anywhere on the sidewalk near the van.

I walked back toward the studio, panting like a woman in labor, trying to blend in with the other pedestrians. When I got right in front of the window, I glanced in and saw Donovan standing at his desk, but I didn't see Nancy anywhere.

My heart thudded in my chest. Where was she? Then I saw her legs sticking out from underneath the gray backdrop. Donovan had his back to her, and as long as he didn't turn around, she'd be safe, but if he did, she stuck out like a sore thumb in her sky-high heels and sunshine-yellow capri pants.

Donovan grabbed something from the desk drawer and shoved it in his bag then headed for the front door.

I breathed a sigh and hoped Nancy had the patience to stay behind the screen.

Donovan stopped short of the door and stood stock still, then shrugged and left.

Before he exited the door, I backpedaled and hid in the alleyway between the buildings. I hoped Nancy continued to stay put in case he stole a glance through the front window. Any movement inside could capture his attention and give her away. I also prayed he hadn't seen my van. Even though I parked several blocks away, it was on the same side of the street he had parked. Now I rethought that color scheme decision. If I was going to keep getting involved in investigations, I might want to repaint it a nice neutral beige color and change the name of my company to ABC Cleaning.

When Donovan was gone, I ran to the front door. It was locked. I pounded on the door, hoping Nancy knew she was in the clear. When she didn't answer, I peered in the front window. Nancy was gone. Or at least I didn't see her legs sticking out from under the backdrop.

"Cece!" Nancy shouted.

I jumped. "Good grief. You scared the bejeebers out of me. Why didn't you follow me out the back door?"

Nancy lifted her leg, revealing a large red welt. "I tripped on my way out. By the time I got up, he was coming in the door. Lucky for me, he got a phone call and wasn't paying attention. I slid behind that thing and hoped he wouldn't see me."

"Let's go home. We've had way too much excitement for one day. The supplies can wait. We'll have to regroup and rethink our strategy."

CHAPTER SEVENTEEN

"People in this neighborhood are so weird. If you don't want the trash company to take it away, don't put it in the trash bin. Sheesh!"
Wickford Sanitation Engineer Jake

Before going to bed, I gathered the household trash and dumped it into the garbage bins, including the three bags from the spa I'd put in the back of the van. Wickford's trash collector would come long before the sun rose. If bins weren't at the curb, tough luck. No second chances. Lightning chased across the sky as I deposited the bins at the curb and raced back inside before the raindrops descended from the heavens.

I made it into the house just as the sky opened up, unleashing rain in a torrential downpour. The rain I'd wished for Phillip's wedding. Thunder kept me awake most of the night—thunder and the fact that one of my suspects was now dead. I had almost dozed off when an idea occurred to me.

I rolled out of bed, grabbed my laptop, and did an Internet search. If I was right, I knew how the drinks were poisoned, and all my evidence now pointed to Flick Donovan. Thunder crashed while I keyed in the search. The lights flickered on and off twice, forcing me to pause while the router reset. The search convinced me I needed to go outside to retrieve the bags of trash from the spa, but it was still pouring. Tree branches slapped against the house, adding to my anxiety.

Around five, the garbage truck rumbled down the street, and I knew I couldn't wait any longer. I slid on a robe, ran barefoot down the stairs, and threw open the front door. Wind and rain assaulted me. I pulled the robe tight and bent to shield myself from the rain as I trekked down the driveway.

The garbage truck squealed to a halt in front of my house, and the worker jumped down and grabbed for a bin at the same time that I threw open the lid.

"Almost missed us, huh?" he shouted over the din of the storm.

I flung bags onto the lawn, searching for the ones I'd brought from Maggie's Salon and Day Spa. "No, I need to find something."

He retrieved a bag from the lawn and tossed it into the back of his truck.

"Stop!" I screamed. "I need that."

"Lady, it's raining cats and dogs. I have a schedule to keep." He ran back to the truck's cab and jumped aboard.

I gathered the scattered bags, shoved them into the bins, and dragged the bins into the garage. My teeth chattered, and water ran in rivulets down my face. Confident the trash wasn't going anywhere, I stripped off my sopping robe and went into the house to change.

By the time I'd taken a shower and changed into dry clothes, Nancy was sitting in my kitchen with a bowl of cereal. Cereal from my pantry. In my bowl. With milk from my fridge.

"Are you enjoying your breakfast?"

Nancy snickered. "We need to talk about the cereal selection."

I rolled my eyes. "Let's not."

"Did you have an early-morning rendezvous with the trash guy?"

"No." I heated water for tea and joined her at the breakfast bar. "Remember when we were cleaning at Maggie's?"

"Yeah." Nancy spooned in a mouthful of cereal and made crunching sounds.

"I couldn't get all the trash bags to fit in her bins, so I threw them in the back of the van to bring home and put in mine. They've been back there since Sunday."

"I saw those but wasn't sure what they were. If I had known it was trash, I would have put them in your bin. Sorry. Sucked that you just remembered them this morning, what with the storm and all."

"Finish your breakfast. We've got work to do." I drained my tea and rinsed the cup.

"What's the job, boss?" She pushed her bowl aside and stood up.

"Not so fast. Rinse that bowl and put it in the dishwasher. If you're going to freeload, the least you can do is clean up." I placed my cup in the dishwasher and stood back.

"Now I see where Michelle gets her attitude. You're getting to be a tyrant," Nancy groused while rinsing her bowl.

"Follow me," I said when she finished.

When we were in the garage, I dumped the bins onto the floor, praying that what I wanted wasn't in the bag the garbage collector had taken.

Nancy watched me with her hands on her hips. "What in the world are you doing?"

I opened the first bag and saw it was trash from my house. "We gotta find the bags from Maggie's." I re-tied the bag and slung it into the bin.

"What? We're rooting through garbage. That's just grossy gross." Nancy puckered her face.

I pushed a bag toward her. "Just do it."

"What are you looking for?" Nancy grabbed the bag with two fingers and pulled it to her.

"Eye drops," I said.

"You can't go to the store and buy your own drops? We gotta dig through trash?"

"No," I said, "I'm looking for a bottle I swept up at Maggie's. When we were at Donovan's studio, I found a bottle in his desk drawer."

Nancy sighed. "I have eye drops upstairs in my apartment too. You want me to go get them?"

"Ugh, just look. I think the killer used them to poison the mimosas." I opened another bag.

"Eye drops?"

"Yes. There's a chemical in many eye drops that causes blood vessels to constrict. I heard about it a while back but paid no attention. I searched the Internet and found that it causes many of the same symptoms that Kayla, Hazel, and Felicity exhibited."

"I'm never using eye drops again," Nancy said.

"They don't have that effect in small doses in your eyes. Just don't go drinking them. Eureka!" I yelled. "This isn't my trash." I dumped it onto the floor and spread it out.

"Oh, ick. There's hair in it. Lots of hair. This is disgusting." Nancy grabbed one of my gardening trowels and pushed around the trash. "Do you see anything?"

"No, it's not in this bag." I took the trowel from her and

shoveled the mess back into the bag. "Let's do another one."

Nancy untied a bag and dumped it onto the floor. It was my garbage.

"Why'd you do that? Don't dump it out if it's my stuff."

"How am I supposed to know what's yours?"

"Just look."

We searched through two more bags to no avail.

I pushed the last bag to Nancy. "This one had to come from Maggie's. Dump it out while I clean up this mess."

Nancy did as instructed, using her foot to push trash around. "I think I found it, but I ain't touching that nasty thing."

"Jeez, you are such a wuss." Ack! If she wouldn't pick it up, I'd have to do the deed. Where was a tissue when I needed it? I forced back a gag and retrieved the eye drops. An involuntary shudder made its way across my shoulders as I swiveled the bottle around where I could read the label.

"Well," Nancy said.

"The same brand I found in Donovan's desk, and a brand that contains the chemical I told you about." I shoved the bottle in her face, which sent her into a panic attack. She jumped back, tripped over her feet, and wound up seated in my garden cart—right on top of an open bag of manure.

I burst out laughing while she pulled herself from the cart, trying to brush desiccated cow dung off her pants without touching it.

I pinched my nose with my fingers. "I'll tell you what's nasty, Nancy." I stopped and doubled over laughing. "Nasty Nancy. *Bwa ha ha*! I crack myself up."

Nancy plastered on a major pouty face, which made me feel bad. Sort of.

I found my gardening gloves on the workbench and slapped at her butt. "You got a little poo here."

"Funny." She reached back and grabbed a handful of manure and flung it at me.

"Oh, that's how you want to play?" I shoveled a hefty portion onto the gardening trowel and hurled it at her, striking the back of her head.

She seized two handfuls and lobbed them into the air, showering me from above. She laughed so hard she snorted, which caused her to laugh harder, then she farted.

"Do you need toilet paper to go with that toot?" I asked.

We both howled with laughter. I never realized I needed a poo fight to release my tension, but even though we were in my garage and it would be awful to clean, it was much-needed laughter with all the stress and questions and fears on my mind.

I composed myself first and hugged her. "I haven't laughed this hard in ages. Thanks."

She pushed me away. "Ew, you got poo on you."

"Duh! Look who's talking."

We both looked like we'd been wallowing in the garden. I grabbed the bag and read the label. "At least it's sterilized."

Nancy frowned. "It's still cow caca."

"Bet you never thought cow dung could be fun." I lobbed another handful past her, missing on purpose. Watching her duck out of the way was almost as entertaining as seeing her covered in poo.

"Stop!" she yelled. "Enough. I look like a giant turd."

I bent over laughing. "We both look like turds."

When I got up, she dropped a handful of manure onto my head.

I shook my head like a dog coming in from the rain, which sent us both into another fit of giggles.

Nancy patted my hair. "I've had mud mask facials, but I don't think manure conditioners will ever become a thing. But your hair has a unique fragrance."

"Like you can talk. Looks like I'll be taking another shower." I grabbed the bottle of eye drops and put it in my pocket. As much as I wanted to linger and continue laughing, I needed to talk to Willow again.

CHAPTER EIGHTEEN

"I still don't understand why Phillip asked Cece to look into Kayla's murder. It doesn't seem right to me." Willow Carson

Willow agreed to meet me at Weezie's Bar and Grill. I was nursing an iced tea when she walked in. Every head in the place turned toward me when she took a seat at the booth where I sat. Conversation ground to a halt. All eyes locked on Willow and me. Cell phones appeared on tables in anticipation of another photo op.

After our encounter at Maggie's, I should have known it would be a mistake to meet her in public, but the truth was I didn't have the stomach to have her at my house again.

"Thanks for coming."

Willow nodded and motioned for the server to bring her the same thing I was having. "I heard on the news that Sasha was . . ." Her voice broke.

I nodded. "Nancy and I found her. We had gone to the restaurant to talk to her, but it was closed."

Willow's eyes widened. "You were there?"

"We went around back to check the kitchen. Detective Zimmerman arrived at the same time. Nancy, my assistant, saw her lying on the floor. We didn't know it was her." I explained about being questioned and released.

"Wow. Just wow. First Kayla and now Sasha. Are they connected?"

The server brought Willow's tea and topped off mine.

"You tell me. What do you know about this?" I pulled the eye drops from my purse and set them on the table.

She picked up the bottle and examined it. "I don't understand."

"At your—" I gulped. "Your um . . . At the club Saturday, Sasha spilled the contents of her purse, and when she had collected everything, she made an issue of not being able to find her eye drops. She said she had recently *lost* several bottles." I put air quotes around the word *lost*.

"The next day, Nancy and I did the annual cleaning for Maggie at the spa. Back in the massage room where your wed . . . your friends had their spa day, I found a bottle of eye drops under one of the massage beds."

"So?" Willow's face held no expression.

"She catered your spa day," I said. "I think this is one of the missing bottles she was complaining about."

Willow handed the bottle back. "You've lost me."

"I visited Donovan's studio yesterday and found an identical bottle in his desk drawer."

"And you think Donovan is hiding her eye drops?"

"No, I think Donovan used her eye drops to poison the virgin mimosas you served at the rehearsal dinner, the spa day, and at the club."

She pursed her lips. "Nope, try again."

"Why? I think it's plausible. And that's not all." I leaned

over the table to keep the prying ears in the next booth from hearing. "I found photos of all of you at the studio."

"Yes. He's a photographer."

"Compromising photos like you were being spied on. These were not photo shoot photos. They were creepy, hidden camera types of photos." I pulled the one I had snagged from the portfolio and laid it on the table, arranging the pieces of her until the almost-nude shot was staring back at her.

Willow grabbed the pieces and ripped them into tiny bits. "This was in his studio?"

I nodded. "Along with several others. They all had the same background."

"This photo was taken in the bathroom at Sassafras and Sage."

"How is that possible? Why were you half-clothed at Sassafras and Sage?"

"It was several months ago. We had a lingerie photo shoot at the restaurant after-hours. The bathroom was where we changed clothes. I'm so confused."

What did I know about modeling? Who knew people took their clothes off in public restrooms? Either way, the eye drops connected Sasha to Donovan, and the photos connected Sasha and Donovan to all the other women. Who planted the hidden camera, Sasha or Donovan? And why?

"There's something wrong with what you're thinking. Donovan wasn't at the rehearsal. I can't imagine him taking photos like those. He's an artist, not a weirdo. Besides, the next day, Sasha wouldn't let him within a mile of the drinks. He's a recovering alcoholic. Plus, there's a lot of animosity between the two of them. She even filed a complaint against him with Glow Girl that could ruin his career. If he had done anything to the drinks, she would have blasted him. She wasn't as protective at the club, because she was busy inside in the banquet room getting ready for our dinner. The drink station was wide open."

I shrugged. "Maybe someone is setting him up. I'm almost positive Kayla's poisoning started Friday night. Why else would she already be showing signs early Saturday morning?" The only ones who hadn't shown symptoms were Willow and Gracelynn. Did they know to stay away from the drinks? I needed to talk to Gracelynn.

The front door of Weezie's swung open and Hazel's two best friends, Bitsy Harris-Dodd and Mavis Blevins, strolled in and sidled up to our booth.

"I see the Wickford grapevine is alive and well." I figured if I got the first shot off, it would defuse the two women and send them packing.

"Well, if it isn't the past and the future bundled into a booth together," Mavis spouted.

I was wrong. They were in for the kill.

"Are you giving Willow pointers on how to keep a man?" Bitsy spewed.

Mavis pointed a manicured finger at Willow. "Take my advice. Don't listen to Cece. It didn't work for her. Oh, wait, you already know that, don't you?"

Willow's face turned scarlet. "I need—I need to leave."

I touched her hand. "Ignore them. The rest of Wickford does." I continued making small talk like we were old friends. Inside, I seethed. I hated showing any kind of friendship to Willow.

Bitsy and Mavis grew bored with us and looked for an empty table. Weezie, the owner, showed up and steered them across the bar. I gave her a thankful smile. I'd have to make it up to her.

"Ugh, those two old grannies will be the death of me." Willow sighed. "I can't go anywhere without running into one of them. It's like they lie in wait for me and then attack. They are sweet as candy when Phillip is around. When he's not, they are vicious and mean. He thinks I'm exaggerating. Maybe we should go. They're sitting over there talking about me."

Self-centered a bit? I laughed, enjoying seeing Willow squirm. "Trust me. He knows you aren't exaggerating. But you better get used to it. As long as Hazel breathes, Bitsy and Mavis will be a force to be reckoned with. The three make up the Wickford triumvirate. You get one, you get them all."

Laughter came from their direction. Mavis and Bitsy were talking to two women at the table next to theirs. Bitsy pointed at Willow, and they all cackled like the dried-up old hens they were.

"Ugh, I don't know how you put up with them." Willow shuddered. "I'm going. You can let them talk about you, but I'm done."

"Good luck with that," I said to her retreating back. "This is only the beginning." I wondered how long Willow and Phillip would make it. I hoped for a long, long time to keep him out of my hair, but I had my doubts. If she folded this easily, she was doomed to a miserable life.

———

I swung by the house and picked up Nancy. "Are you ready for another adventure? Felicity called. She's arranged for me to meet Gracelynn."

"Oh yeah, now you want me to go." Nancy pouted because I wouldn't let her go to talk to Willow.

"I'm sorry, but Willow is still a raw spot for me. It's difficult to sit across from the woman who lured my husband away, so excuse me for not wanting to share my distress."

"Whatever. Let's ride. I'll drive—in case you want to take a jaunt past Alder's house." Nancy winked.

"You can drive, but we aren't going by Alder's. I'm done worrying about what's going on." What I didn't tell her was I had found another voice mail and a text from him. Our timing was all haywire, and I blamed his ex-wife. I wondered if someone had put a hex on me. It could happen.

My suspect list continued to narrow. Sasha was dead. While it didn't mean she didn't kill Kayla, it meant she didn't put that chef's knife in her own back. Donovan still looked like a creeper in my book, but Willow swore he would never take those kinds of photos. Plus, he didn't have access to the drinks Friday or Saturday morning unless he somehow bypassed Sasha's protective guardianship of the brunch table.

I was lost in my thoughts when Nancy slammed on the brakes and sent me flying against the seat belt. "Hey, careful."

"Duck, duck, duck," she said.

"Goose!" I yelled.

"No, I mean get down in your seat. Quick!"

I slid down so fast I almost strangled myself with the seat belt. "What the devil is wrong with you?"

"Alder's on his front porch with the ex."

Nancy's words fell on me like the cartoon anvil—dropped from the cliff on the unsuspecting victim. Joyce was still here. This was more than a friendly visit. If Nancy wasn't with me, I'd march right up to the porch and let Alder have it. He had it coming, and I was ready to unleash it.

"What are you doing here?" I snapped. I didn't know who I was madder at, Nancy, Alder, or myself. "Didn't I tell you not to come?"

"Too late. Surprise!" Nancy floored the Jeep. At the end of the block, she hung a left and hollered, "All clear!"

I sat up in the seat and readjusted the seat belt. "Never do that again."

"Blah, blah, blah." Nancy plugged her ears with her pointer fingers. "Can't hear you talking."

I grabbed the steering wheel. "Have you lost your mind?"

"You are seriously no fun." She took the wheel and proceeded to Barney's Rise and Shine, where we were meeting Felicity and Gracelynn.

"Did Alder recognize your Jeep?" I asked.

"You're done with that, remember? Now let me concentrate on driving us to our destination."

When she wheeled into the parking lot, I saw Gracelynn and Felicity arguing at the side of the building. "Nancy, see if you can get closer."

She did. She pulled the car into the spot right next to them.

"Oh, for crying out loud," I said.

"You told me to get closer. Any closer and I'd run them over." Nancy threw the shifter into neutral and killed the engine. "Want me to move?"

Felicity paid us no mind and continued arguing.

"No, don't worry about it." I unbuckled and jumped from the Jeep.

Before I could go around to where they were, Nancy rolled down her window and yelled, "Hey, girls. What's going on?"

That caught their attention. When they saw me come around the Jeep, Gracelynn looked at Felicity then took off running.

"Nancy!" I screamed. "Go after her. I'll stay here with Felicity."

"Not in these heels!" Nancy yelled. "I'll break my neck."

I rolled my eyes and took chase. Gracelynn sprinted down the sidewalk. Lucky for me, several people milled about, and she kept having to slow down to keep from mowing them over. I zigzagged, trying to maintain a visual. I lost sight for a minute, but when she crossed the street, I crossed too, dodging between honking cars.

I had recently started working out at the gym again, and my stamina was returning, but running on a treadmill and running on a city street were two different animals. My breath came in hitches as I continued after her. She turned down an alley, and I followed.

The alley dead-ended, and she slammed into a fence with an *oompf*. She grabbed a trash bin and pushed it closer to the fence.

"Stop. I just . . . want to . . . talk."

She turned and slid to the ground, panting. "What . . . What do you want? Why are you doing this?"

I bent over and held my knees, willing my breathing to return to normal. "I just want to talk. That's all."

"What's all the racket?" a voice yelled from a window above.

"Nothing. Everything's fine." My heart pounded from exertion. I definitely needed to up my game at the gym.

"Don't make me call the cops!" the voice shouted.

Somewhere in the distance, a dog barked, causing the neighbor dogs to join in.

With the distraction, Gracelynn rammed into me, knocking me to the ground. By the time I caught my breath and picked myself up, she was long gone. I limped back to the street and looked both ways. She had blended in with the pedestrians and disappeared.

I hobbled back to the parking lot where Nancy was chatting with Felicity.

"Where is she? Did you lose her?" Nancy asked. "And why are you limping?"

"I cornered her in an alley, then a neighbor distracted me, and she got away. She plowed right through me." I walked over to the Jeep, sat down, and checked my elbow for abrasions.

"I swear," Felicity said. "You'd think she's guilty the way she's acting." She promptly keeled over.

I ran to her, kneeled, and checked her pulse. "What's been going on here?"

Nancy raised her hands in an "I'm innocent" gesture. "Beats me. She's been acting loony since I got here."

"What do you mean by loony?" I pulled off my jacket and slid it under Felicity's head.

"She acts like she's drunk," Nancy said. "Before you came back, I had her sitting on the curb with her head between her knees, but she insisted on walking around. That's what she was doing when you came back. Talking crazy talk about Gracelynn killing Kayla."

Felicity roused. "Where am I?"

"You're okay. We're in the Barney's parking lot. Can you sit up? What happened?"

Nancy helped Felicity to a sitting position and leaned her against the Jeep.

"I don't know." Felicity rubbed her head and moaned. "One minute Gracelynn and I are talking, and the next minute I'm dizzy and feeling like I will be sick."

It sounded like she was exhibiting the same symptoms she had the day of the wedding. The same symptoms as Kayla and Hazel.

Willow had basically told me Donovan could not have introduced the poison prior to being at the country club. Which meant Willow was incriminating herself, or Gracelynn was guilty. With the way she was acting, I'd place my bets on Gracelynn.

"How long have you been sick?" I asked.

"It started this morning, right after I woke up. It might be a hangover from last night. I went to happy hour, but I only had one cocktail and switched to ginger ale.

"I came here for breakfast and just had toast and a glass of orange juice because I was feeling so crappy." Felicity groaned. "You don't think someone poisoned me, do you?"

"It's possible. The symptoms are similar," I said. "Who were you with last night?"

"Gracelynn and Willow. I invited them like you suggested. Especially with Sasha dead, I felt like we needed a giant group hug." Tears welled up in her eyes, and she shook her head. "I can't believe either of them would hurt me, much less kill Kayla."

I touched her shoulder, and she leaned into me, sobbing against my shoulder. "Shh. It's okay. You should go to the police."

Her body trembled. "I can't. I just can't. They're my best friends. Neither of them would ever hurt anyone."

Not only had one of them hurt someone, it looked like they tried to incriminate Sasha or Donovan. Gracelynn had run both times I'd tried to talk to her, and she'd been at the restaurant when the photos were taken. All the women had been. But maybe Willow was being deceitful too. It wouldn't be the first time she'd done something underhanded.

"Do you have any idea what might motivate Willow or Gracelynn to do something like this?" I had my suspicions, but I wanted to hear Felicity's thoughts.

She shrugged. "I still don't believe it's possible."

"Let's say hypothetically one of them did. I'm not saying make an accusation—just think about what could cause either of them to spike your drinks. Can you at least do that?"

"Maybe." She paused. "Oh, I don't know. This is hard, thinking one of your best friends is a killer."

This woman needed to concentrate. Someone had killed her friends and tried to poison her. "Remember, we're not accusing, just speculating on a motive."

"Okay. I can do that. I know Willow, Kayla, and Gracelynn were competing for the same modeling job. Willow was jealous of Kayla because of—" She stopped.

"Go on. Willow was jealous because of Phillip. I get it."

Felicity forced a slight smile. "Yeah, Willow was crazy jealous. She accused Kayla of putting moves on him."

"That's the stuff we need to look at." But it didn't jibe with what Willow had said. "What about you?"

She bristled. "What about me? I didn't do anything."

"I'm not accusing you. I'm asking if Willow or Gracelynn would have any motive for hurting you."

"Duh. Yeah, I get it. I don't know. Willow is jealous of everyone where Phillip is concerned. I guess that could include me. Gracelynn worried about what everyone else has. I had recently gotten a job that upset her when she got turned down. I can't believe she would resort to that. But it makes sense. She could have spiked my orange juice this morning."

"Why were you and Gracelynn arguing when we pulled up?" I asked.

"She changed her mind about talking to you. I tried to convince her, but as you saw, she bolted," Felicity said.

I patted her shoulder. "Are you feeling better?"

She nodded and got to her feet. "I'm fine."

"Are you sure? Get yourself checked out." I stood up.

"No, I'm good, really. I'll call my doctor if I start feeling bad." Felicity turned and walked away.

"Is she going to be okay?" Nancy asked. "She was loopy."

"I think so." I brushed off my pants. "She's a stubborn one. Give me a second, will you?"

Felicity had gotten in her car and fastened the seat belt. I waved for her to wait. "Do you have Gracelynn's address?" If I visited her at home, she might be more comfortable talking to me.

"Sure, she lives not too far away." She pulled a scrap of

paper from her glove box and jotted down the address. "Do you think it's wise to go to her place?"

"I'll be okay," I assured her, but maybe I was assuring myself. I knew better than to confront a killer, but I didn't know for sure Gracelynn was a killer. Yet!

CHAPTER NINETEEN

"It's never a good thing when Mr. Cavanaugh shows up unannounced. Who am I kidding? It's never a good thing when he shows *up*."
Beatrice Giovannetti

When Nancy and I got back to my house, Phillip's car was in the drive and he wasn't in it, which meant he was in my house.

He was sitting at the breakfast bar when I walked in. Beatrice gave me a worried look and mouthed, "Sorry."

After Phillip first left, he kept showing up unannounced and letting himself in. I changed the locks. He got better about calling first. It still annoyed him he didn't have free access, but since our divorce was final, I didn't care. Part of my settlement was our family home, so he could deal with it.

"What did you say to her?" Phillip's eyes drilled into mine.

"Who?" I placed my purse on the countertop.

"Willow," Phillip said between gritted teeth. "Don't act innocent."

"I've got work to do. Catch you later." Nancy retreated from the room.

"I'll be upstairs vacuuming," Beatrice said.

I waited until Beatrice left. "What are you doing here? And what's this about Willow? I just saw her."

"What did you say to her?" he demanded. "She came home bawling her eyes out."

What did I say to her? "Oh, you jerk. Sasha died. Nancy and I found her. If Willow is upset, it was because of that, not anything I said."

Phillip paced the kitchen with nervous energy. His standard tell when he was about to go ballistic.

"Sit down," I said, needing to defuse the situation. "You're angry, and I have no clue why."

He turned around so fast I jumped. "You think so. Of course, I'm angry. I'm livid. You've gone too far. I get that you're upset I'm getting married, but that doesn't give you a right to take it out on her. By the way, our deal is off. If you want your van paid for, you can do it yourself. This nightmare is dragging on too long."

His outburst caused my last nerve to unravel. "No way! We made a deal, and you're sticking to it. As far as Willow goes, you better explain because I am clueless. If I upset her, you need to tell me what it was. If it's like the tale she told about me assaulting her, she's making up another whopper."

He slammed his hand on the counter. "She called off the wedding. She said she's making a tremendous mistake and wants to call it quits before it's gone too far. Tell me you had nothing to do with her decision."

For a second I wanted to laugh. Served him right. "Oh, calm down. I know who upset her, and it wasn't me."

"Right," he said with a smug tone. "The honorable Cece Cavanaugh would never undermine my relationship with Willow."

"It was most likely your mother's goon squad. Willow and I met at Weezie's to talk about some things I found out. While we were there, Mavis and Bitsy saw us together. They roughed her up."

Phillip rubbed his jaw. "And you let it happen? You let the two of them intimidate her?"

Wow, he had some nerve. "I'm not her mother, though I am old enough to be. But she got a splendid picture of what marrying you would be like for her. Mavis and Bitsy aren't going to let up, and Willow must have realized it. You want to chew someone out, go talk to them. Maybe you'll get an apology and a promise that they won't bully her," I said. "Good luck. Those two, along with your mother, have no mercy."

He sank onto a barstool. "I swear. It must have been bad. I've never seen Willow so upset."

"It made me cringe, and I'm used to their antics."

"I don't suppose you'd talk to her, would you?"

This time I laughed. "Not on your life. And our deal is not off. Now get out."

———

I made my way through the hedge separating my yard from Angie's. It had been too long since I'd talked to my bestie, and I needed a bit of encouragement from her. She was sitting on her patio drinking iced tea when I popped through the opening we'd created from all our years of cutting through the hedge to get to one another's houses. We lived the adage that back door friends were best.

Angie's husband, Dave, and Phillip had long since given up scolding us for ruining the landscape, not that it mattered what Phillip thought now.

"Howdy, neighbor." Angie motioned to the door. "Grab a glass of tea and pull up a chair. I need company and girl talk."

Once I sat down, we both started talking at once.

"You go first," she said.

"No, you go first."

"I'm bored out of my skull," Angie moaned. "I'm stuck on that dispatch desk and itching to get back on the street."

"Don't rush things," I said. "You need downtime before the baby gets here."

"I know." Angie rubbed her belly. "She's kicking like a mule these days. And the heartburn is a killer."

I smiled, remembering both my pregnancies. "Has she had the hiccups yet?"

"All the time. I think she'll be a drinker." Angie laughed. "Speaking of, I can't wait until we can do a night out at Weezie's after she's born. I miss my alcohol. What's going on with you?"

I hadn't talked to Angie in a while, and I needed her advice, but I was treading on thin ice. If she determined I was working against Detective Zimmerman, she'd clam up and tell me to mind my business.

"Have you heard anything on the investigations?" I asked.

Angie's hand slowed on her tummy. "I heard that you were at the crime scene when the second body was discovered."

"I had gone to see her. When the restaurant wasn't open, Nancy and I went around back. That's when Zimmerman rolled up." I wrinkled my nose. "That guy is a jerk."

"You're telling me. I can't get anything out of him. He's locked down the investigation and accused me of sharing information with you."

I laughed. "We both know that's not true."

"What have you dug up?" Angie asked.

My mouth dropped. "Me? Nothing."

Angie chuckled. "Don't give me that. You are in this so

deep. I can tell. You get involved when it's people you *don't* know. You're snooping around this one because of Willow, Hazel, and Phillip. So, fess up. Give me the *deets*."

I feigned ignorance. "I'm clueless."

"Cece Cavanaugh, spill it." She stared at me until I broke eye contact.

"Okay, but you better not breathe a word of this to Zimmerman. He'll hang me out to dry."

I told her what I had been digging into for the last couple of days, including my deal with Phillip.

"Whoa, you're in deeper than even I could have imagined."

"Right? I keep hitting a dead end. Everything seems to point to Gracelynn. I imagine that's why she won't talk to me." I took a sip of tea. "Or Willow, but other than the cheating-with-my-ex-husband thing, she seems like a likable person. At least to where I don't want to rip her face off any longer."

"Why Gracelynn?" Angie asked.

"So far, she's been unwilling to talk to me. I think that says something. Flick, Willow, and Felicity eventually opened up."

Angie's mouth dropped open. "You talked to Willow? That's a breakthrough given your little meltdown at the spa in front of all of Wickford."

"You saw the newspaper?"

"Yup," Angie said.

I cringed, remembering the incident. "It wasn't the entire town of Wickford."

"No, just the gossip-mongers." Angie burst into laughter. "You always have the best timing."

I hoisted my middle finger in the air.

She placed both hands over her belly. "Not in front of my child, please."

We sat for a while just enjoying the sounds of nature. Our properties both backed up to a small nature preserve with a lake and walking trails. There was a time when the four of us, Dave, Angie, Phillip, and I, had spent many an evening sitting on either our patio or theirs, while the guys grilled and Angie and I caught up on our girl talk. When my kids were little, they'd be playing in the yard chasing fireflies, or practicing their tumbling skills. Times had changed. My kids were grown, and it wouldn't be long before Angie and Dave would welcome their little one.

Angie broke the silence. "Watch for the unexpected."

"What?" I asked.

"The unexpected. The person you least think did it. Gracelynn is too obvious."

I wasn't sure what shocked me most, Angie helping me figure out the killer or telling me that Gracelynn was too obvious. "Tell me more."

"Watch your back. Keep your eyes open for the least obvious and start there," Angie said.

"Well, the least obvious is Hazel. Wouldn't it be a hoot if the old witch was guilty?"

Angie shook her head. "You can't get that lucky. Hazel's a tyrant, but she's not a killer. Same with Phillip. Don't spin your wheels with them. They have nothing to gain. Neither one of them knew Kayla or Sasha well enough to have a motive. Start with the least obvious person who had a motive. Narrow down the suspect list."

"I can't believe you're saying this." I reached across the table and put my hand on her forehead. "Are you feverish? Hallucinating?"

Angie's smile faded. "I can tell you not to get involved with this, but I know you will. I want you to go into it with your eyes open. You've had too many close calls."

I leaned back in my chair, not sure I'd heard her correctly. "You're telling me to do this? Why the change?"

"I'm not telling you to do anything, Cece, but this is too juicy for you—knowing you—to ignore. And secondly, Zimmerman gets on my nerves. He's bucking for a promotion. Anyway, with Alder on leave, Zimmerman's strutting around like he owns the detective bureau."

I curled my lip. "Don't even talk to me about Alder."

"Still haven't heard from him?"

"Oh, I have. We keep missing one another's calls, and when he calls, he leaves generic messages." I felt tears sting my eyes, and I swiped them away. "He hasn't bothered to tell me his ex-wife is in town, much less that she appears to be living at his house."

"What? How do you even know his ex-wife?"

I explained about the neighbor Nancy and I had run into and her big news about taking soup to Becca's mom. "And if that's not bad enough, every time I get in Nancy's Jeep, she has to take a spin through his neighborhood. The last time, he was sitting on his front porch with Joyce like an old married couple enjoying their evening."

"I do not understand what's going on, but I will give you the same advice I gave you about this investigation. Watch for the least obvious reason. I mean, you're making yourself nuts worrying about the most obvious reason she'd be in town. Think about it. They divorced over twenty years ago. Why now? Alder's never had a serious relationship since they split up. Now he's found you. Why would he screw that up?"

I shrugged. "Maybe he—"

"Maybe he nothing. Don't be such a putz. Either trust him or not. Your choice."

I laughed. "I trusted Phillip and you see where that got me."

Angie smacked her forehead. "Alder is not Phillip. Not

even close. Don't screw this up, Cece. Call him. Text him. Go over there. Do whatever it takes. There is a logical explanation. I've worked with Alder for a long time, and he's one of the good guys."

I raised my hands in surrender. "Okay, okay. You're right. In the meantime, I need to distract myself to keep from going crazy."

Angie laughed. "And what better distraction than a murder investigation."

"Two," I said. "Make that two investigations."

"I will be sorry for encouraging you, but Zimmerman needs to be taken down a notch or two."

"Aye, aye." I saluted. "I'll do my best."

Angie reached across the table and grabbed my hand. "Be careful. I mean it. Don't get yourself in a mess like the last time. You find anything out at all, you bring it to me. I'll go around Zimmerman and take it to the captain."

"Can do. Okay, I'm headed to talk to Gracelynn. I'm feeling more confident that she might not be a suspect, but there's also a reason she keeps pulling a disappearing act."

I waved goodbye with Angie calling warnings over my shoulder.

CHAPTER TWENTY

"It's time I leveled with Cece regarding Joyce. I've dreaded this talk, but I need to have it."
Case Alder

I had stalled. Stalled in my relationship with Alder. Stalled in my quest to find out who killed Kayla and Sasha. Sure, I was getting information, but not quickly enough, and nothing pointed to one person. I wanted to drop everything. But Mama didn't raise a quitter. The idea of quitting made me dig my heels in deeper, and that was what I intended to do.

Despite my talk with Angie, as I trotted across my backyard, my anger spiked. I had no intention of waiting for Alder to tell me what was going on with Joyce. It was time to shake things up in our relationship. This time I didn't need Nancy. Phone calls and text messages didn't work. I needed a face-to-face with him. I didn't fight for Phillip, but I decided waging a battle for Alder was exactly what I wanted. To heck with his ex-wife. I wanted answers.

I slid open the back door to retrieve my keys and purse

from the kitchen. A bud vase with a single red rose sat on the counter next to a bakery bag from Oppenheimer's.

And Alder sat at my breakfast bar.

I did a double-take, my mouth hanging open like a yawning dog.

Beatrice had plated a batch of chocolate chip cookies and fixed two glasses of iced tea and had them waiting. "If you don't mind, I'm calling it quits for the afternoon," she said, untying the apron.

"Uh, no. Go ahead," I said, finding words.

She hung the apron in the pantry, grabbed the bakery bag, and said, "Thanks, Detective." Then she winked. Of all the nerve. We needed to talk about consorting with the enemy.

I didn't know whether to hug Alder or slug him, but darned if he didn't look good sitting there decked out in blue jeans and a blue-checked shirt that matched his eyes. I blinked and forced myself back to the matter at hand, which was *not* how attractive he was, or how my heart fluttered when his mustache wiggled, or how it parted to show the tiny scar on his upper lip.

"I owe you an explanation—" he started.

"Ya think?" I blinked again. My plan for waging a battle slipped away. "You've been missing in action." I wanted to launch into him about his ex-wife, the vagueness of his texts and voice mails, and his unexplained leave of absence from work that he'd not bothered to share with me, but his eyes looked sad and tired. The slump of his shoulders looked like he carried the weight of Wickford. This was not the good-natured man I knew so well. He was a tormented man. He was breaking up with me. He had summoned the courage to tell me in person.

"Just get it over with," I said. "I can take it."

He grabbed my hand and pulled me to him, burying his

face in my shoulder. I wanted to wrap my arms around him, but I pushed away.

"Don't," I said. "Don't make this worse. I know about your ex-wife."

He drew me tighter. "It's not what you think. Let me explain. I'm not that guy. You know that."

"I want to believe you. I really do." I didn't push back this time.

His tenseness eased, and I felt his sigh against my neck.

"You better have a good explanation." I let my fingers play across his broad shoulders.

"I do have a good explanation," he said.

"Then break up with me and leave. No. Why don't you just leave? I don't need or want to hear the sordid details." I spied the flower he'd brought out of the corner of my eye. A single red rosebud identical to the one he'd bought me a year ago when our relationship was just starting to blossom. The irony hit me like a brick. Our relationship had come full circle, right down to the bud vase and rose. The beginning and the end. Right back to square one.

"Cece, I am not breaking up with you." Alder pulled me into his lap. "You're the best thing that's happened to me in years. But this situation is complicated, and I need to tell you what's happening. The entire story, because I need you to trust me."

"Trust?" I laughed. "That's hard to swallow given that your ex-wife is living with you."

Alder rubbed my back, and I sensed he was struggling with words.

"It's difficult." He paused, his hand slowing on my back. "Your world blew up when Phillip was unfaithful. The same as mine when I learned that Joyce had cheated with my best friend. I am not getting back with Joyce. That has never been a choice. Never will."

I scoffed. "It appears that way."

Nancy trotted in the sliding door. "Hey. What's on our—" When she saw Alder, her eyes grew to the size of dinner plates. She took two steps back, tripped, and went down like a flailing crab—arms and legs flying in all directions. "Ooopf!"

I ran over and kneeled by her. "Are you okay?"

"Yeah." She winked several times in Alder's direction. "What's happening?" she whispered.

I shrugged. "Tell you later," I mouthed, helping her to her feet.

Alder covered his mouth with his hand, hiding a smile.

"Hi, Detective." Nancy wiggled two fingers in his direction.

"Hi, yourself," he returned the greeting.

"I'll come back." Nancy backed out the door and pulled it closed.

"Sorry about that," I said.

"Is she ever going to move out of here?" he asked.

"You're changing the subject." I redirected the conversation. "You were about to tell me why you aren't breaking up with me while your ex-wife has taken up residence in your house."

Alder raked his hands through his hair. "Okay, you're right. I don't want to have this conversation, but here goes."

My heart thudded in my chest.

"Joyce is sick. Very sick."

"And that necessitates her living with you?" I asked, not sure how his ex-wife being ill morphed into her moving into his house when she lived in Belgium.

"She's back in the states for an experimental treatment and needed someplace to stay." He frowned. "I don't owe Joyce a thing. Nothing. But I owe Becca. This is her mother, and I can't make Becca go through this alone. So, they're both staying with me."

"That's why you took a leave of absence?"

He nodded.

"Why didn't you tell me?"

"It all happened so fast. Joyce called Becca Friday and broke the news. Joyce wanted to stay with Becca while she underwent treatment. Becca lives in a six-hundred-square-foot apartment. Neither of them would be comfortable, and Becca has a full-time job and classes. I couldn't let her take this on alone, and she was too stubborn to ask for help. It was easier for me to take leave without repercussions."

I understood his predicament. If Phillip were ill, I wouldn't want either of the girls to take on the task of taking care of him, but I didn't think I could. Maybe because our split was so fresh, but I wouldn't have to worry as long as Hazel was in the picture. Not that she would take care of him, but she'd hire the best nurse her money could find. Even with Alder's explanation, it still didn't explain why he'd not told me up-front about Joyce.

"I can see from your expression you have doubts," he said.

I didn't realize my face had given me away. I tried to smile, but it felt fake. "I don't get why you didn't tell me."

"Becca panicked when she realized how serious it was. She waited until Friday night to tell me, and we went into prep mode. I knew I needed to take time off work. My boss rushed my leave through, then we had to contact a medical supply company and get a hospital bed and equipment. It's been a nightmare of phone calls."

Part of me was disappointed, and the other part understood. "I would have helped. I know people. I could have helped get things set up. I'm familiar with home healthcare options," I blabbered, still uncomfortable knowing his ex-wife was living in his home. Uncomfortable about being jealous when she was so ill. Uncomfortable that he hadn't confided in me sooner.

He took my hand. "It wasn't right to ask you. It's not right for you or my daughter. You and Becca have never met, and it's not fair to bring you into this very private moment for her when she's dealing with the reality that she may lose her mother."

I nodded my understanding.

"When you meet Becca, I want it to be a positive moment for both of you. There is no doubt you two will hit it off, but now is not that time. We'll get there, but I need to respect her time with Joyce."

I placed my hand on his cheek and kissed him. "You're a kind man. I'm sorry I doubted you."

"I want you to remember, I'm doing this for Becca, not Joyce. Well, a bit for Joyce, but not in *that* way. Not in any way that's meaningful or meant to resurrect our relationship, and she knows that. She's not here for me. She's here fighting for her life. And I aim to fight for her to get the best shot she can. For Becca."

All of my doubts and concerns faded away. My heart understood this good man standing in front of me was a keeper.

"Now we need to talk about your investigative skills," he said, his mustache lifting.

I stepped back and narrowed my eyes. "You've been talking to Zimmerman?"

Alder laughed. "I was talking about your not-so-stealthy stakeout at my house, Ms. Snoopy Pants."

I scoffed and curled my lip. "Ms. Snoopy Pants?"

"Velma is the self-appointed neighborhood watch captain of my street." His sly grin made my heart flutter.

Busted. Nancy and her big ideas. Next time I'd leave her at home. Not that I intended for there to be a next time.

"She told me all about you and Nancy staking out my house."

"Nosy old biddy. And we weren't staking out your house. I was concerned about you." I shook my head. "Nancy is not very subtle."

"Um, Nancy might be an accomplice, but you, my dear, are the guilty party. And I . . . Wait! What does Zimmerman have to do with this?" Alder smacked his forehead. "Let me guess. Don't tell me you got involved with his investigation."

"Investigations," I corrected. "There was a second murder."

"Cece, for the love of all that is holy, do not get involved. Zimmerman means business, and I can't protect you."

"Yeah, Angie's worried Zimmerman is out to make a name for himself at your expense."

"Trust me, I can handle Zimmerman. Just stay out of his way, okay? He's like a chihuahua with no teeth. He may not bite you, but he'll make so much ruckus, you'll wish he had just to get it over with. Until I get back to work, I can't do anything but tell you to steer clear." He wrapped his arms around me. "You have a knack for trouble, but you need to take this seriously. Understand?"

I didn't answer. I didn't tell him about my pact with Phillip. He wouldn't understand my need to see this through. I didn't want to make trouble for Alder, but I had a stake in seeing this investigation wrapped up and justice served to the guilty person or persons.

CHAPTER TWENTY-ONE

"When a middle-aged woman walks into your studio dressed like a streetwalker, nothing good can come of it."
Flick Donovan

I punched Gracelynn's address into my GPS and pushed aside my talk with Alder, satisfied and relieved by his explanation. Gracelynn was the missing piece. Nancy had wanted to join me, but I'd told her I'd have more luck on my own.

I pulled into the parking area at Gracelynn's condo and crossed my fingers. It still embarrassed me that I'd let her take me down and get away. But age was against me. That girl could run.

I stood at her front door, checking to make sure she didn't have one of those security doorbells. If she saw it was me, she'd probably not answer the door.

Before I could knock, the door opened, and a small puppy on a leash emerged. Gracelynn stood at the other end of the leash, gaping at me. The puppy erupted in a fit of barking and jumping. I bent down and scratched it behind the ears until it settled down.

"You again?" Gracelynn scooped up the puppy.

"Wait," I said. "Hear me out. Please?"

"Felicity told me about you."

"Yeah, I bugged her until she gave in too," I said.

She shrugged. "You are persistent. Come on. I need to walk Petal."

I worried all the way over about going into her house. Walking with her and her dog set me at ease. What was she going to do? Kill me in broad daylight? Besides, she owned a puppy. How bad could she be? Angie seemed to think Gracelynn was too obvious, and I trusted Angie's street smarts. She'd been a cop for over twenty years, and she knew criminals.

We set off down the sidewalk with Petal sniffing and trying to eat everything she encountered.

"What is this all about?" Gracelynn demanded. "I don't understand why you're digging into this. You don't work for the police. Are you just being nosy, or do you have an ulterior motive? Are you trying to break up Phillip and Willow?"

"The simplest answer to all your questions is I have a vested interest in wrapping up this investigation. Phillip and I are divorced, but our family name is associated with this investigation."

"Worries of the rich," she said with a sneer in her voice.

"Not with me. I lost everything when Phillip and I divorced. I have two daughters I'm concerned about. They have to live with this nightmare."

"What do you want from me?" She pulled a dog treat from her pocket and fed it to Petal.

"What's your take on Flick Donovan?" I asked.

She laughed. "He's a chameleon. Blends in with the background. He's a player but disguises himself as the perfect boyfriend. All the while he's hitting up your best friend. I don't have a high opinion of him."

Petal leaped and jumped at my feet. I bent and rubbed her head. "Yet, you still model for him?"

"He's an ace photographer. My career is new. I can't afford to dump him. He has an eye for art, and his photography skills are second to none. No, if I found another photographer, I'd be setting my career back years." She shrugged. "It's pathetic. As much as I hate to admit it, I need him to advance my career. If I get this new modeling contract, I'll be working with him exclusively for a year."

"Is this the job you, Kayla, and Willow were vying for?"

"Yeah," she said.

So, the odds just got better.

"Why wasn't Felicity in contention?" I asked.

"Oh, she was, but she got cut early on. And she was not happy about it. We hear all about how unfair it was all the time. She's stuck in pity-mode."

Interesting.

At the corner, Gracelynn and Petal turned left. "The dog park is at the end of this block. I'll let Petal loose, and we can find a bench and sit."

I followed, planning what I would ask next.

At the park, Gracelynn unhooked Petal's leash. Petal took off like a crazy dog, zooming all around the fenced-in enclosure.

"Petal will wear herself out and sleep the rest of the day. Puppies are a lot of work."

Never having had a dog, I took her word for it and nodded. With Michelle going off to college next year, I might have to consider getting a dog. Not a puppy, but an older one for company. Angie would have the baby. Nancy and Grant were an item—Nancy might move out if things with her and Grant got serious. My only company would be Beatrice, and she only came three days a week. That left four days in an empty house. My mood plummeted.

"Did Donovan ever seem like he . . ." I stalled, not sure how to ask if he was into the more promiscuous types of artistic expression.

"Like what?" she prodded.

"Did he take *other* kinds of photos?"

"Besides the ones Glow Girl hired us to do? I don't understand." She paused when Petal came up to the bench and sat down, waiting for a treat. Once the puppy had gobbled it down and raced off, Gracelynn turned to me. "Ew, do you mean porn?"

I nodded.

"No. That's disgusting. I would never pose for that. Talk about kill my career before it got started."

When I didn't comment, she grabbed my arm. Her expression bore a sense of panic. "What are you not telling me?"

I explained about the secret photos without telling her where I'd found them.

"Sasha told me she'd found a hidden camera in the restroom, but she never said it had photos of us. How could she not tell us that?" Tears filled Gracelynn's eyes. "Do those photos have anything to do with Sasha's death or Kayla's?"

"It's possible."

"Who had those photos? Where did you get them?" Gracelynn demanded.

I was hoping she wouldn't ask. "I saw them in Donovan's studio." I left out the part about snooping.

"What? That's ridiculous," she said. "Flick would never put his career in jeopardy to do something like that. Someone else had to plant that camera—maybe intending to set Flick up. O-M-G! I wouldn't put it past Sasha given the bad feelings between them. She told me she'd get even with him, but I thought she carried out her threat by reporting him to Glow Girl."

"That doesn't explain what happened to her," I said.

"Ugh, you're right. If Flick found out what she'd done, he would have been irate, but he would never hurt her."

Petal collapsed at Gracelynn's feet, panting like a . . . well, like a dog.

"Let's get her home." Gracelynn picked up her puppy, and we left the park.

When we arrived at Gracelynn's condo, I said, "Can I ask you something else before I leave?"

"Sure." She opened the door and put Petal inside. "Go get a drink, silly puppy."

"The morning I saw you and Felicity in the parking lot at Barney's. You all had been to happy hour the night before. Whose idea was that?"

"Felicity. Normally, Willow is the organizer of our group. If it weren't for her, we'd all be sitting around twiddling our thumbs. But Felicity thought we needed to talk about Kayla and Sasha and share our feelings."

"When did she get sick?" I asked, remembering how ill Nancy said Felicity had been.

"Felicity? I don't recall that she was sick. She didn't even drink much the night before," Gracelynn said.

"Um . . ." I wondered. "Did Felicity tell you she had told me she'd ask you to talk to me? That's why I showed up."

"No. I had no idea. I thought you were following us. She told me and Willow we shouldn't talk to you."

Either she or Felicity was lying. I swatted a fly that had landed on my arm.

Petal scratched at the door. "I better get inside before she ruins the door. She's not very patient."

"Wait. Did you and Kayla argue over Flick?" I asked.

Gracelynn's eyebrows quirked. "No. We had our difficulties. But Kayla and I had a different taste in men. Who told you that?"

"Felicity."

"No, she's the one who got her panties in a twist over Flick. Everything was always about Flick. They broke up over six months ago, but she still can't let it go."

I told her bye and headed to my van. Now I had an alternative theory about who killed Kayla and Sasha.

As much as I didn't want to, I needed to talk to Flick Donovan. After Angie's warning about being careful, I didn't want to go alone. While I didn't think Donovan was the murderer, I had yet to rule him out. After driving by his studio and verifying he was there, I called Nancy and asked her to meet me.

In less than forty-five minutes, Nancy pulled to the curb behind my van. When she exited her Jeep, I did a double-take. Goodness only knew what she'd been doing when I called. She looked like a twenties flapper—only in pants instead of a dress. Her pants and top had more dangly fringe than I'd ever seen. She wore hot-pink-and-white-striped stilettos. Where did she find these outfits? She almost undulated as she walked, the fringe syncing with her strut.

"What are we doing this time, boss?" she asked as she climbed into the seat next to me.

I frowned. "Don't call me boss, okay?"

"Okay, boss."

"I'm serious," I said.

She turned her lips into a pout. "Sorry."

"I'm going to talk to Flick about the camera that Sasha found in the restroom at Sassafras and Sage."

"How is that connected to the murders?" Nancy asked.

"I don't know, but it is. I wonder if Sasha installed the camera and planted the photos to discredit Flick. Gracelynn told me that photos like that could ruin his career if they were found out. Sasha definitely had it in for him. The whole woman-scorned thing," I said.

"So, who killed her?"

"I don't know."

"Umm. We'll just see what the freak says about that," Nancy said.

"Not we—me," I said.

"No fair. Why'd you even call me if I don't get to help?"

"Look, I'm running around questioning people. Maybe our last fiasco taught me we need to be watching out for one another. If Donovan is the killer, I won't put both of us in peril." I stopped for a breath. "You stay out here and be my eyes and ears. He only has two exits. The front door is in plain sight, or the back door. If he comes through the back, he'll come out of the alley. You'll have eyes on both places. Does that make sense?"

Nancy sank back into the seat. "I guess."

"Keep your eyes open. If something doesn't seem right, call 9-1-1." I opened the door and had one foot on the pavement.

"Wait!" Nancy yelled. "I've got an idea."

I pulled my foot back in and shut the door. "What?"

She turned to face me and had the biggest grin plastered on her face. "You wanna find out if he's into kink, right?"

"Huh?" I asked, not sure what she was getting at.

"You're just going to waltz in there and ask him if he's into taking sleazy photos of women in restrooms? You think he'll roll with that and admit it?"

She had a point.

"I don't know," I said.

"He'll deny it. Then where are you? Huh? I'll tell you

where. Right back where you started. Only this time, he clams up and won't tell you squat." Nancy's grin turned into a smug smile.

"You got a better idea?"

"Duh. Me and the *girls* got a plan." She shook her chest and made the fringe shimmy.

I slapped my head. "Let me hear it. From start to finish, and don't leave out anything. I don't want you getting in over your head. I put you in danger the last two times, and I'm not doing that again. We need to work smarter this time."

"Take your van up the street and park it out of sight," Nancy said.

I shook my head. "I'm not good with leaving you on your own."

"No, you come on back and sit in my Jeep. It blends in. You can keep an eye on everything. If he tries anything funny, you can jump him."

A vision of me hopping on his back like a cowboy riding a bronco ran through my mind. "Not going to happen. I'll call 9-1-1, but I'm not jumping on anyone."

"I didn't mean literally, silly." Nancy cackled like a hen forcing out a jumbo egg. "Call 9-1-1, then waylay him. Stall him until the cops get here."

"Okay, that sounds better," I conceded. "What's your plan?"

"You can't go waltzing in wearing your suburban mom wardrobe and ask this guy if he takes 'girly' pictures or if he's into kinky business." Nancy shook her "girls" again. "This is where I come in. Suppose I'm looking for *that kind* of photographer. Like I want to expand my portfolio."

I smacked the steering wheel. "No way. Do you understand the risk you're taking? If that guy is a creeper, you can't do this."

"That's the beauty of you watching from here. If he gets

out of hand, you got my back." She threw her hand in the air for a high five.

I reluctantly slapped back. "Let's do it. I'll go move the van, then we'll get this show on the road."

When I returned from parking the van, Nancy was not in the Jeep. I hadn't given her specific instructions to wait for me. No telling what she was doing. I climbed into the driver's seat. Nancy had left a note on the steering wheel. WISH ME LUCK. KEYS ARE IN THE CONSOLE. I CAN DO THIS, CECE.

I turned to face the front window of Donovan's studio. The way the sun glared, I couldn't see inside, but I had to have faith in Nancy. The minutes on the clock ticked by, and the longer I sat waiting, the more worried I became.

What was she doing? What was he doing? My eyes grew dry from keeping them trained on the window. I couldn't even detect movement because of the stupid reflection.

My intuition nagged at me to intervene, but Nancy's note held me back. I needed to give her the opportunity to do this. My left leg bounced up and down. My eye twitched. A feeling of dread washed over me. I had to do something; I couldn't take sitting here any longer. I glanced at the clock, and fifteen minutes had passed since I'd returned to the Jeep.

I'd give her a few more minutes, then I'd at least get out of the Jeep and move closer to the building to see if I could get a view inside the studio without all the reflection.

The next five minutes seemed like an hour. When the time was up, I jumped from the Jeep and ran across the street. As I got closer, I changed my angle and saw Nancy inside, but I didn't see Donovan.

The front door opened, and he stood there with a scowl on his face. "Why don't you come in and join us, and you can explain what you're up to."

My shoulders sagged. I considered running, but Nancy was inside. No telling what he'd do to her. I had to stay. I'd left my cell phone lying on the dash of the Jeep while I watched the time click away. I glanced behind me, trying to estimate if I could make it back to the Jeep, get the door unlocked, and get inside before Donovan could catch me. Did I risk it? If I couldn't catch Gracelynn, what chance did I have against Donovan?

None.

I followed him into the studio, dragging my feet as slowly as possible. Nancy sat hunched over on a bench.

"Why don't you join your friend over there and fill me in?"

I tromped across the room and sat beside Nancy.

"Sorry," she said. "I didn't fool him for a hot minute."

"Figures," I mumbled, relief that she was okay settling over me. But then came a wave of panic. It didn't mean we would stay okay.

Donovan pulled the chair from his desk and scooted it in front of the bench where Nancy and I sat. "You two want to give me one good reason I shouldn't call the police?"

"Police?" I let my voice rise in a shocked tone. "Why would you call the police?"

"Why wouldn't I?" He pointed a remote at the TV hanging on the far wall and it flickered on. He pressed another button, and a video of me rummaging through his desk played.

"Oh," I said. "I can explain."

"I hope so, because this disturbs me." He fast-forwarded the video to show Nancy rushing behind the backdrop. Then he zoomed in on her yellow-capri-clad legs and stopped the video on that image. "You're lucky I was preoccupied that day. I felt like something was off, but I was late for an appointment."

"Looks that way," I said.

"You two are lousy burglars, so what gives?" Donovan

turned his gaze on me. "I take it you are the brains of the operation. What were you looking for?"

Nancy stuck her tongue out.

I elbowed her in the ribs. "Stop it."

She leaned over and whispered, "He's one of the good guys."

"He had me fooled," I said.

Donovan cleared his throat. "I'm waiting."

I weighed my options. I could tell the truth—novel idea. Or I could create a whopper story, but I wasn't sure I could top whatever Nancy had done, and if Nancy's double Ds didn't help her, my barely Bs were useless. I looked down at my chest and sighed. No help.

Donovan didn't look like a killer, and he hadn't roughed Nancy up. He hadn't called the cops on us when he saw the video to report us for burglary, and he hadn't come after me. He could have found out where I lived by calling Willow. I opted for the truth.

I took a deep breath and lobbed my first question, watching for his facial expression. "Did you put a hidden camera in the restroom at Sassafras and Sage?"

He squinted one eye and hiked his lip in a puzzled expression. "What?"

"The video." I gestured at the screen. "You're a camera expert. You could slip into Sassafras and Sage and hide one with no problem."

The color drained from his face. "Hidden cameras? In a bathroom? What kind of cretin do you think I am?"

"That's what I want to know. You like photographing the ladies. Do you like taking *other* kinds of photos?"

Nancy gave her *girls* a shake to emphasize my point.

"Wait, you sent her in here pretending to want porno photos to see if I was a perv?"

I glared at Nancy. "Porno photos? You couldn't find a better idea than porn?"

She shrugged. "It was worth a shot, but he didn't fall for it. That's why he's a good guy."

"I *am* a good guy," Donovan said, drawing the attention back to him. "And this guy wants answers. Why were you rifling through my studio? Why did you accuse me of planting hidden cameras? I'm assuming this has to do with Kayla's and Sasha's deaths."

I nodded. "Before Sasha died, she found a hidden camera in the bathroom at Sassafras and Sage, and it coincided with around the time you did the photo shoot there. The photo shoot you suggested."

"And you think I planted it there? Were there photos?"

"Yes," I said.

Donovan leaned forward and grasped his head with both hands. He mumbled to himself about being ruined.

I went to his desk and found the portfolio with the torn photos and nudged him on the shoulder. "Here, I found these the other day. I swear I didn't come in here looking for them, but I found them when I was looking through your portfolios."

He took the pieces. "From Sassafras and Sage?"

"Yes. I can put them together and show you," I said.

He shook his head. "No need. I can tell by the pieces. I swear to you, I didn't take these. These would ruin me. If Glow Girl or any other client saw these, I'd be toast. The security cameras I have in the studio are legit cameras installed by a professional company. I have thousands of dollars of equipment in here and can't take a chance on it getting stolen." He craned his head around. "You found these in one of my portfolios?"

"Tucked in the back of one."

He slowly shook his head. "How did you know they were there?"

"I didn't," I said. "I stumbled across them."

He sat up straighter in the chair. "What *were* you looking for?"

I felt heat rising to my face, and the surge of another hot flash washed over my body. "Evidence."

"Evidence of what?"

I glanced at Nancy, who until now had remained silent.

"You need to tell him everything," she said.

Donovan looked at Nancy and smiled. "You should listen to her. Tell me everything, because you digging through my stuff is not acceptable. I've given you a lot of leeway, so don't make me regret not calling the police." He patted his pocket. "I still can. I've got you dead to rights on my security camera."

I joined Nancy on the bench. "I don't even know where to start, but I'll start with your relationship with all those women in the wedding."

"I don't know what they told you, but I didn't have anything serious with any of them. With Felicity, but that's over," he said. "Sasha and I had a fling. I told you about that. She couldn't let it go, but I moved on. She's still holding a grudge big time. She's been talking to the powers-to-be at Glow Girl, trying to get me fired or at least discredit me."

"Did one of them take it too seriously? Enough to kill Kayla and Sasha?" I asked.

"I haven't said anything, but Kayla and I had recently started going out." He pointed an index finger at himself. "We were keeping it quiet. I didn't want Willow or Gracelynn thinking it would give Kayla an edge when it came to the new job they were competing for."

"Would it have?" I asked. "Given her an edge."

He shook his head. "No. I don't have that kind of clout with Glow Girl."

"You're a regular ladies' man." Nancy made a barfing sound. "Did they know you didn't have any influence?"

"I don't know," Donovan said. "That's why we were keeping it quiet."

"If you didn't take those photos, who did? And why would they turn up in your portfolio?"

"How do I know you didn't put them there?" Donovan asked.

"You have the proof on your video that I found the photos," I said, puffing up like a know-it-all. "It should show I didn't put them there."

"Excellent point," he said. "We can fight about this or we can figure it out. What else do you know?"

"Psst," Nancy said, drawing my attention to her.

I rolled my eyes. "What?"

"He can help us." Nancy nodded her head in Donovan's direction. "We can use all the help we can get."

"Do you think the same person who killed Kayla also killed Sasha?" Donovan asked.

"That seems obvious, but why? If you didn't do it, I'm down to Willow, Felicity, or Gracelynn. Which one of them is capable of murder? Or could they be in it together?" Perspiration trickled down my back. My hot flash had subsided but threatened to return. I picked up a brochure from a nearby table and used it to fan myself.

"Who knows with those chicks? They were always squabbling." Donovan's phone rang, and he excused himself to take the call out in the hallway.

"Waddya think?" I asked Nancy. "Is he telling the truth?"

Nancy pursed her lips. "Um. If he had something to hide, he would have called the police on us already."

I laughed. "He might do that right now."

"Doing what?" Donovan walked in the door and stepped to his desk. "Excuse me a sec. I need to get a pen and schedule an appointment."

He picked through his desk drawer. "What's this?" He pulled the bottle of eye drops from his desk and held it up. "These are the same ones Sasha was addicted to."

"They were there when I looked through the desk." I hoped my embarrassment didn't show on my cheeks. "What's the deal with them? She made a fuss over losing a bottle of them the day of the wedding. I found a bottle like that at the spa."

"Sasha had chronic dry eye. She used those things like some people use lip balm and always had a bottle in her bag or pocket—often interrupting our photo shoots to put them in." Donovan stopped and rotated the bottle in his hand. "I don't understand the significance."

"I'm beginning to. I think eye drops were used to poison Kayla," I admitted. "If you caught me and Nancy on your fancy security camera, you probably have whoever put the photos in your portfolio and the eye drops in your desk, right?"

Donovan scratched his chin. "Kayla was killed with eye drops, and you think someone was trying to set me up? This sounds crazy. But Felicity . . ."

"Felicity what?" I asked.

"It sounds far-fetched, but what if Felicity found out I was seeing Kayla?"

"Gracelynn and Kayla had some sort of disagreement back when you did the photo shoot at Sassafras and Sage," I said. "Felicity told me it was over a guy. Could that have been you they were arguing about?"

"That's about the time I started seeing Kayla. If Kayla told Gracelynn, I know Gracelynn would have told Felicity. No telling what went through her mind."

I nodded. "Someone is setting you up. The question is, would she frame you for murder? You have nothing to lose by checking, do you?"

"Let me check the videos. They only go back thirty days." Donovan jotted a note on a legal pad.

"How long will that take?" I asked. "I'm running out of time."

"I'll get on it, but give me a day or two. My schedule is packed. I have this shoot today, then tomorrow my folks are in town all day."

The studio door opened, and a woman entered. A small boy followed her, dragging a ratty teddy bear.

"My next client is here. I'll work on this, and I'll get back with you." Donovan tousled the child's hair. "Hey, buddy. You ready for today?"

The boy whimpered and Donovan kneeled. "You be a big boy and let me get these photos, and I've got a surprise for you. Do you like to color? I have a new coloring book with your name on it."

The boy nodded.

"Mom, why don't you take him behind that screen? There are four outfit changes for today's shoot. Let's start with the tux."

The mother and child disappeared behind the screen.

I gave Donovan my number. "Call me when you find out."

Nancy and I headed out the door and Donovan said, "Nancy, when you're ready for actual photos, you come on back. Okay? You've got glorious bone structure."

Nancy preened. "I always wanted to be a model."

I slugged her in the arm. "Down, girl. He's not making you a model. He's going to snap a couple of photos. Come on, we've got work to do."

CHAPTER TWENTY-TWO

**"I hate it when Cece doesn't trust me enough to bring
me along when she talks to perps."**
Nancy Lustbader

"What are you working on today?" I asked Nancy. We sat on
my patio discussing our schedule for the day, eating bagels
and cream cheese, courtesy of Grant Hunter. He'd dropped
them off on his way to work.

Nancy dunked a bagel in her coffee. "I need to run out to
Hunter Springs to check some units."

"Is that code for you're meeting Grant out there? I saw
you two in my driveway playing kissy-face when he brought
the bagels."

A blush spread across her face. I didn't think I'd ever seen
the woman self-conscious before. In fact, I would have sworn
embarrassing her was an impossible task.

"No, silly. He probably won't even be there." She winked
as she took a sip of coffee. "But maybe I'll get lucky."

"Or he'll get lucky, right?" I laughed at my wittiness and

changed the subject. "What's your take on Flick Donovan?" After Nancy and I had left his studio, she went on her way and I came home. Her way apparently included a stop at Grant's because she hadn't come home before I'd gone to bed.

"I don't think he's guilty, but I still don't get why someone would hide a camera in the restroom at Sassafras and Sage and then hide the photos at his studio," Nancy said.

"What if the police had searched his studio and found those photos?" I took a bite of bagel. "And the eye drops weren't a coincidence."

"He'd look guilty as sin," Nancy said around a mouthful of bagel.

"Unless . . ." I jabbed my finger in the air. "What if the person did it to discredit Sasha? If those photos had leaked, her restaurant's reputation would be ruined."

"How does it tie to Kayla?" Nancy asked.

"Good question. You know, all along I've been thinking it was Gracelynn, but Felicity has been awfully forthcoming with information. Plus, she's lied to me a couple of times. I think this all has to do with the job they are vying for. Felicity was out of contention early on. What if she's holding a grudge against Flick for their spoiled relationship and the other women because of the job? What better way than setting Flick up? But something is not right, and I can't put my finger on it."

Nancy rolled her head in a circle. "You're making me dizzy."

My cell rang and displayed Phillip's number.

I answered. "What?"

"I'm sending you video from the club's security camera. Geoff had backup copies," Phillip said.

"What does it show?" I asked.

"See for yourself. I have to go." He disconnected.

I opened the email he'd sent and clicked on the first file. The video loaded, and I pressed the play icon.

Nancy peered over my shoulder. "What are we watching?"

"Footage from the country club the day Kayla died," I said.

The shot showed the door leading to the restroom where I found Kayla and the door leading to the small patio area. As the video played, Kayla came into view. She swayed as she walked, appearing to slide her hand along the wall for support. It took her several tries to open the door, but she finally managed and disappeared inside.

"She looks tanked," Nancy said.

"That's how she was at the spa, only she's more unsteady this time."

A few seconds later, Hazel appeared, coming from the same direction Kayla had come. Her dress was intact and her hair immaculate. The essence of Wickford elite, if you could ignore the awkward gait and sluggish stride. Or the essence of Wickford elite after a few too many cocktails. She passed the restroom door without a bit of hesitation, fanning her powdered face with her ridiculously overpriced clutch.

"She looks like she's about to lose it," Nancy said.

That was not a phrase I'd ever heard about Hazel unless it was a comment about her temper, which she lost often. Usually on me. Or anyone who got in her way.

"Lordy, is she heading to the men's room?" Nancy leaned in closer. "I've done that a time or two when I had too much to drink. Well, one time was because I couldn't figure out what a *Sheila* was."

I stared at Nancy. "Seriously? You went in the *Bloke* door?"

Nancy shrugged. "I had to pee."

"You're a train wreck," I said.

"You could do some serious blackmail with this video. Take that old crone down a notch or two," Nancy said.

I laughed. "Don't think it hasn't crossed my mind. Except she isn't drunk, so it's kind of not a fair fight."

"Look! Look!" Nancy pointed to the screen.

Hazel approached the back door—the one leading to the small hidden patio—

and pushed it. When it didn't open, she put her shoulder into it and pushed again.

"Why doesn't she push the exit bar?" Nancy asked.

I pulled my phone closer for a better look. "This is like watching a comedy act."

Hazel continued to ram her shoulder into the door.

"If I had to guess, I'd say she thinks she's at the restroom door. It sticks, and you have to put some muscle into it to get it open," I said.

Hazel pounded on the door then slumped against it. When she did, she fell against the push bar and the door flew open, and down she fell. She lay there for a few minutes, half in and half out of the doorway. Slowly, she crawled to her knees and tumbled out the door. The door slammed behind, cutting off our view.

"Wait. What happ—" Nancy said.

"Crap! Hold on." I selected the second file Phillip had sent.

This camera view focused on the exterior of the fire door. The door flew open, and Hazel rolled on out like a tumblebug. She lay there in a fetal position.

"Is she asleep?" Nancy asked.

"No, probably just stunned." Man, if only she were drunk, I could get so much traction out of this video. If I were that kind of person.

"That's a wicked grin on your face," Nancy said.

I shrugged. "At least I know she's okay, so I don't feel so bad. But this video is priceless."

Nancy giggled.

"This still doesn't explain her appearance when I saw her face-plant on the garden walkway," I said. "This has only got to get better."

Hazel pulled herself up, brushed herself off, and promptly tripped and fell against the same bench where I had gone down. Instead of getting up, she wallowed around grabbing at branches, trying to get purchase on something solid. When she finally grabbed the arm of the bench, she jerked herself up and snagged her dress on a rose bush. She reached around and jerked the offending limb. The thorny bush wasn't about to surrender. Hazel was in a serious conversation with the bush, probably threatening to exterminate all its relatives.

"I wish this video had sound or I could read lips," I said. "She rarely curses, but when she does, it's entertaining to watch her be all self-righteous when the cursey words are flying out of her mouth."

Her sleeve snagged when she jerked a second time. The more she fought, the more tangled it became. She swatted and slapped to no avail.

She grabbed the sleeve and yanked, liberating it from the bush, but doing major structural damage to the fabric. The sleeve, free from the dress, slid down her arm. Hazel reached up, patted her hair into place, and staggered down the walk and out of sight.

"Holy crap! What I wouldn't give to send an anonymous copy of this to the *Wickford Daily News*." I closed the file and laughed. "This is priceless."

"What does it prove?" Nancy asked.

"Hazel didn't follow Kayla into the restroom, and Hazel's condition wasn't caused by an altercation—unless you consider her fight with the rose bush. I'm more convinced than ever that Kayla and Hazel were poisoned."

My cell rang again.

I answered without checking the caller details. With my

name and phone number plastered on the side of my van, plus all the promotional flyers and business cards I constantly passed out, any caller could be a potential customer.

Nancy picked up the newspaper and paged through it, pretending not to listen, but not doing a very good job.

"That was excellent news," I said after disconnecting.

"Who was it?"

"Felicity. She and Gracelynn are at a photo shoot and she invited me to come watch." I had a sudden vision of holding the title to my van, knowing that I owned it outright.

"What's so great about that?" Nancy asked.

"Since I talked to Donovan, I'm feeling more and more like Felicity is my prime suspect. This way I can talk to her with other people around."

"You comfortable with that?"

"Sure. There will be others there. And Gracelynn is off my radar."

"Where?" Nancy asked.

"You know the old barn up on Route 7?"

"That place is so cool. They did a movie out there a couple of years ago," Nancy said.

"I know. Michelle had her senior photos taken out there. Her entire class did. It's kind of a legend around here."

Nancy followed. "Can I come? I'll even drive if you buy gas."

I scoffed. "Thought you had a rendezvous with Grant."

"I told you he'll probably be gone by then. You could swing by and pick me up." Nancy dropped the newspaper on the table and headed into my pantry.

"No, I don't need an audience." I nudged her out of the way. "What are you looking for?"

"A snack," she said.

"You just ate two bagels and half a tub of cream cheese," I chided.

Nancy stuck out her tongue in response. She grabbed a bag of chips and a bag of cookies off the shelf. "For your information, I'm taking these with me in case I get hungry later."

I snatched the cookies back. They were my favorite and cost a fortune. I rarely splurged on snacks, but I made an exception for soft-baked butter cookies from Oppenheimer's. "Not with my cookies."

"Okay, okay. I'll leave them here if you let me go with you," Nancy begged.

"You're leaving them here, regardless." I tucked the cookies out of sight and shut the pantry door. "And no, I think Felicity will be more willing to talk if it's just me. I don't want to spook her. After I'm done out there, I can swing by and give you a hand."

Nancy wrinkled her brow. "No, thanks. I don't need your help. Don't want you accusing me of not pulling my weight."

"You remind me of Michelle when you pout." I rolled my eyes. "And you know better. I offered you a raise, didn't I?"

"Yeah, it's not like I've seen it yet," Nancy said.

"And you won't if I don't figure out what's going on with Kayla's and Sasha's murder." I hated that Phillip had me backed into a corner with this stupid deal, but I had a lot riding on it, and I'd be darned if I would give it up without a fight.

"You don't think it's a trap, do you?" Nancy asked.

"No, it's a photo shoot," I said.

"Be careful," Nancy said.

"I will. If it feels off, I'll come home," I said.

"After she kills you?"

"Oh, please. There will be other people around. I promise I won't go off with her by myself. I told her about Michelle being interested in modeling. She said the next time she had a photo shoot, she'd let me know. It's just a follow-up to our conversation."

———

I turned off the pavement onto the rutted dirt road that led to the old barn. It had been pristine white back in the day, but now it was a dirty gray, with peeling and faded paint. Several decades had passed since the building had seen a fresh coat. Barely visible from the road, the barn sat back off the main highway and was legendary in Wickford.

Every year families came out here in the spring for family photos. The huge barn sat nestled in a field overgrown with redbud and dogwood trees, and the old farmer who owned it had long since given up trying to maintain it. If people got too crazy out here, and he got complaints, he'd run them off, but mostly, he just ignored everyone and let them use it.

The ancient building had a second-floor hayloft with a door where the farmer used to load square hay bales with the help of a conveyor system. The conveyor was gone, but the second-level door made an exceptional photo opportunity. Over the years, I had seen many engagement and wedding photos of cheerful couples sitting in the loft waving from the door. It was a miracle no one had fallen, but I assumed it was a risk the farmer was willing to take.

I pulled behind the barn. Two cars and an old pickup sat in the barn lot. Throwing the van in park, I jumped out and jogged toward the barn.

"Felicity!" I yelled. As I approached the door, a shiver traveled down my spine. I was excited about seeing a photo shoot in person, but I also had some hard questions for Felicity and that made me anxious. How would she react? Did I have the guts to confront her? Should I wait until the shoot was over, but before everyone packed up and left? As much as

I hated to admit it, Nancy was right—I shouldn't have come here alone. I could call her and ask her to meet me here like I did with Donovan at his studio.

No, that would just prove her right, and she'd get all big-headed about it. I had come too far to back down now. I took another step and stopped. But no one had seen me. Now seemed like a perfect time to get back in the van and leave. The voice in my head laughed at me for being chicken.

Stop it. There are three vehicles here. At least two other people, not including Felicity. Confront her and get it over with. Get the answers you need to get this wrapped up once and for all. Nothing bad will happen. Yeah, but that's probably what Sasha said right before she felt the knife in her back.

That was all it took. My heart kicked into high gear, thudding against my chest. I clicked the remote on the van and ran back. The wind had picked up, and bits of straw and debris swirled around my feet. A moaning sound came from the barn as the wind pounded against it. Little hairs on my arm stood at attention.

As I reached for the door handle, I heard a voice behind me. I screamed and froze, waiting for the knife or the bullet. When I realized it was Gracelynn, I slumped against the van, adrenaline rushing through my veins.

The large double doors were shut. Gracelynn and Felicity stood in a regular passageway doorway, waving. Felicity wore a billowy white cotton dress with a tangle of flowers woven in her hair, which was curled into ringlets falling gently onto her shoulders. Gracelynn wore a flattering off-white A-line dress covered in delicate Chantilly lace. Her gorgeous hair had been swept up, with soft tendrils framing her face.

"Come in and get out of the wind. It's crazy out here," Gracelynn said.

I clicked the van locked and joined them, the coolness inside the barn a welcome relief from the blistering wind.

Contrary to my belief that the farmer had abandoned the barn, it still appeared to be in use. The entire barn was decorated for a wedding—a beautiful, rustic wedding—complete with tiny fairy lights strung from the rafters. Garlands of magnificent white silk, blossoms, and tulle graced several old farm implements. A few photo backdrops were in place at various locations in the barn, with lights and reflectors set up. Several old tractors looked in various stages of disrepair. The machine-related smells associated with the other pieces of random farm equipment irritated my nose.

A wooden stairway led up to the loft, and in the opening, I saw rows and rows of tidy hay bales matching the ones on this level. Sunlight glinted in from the loft opening, and the breeze rustled the hay. Small bits of which floated from the loft.

"Oh, my word, it's beautiful. It's amazing." I twirled around and took in the scene a second time. "Who would have known from the outside how lovely it is?"

"Glow Girl rented it for the month. We're shooting a campaign for one of the chain bridal shops," Gracelynn said.

"I thought you'd like it." Felicity sat on a bale of hay. "I would have invited you sooner, but it's been so hectic. Today we're doing a few re-shoots, so it won't be nearly as chaotic. But I just got a text. The others are running late. Once they get here, it will go quick."

"Is Willow going to be here?" I didn't know how I felt about Willow, but I didn't want to socialize with her. Much less watch her strut around in bridal attire. And given the fact that she'd called the wedding off, I sure didn't want to be a shoulder for her to cry on or vent to. We were not pals and never would be.

"No, she didn't need retakes. Her photos always turn out gorgeous," Gracelynn said.

I sniffed the air. "You'd think they could do something about the smell. It kind of ruins the vibe."

"I don't know what's up with that. It's terrible." Gracelynn sniffed the air. "This is the first time I've really noticed it."

"Make yourself comfortable." Felicity patted a bale next to her. "We shouldn't have to wait too long. Everyone's eager to get this wrapped up."

"Is it okay if I look around?" I wanted this over with, but now with everyone lagging, I'd be here forever, and there was no way I'd ask Felicity these questions when it was just the three of us.

"Knock yourself out." Gracelynn opened a cooler next to the bale where Felicity sat and pulled out a bottle of water. "Anyone want one?"

Something about what Felicity had said niggled the back of my brain, but I couldn't quite catch what it was. I hesitated. I had no intention of drinking it. "Sure."

Felicity shoved her hand in the cooler and withdrew a bottle. "Yes, I'm parched."

Gracelynn twisted off the cap and handed a bottle to me then took one for herself.

I walked around the barn, admiring the various vignettes that had been created with the backdrops. Who knew hay and farm equipment could be turned into wedding décor with the addition of some tiny lights, swags of flowers, and canning jars? For a moment, I let myself dream that Jessie and Brad might opt for a rustic barn-themed wedding. They'd been dating for ten months. Jess had never dated anyone that long. A mother could dream.

Gracelynn came up beside me. "I'm surprised to see you here."

I put my dream on hold. "Felicity invited me to watch the photo shoot."

"Really?"

"Yes." I looked at Gracelynn, gauging how much I could trust her. She seemed sincere, and her boss had said what a tender heart she had. The only negative I'd heard about Gracelynn was from Felicity. I felt confident Gracelynn was not the killer. And even more confident in my suspicion of Felicity.

"Who else is here?" I asked.

"Just us. Felicity said the others are on their way," Gracelynn said.

"There were two cars and a truck outside. Who does the third one belong to?"

"The farmer, I guess. It's been here every time we've come out."

"It's just the three of us?" I asked.

Gracelynn's perfectly manicured eyebrows scrunched together. "So?"

I meandered toward another vignette, farther from where Felicity was seated, hoping Gracelynn would follow.

She did.

"What's going on?" She took a long drink from the bottle.

"How much do you trust Felicity?" I asked.

"What do you mean?"

Dust in the air caught in my throat and sent me into a coughing fit. I glanced at Felicity, who was still sitting on the hay bale across the barn. She leaned forward, tilted her water bottle, and drank, then smoothed her white cotton dress over her legs.

I was seconds away from taking a drink when my coughing abated. I cleared my throat and continued walking.

"We've got plenty of water." Gracelynn tipped hers and took another drink. "Don't be shy. This dusty old barn can get to you, especially when it's windy. Felicity always brings plenty of water for us."

"Felicity brought the cooler?" A rush of fear zipped through me. "Don't drink any more water."

"What are you two talking about?" Felicity asked from across the barn.

"Just admiring the setup," I said.

Gracelynn stared at her water bottle. "Why not?"

"I know this will sound crazy, but hear me out before you say anything." I took the bottle from her hand. "I think Felicity killed Kayla and Sasha."

Gracelynn turned and looked at Felicity. "No! No way. You're wrong."

"Shh, not so loud," I whispered, glancing at Felicity.

She looked gorgeous, the perfect example of a laid-back country bride. Could this woman really be a killer? Could I trust Gracelynn to keep her mouth shut? And where was everyone?

"I don't think so. It all adds up. Look, I don't have time to explain it all now. But I promise, as soon as your photo shoot is over, I will. Speaking of that, who all is coming today?" I asked, swatting at an annoying fly that kept buzzing around, trying to land on my face. I hated barns. They scared me with all the creepy-crawly critters. Not to mention the smells and snakes. This barn was especially smelly with the chemical machine odor permeating the air.

"I don't know. Felicity called me this morning and said Flick had called her and said we had several shots that needed to be redone. She didn't say who all needed to have re-shoots," Gracelynn said.

I dropped the bottles I'd been holding. "We have to go. Now!"

"Where're you going?" Felicity said in my ear.

I jumped. I hadn't noticed she had left the bale of hay she'd been sitting on.

"Um, I need to get home. I didn't realize this would take so long. Maybe I can come back some other time," I said.

"When's Flick getting here?" Gracelynn fanned her face. "It's too hot to stand around waiting on him. My hair is wilting."

"He's not coming." Felicity's faced hardened. "The re-shoot is off."

"Why?" Gracelynn said.

"He just called. From the police station." She blinked rapidly and her frown deepened. "He's been arrested for killing Kayla and Sasha."

"What? Why would he do that?" Gracelynn cried in disbelief. "Why would he call you?"

I wasn't buying it. "Come on, Gracelynn. We need to go," I said.

"No, I want to hear this." Gracelynn planted her feet in a stubborn stance. "He would never hurt Kayla. This better be good," Gracelynn said.

"Yes, it better be good," I said. "Donovan told me he and Kayla had recently started going out," I said.

"They have not!" Felicity screamed. "Flick loves me."

"Felicity, you know better. You've got to stop obsessing over him." Gracelynn reached for Felicity's arm, and Felicity slapped her hand away.

"I'm not obsessing. It makes sense. Think about it. He knew I would have been in contention for the contract with Glow Girl had it not been for Kayla. She's been complaining to Glow Girl about him. He probably thought if they gave the campaign to her, they'd dump him as the photographer," Felicity said.

"That makes no sense. *Sasha* reported him to Glow Girl, not Kayla," Gracelynn said.

Felicity sniffled. "Kayla did too. Willow told me at happy hour."

"I don't remember her saying anything about that," Gracelynn said.

"You were in the restroom."

"I don't believe you," Gracelynn said.

"How was Sasha involved?" I asked. I kept tripping over a piece of information and could not for the life of me bring it to the front of my brain. I was living proof that brain fog from menopause was real. It was as real as the hot flashes and insomnia I suffered from regularly.

Felicity shook her head. "She set him up. She told me she put that camera in the restroom."

"Why?" Gracelynn demanded.

Felicity's chin trembled. "She was going to send the photos to Glow Girl, but I couldn't let her do that. I had to protect Flick. What I don't know is how those photos wound up at his studio."

Gracelynn's eyes widened. "You killed Sasha. Did you kill Kayla too? But you got sick at the club too."

"All an act," I said. "She was never sick, were you?"

I didn't get an answer because Gracelynn's knees buckled, and she went down in a heap of satin and lace in front of me. When she did, Felicity made a break for the door.

I wanted to get the devil out of the barn, but I couldn't leave Gracelynn. I kneeled beside her. "Hey, are you okay?"

When she didn't respond, I screamed, "Felicity, help me! Something's wrong—"

"She'll only sleep for a little while." Felicity smiled and slammed the door, cutting off the daylight, the only light now coming from the fairy lights overhead and the sunlight coming from the big hayloft door upstairs.

I pushed against the door, but it didn't budge. The rusty hinges groaned against my weight.

"Hey!" I pounded on the door until my fists throbbed.

"Felicity, help me. What did you give her?" I continued to flail against the door.

"You should have left well enough alone!" Felicity screamed. "You were too nosy. Always coming around with your questions. Even Flick called me yesterday and made accusations."

I backed up and ran full speed, ramming the door with my shoulder. "Come on. Let us out. Let's talk about this."

Felicity sobbed against the door. "No, it's too late. I've done too much to take it back."

"Please, listen to me," I pleaded. "It's not too late. Tell me what you gave Gracelynn. Was it in the water?"

A car engine started. Tires crunched across the gravel and the sound grew distant. *She's leaving us here.*

I checked Gracelynn to make sure she was breathing and that her pulse was good, then I picked my way up the stairs to the loft and ran over to the opening. Sure enough, I could see Felicity's car driving down the rutted road toward the highway.

All the things I'd been trying to remember tumbled into place like a giant jigsaw puzzle finally coming together. She hadn't been on a shoot today, at least not one with Donovan. He'd said yesterday that his parents were coming to town, and he was taking them out for the day.

I pulled out my cell to call Nancy, only I had no bars. Thank goodness she knew where I was. Eventually, when I didn't come home, she'd come looking for me. It might mean spending the night in the barn if she came home late.

I walked around the loft, trying to find a signal to no avail. I even stuck my hand and phone out the loft door, hoping for one measly bar to make a call. My only option was to find a tool in the mishmash of equipment to pry the door open.

On my way down the stairs, I smelled smoke.

CHAPTER TWENTY-THREE

"Who suspected it would be so easy to get Cece out to the barn on the promise of seeing a live photo shoot?"
Prime Suspect

Tiny flames licked the base of the wall next to the door. The double door looked like a safe bet, no flames lapping at them. I grabbed a handle and pulled. It creaked and groaned, but I couldn't push or pull them open.

I checked on Gracelynn again. Sleeping like a baby.

"Gracelynn, wake up, honey." I patted her face gently, trying to rouse her.

No response.

I pulled a handful of ice from the cooler and massaged her face with the cold cubes.

Still no response.

I grabbed under her arms and pulled her farther into the barn, away from the burning door. When I was satisfied she was out of immediate danger, I made her comfortable and concocted a pillow out of hay for her head. I suspected

Felicity had given her a double dose of sleeping pills disguised in the water bottle and thanked my lucky stars I hadn't touched mine.

I noticed a long rod with a hook hanging on the wall. I dropped my purse on a hay bale, snatched the hook off the nail, and jammed it in a tiny slit between the doors, pushing and twisting to get leverage to force the doors open. Nothing.

I tried another door with the same result. The chemical odor I'd smelled earlier was stronger at this end of the barn. A jolt of white-hot fear raced through my limbs when I recognized the smell—kerosene. My Grandpa Earl used it to burn brush when I was a kid. I remembered him pouring it around the base of the brush then standing back and throwing in a match to ignite the pile. There were two cans marked KEROSENE next to a workbench. I lifted each one. They were both empty.

When I checked my phone for a signal—still nothing. Why hadn't I listened to Nancy? Though, if I had, we'd both be in a barn with tiny, mesmerizing flames inching their way toward the stacks of dry hay. Hay that Felicity had doused with kerosene.

The cooler still had ice and two bottles of water, which I poured onto the stray flames to keep them from getting to the bales.

The smaller door was hot to the touch, so I didn't dare try to pry it open for fear the fire would *whoosh* into the building and the entire thing would go up in flames and toast us like marshmallows.

I gave the double door another whack with the hook, venting my anger against the wood over and over and over in frustration. When it didn't budge, I sank to the floor and let the tears flow. I couldn't sit by and let the barn burn down around us. With Gracelynn passed out cold, it was up to me to find a way out.

There were several stalls in the middle of the barn. I hurried down there looking for an exit. When I was a kid, my Grandpa Earl's barn had a door in each stall leading outside to a fenced enclosure. I ran from stall to stall trying doors. I pushed against the ones that weren't blocked by bales of hay stacked to the ceiling. None of them budged. I changed my tactic and searched for a horse blanket or something to smother the fire, anything to keep it from blazing out of control. Instead of a blanket, I found a hydrant with a hose attached between the first and second stall. I said a prayer and lifted the rusty handle as far as it would go. Nothing. Then a trickle emerged. The trickle did not change as I tugged the hose closer to the fire—brief spurts and glugs as I pulled. Nothing like the stream I needed to extinguish the flames, but I had to wet down everything. I didn't remember the flash point of kerosene, but I knew the flames didn't have to reach the hay for it to ignite.

I tugged the hose closer to the flames, and it stuck on something, nearly jerking me off my feet. It had tangled itself good. I reared back and pulled as hard as I could. The tangle loosened, and the flow increased a bit. The flames kept growing closer. Sweat clouded my vision and poured down my face. My perspiration-soaked clothing clung to me.

Flames crawled up the walls at the far end of the barn where I had entered. My trickle of water would be useless against it. The best I could hope for was a passing neighbor who would see the fire and call 9-1-1 before the kerosene ignited.

I aimed my hose at the ground and kept soaking the bits of straw and debris, alternating between spraying and stomping out the flames with my shoes. My arms grew weary from tugging the heavy hose. Smoke wafted across the ceiling, and my lungs ached from inhaling the scorching air. I pulled off my shirt and trickled water on it, letting it soak through, then placed it over my nose and mouth and tied the sleeves behind my head.

Relief was instantaneous and gave me a burst of energy until I realized I was losing the battle. I drenched the hem of Gracelynn's dress and placed it gently over her nose and mouth. Fire crept toward us on both sides. The temperature in the barn had risen several degrees, and it would only be a matter of time before the whole barn burst into flames.

If I abandoned fighting the fire, I could go up into the loft and get fresh air from the hay-loading door, but I'd have to leave Gracelynn here. There was no way I could drag her up the staircase. The downside was the fire would continue to grow until it ignited the hay then spread to the hay stacked in the loft. I could jump from the second story onto a graveled barn lot and try to go for help. A broken leg or two would be better than burning to a crisp in the barn. If I could hold out until someone notified the fire department, it would be worth the risk.

I dropped the hose and climbed the stairs. When I reached the top, I untied my shirt from around my face and put on the wet mess. Lord knew I didn't want to be found in a heap in the gravel in my bra with my shirt tied around my face. If Hazel thought my van was an embarrassment, she would die of mortification when that photo hit the Wickford gossip column.

The highway was empty—not a car, truck, or tractor in sight. My hopes of a quick rescue went down in flames. Or up in flames was more like it. I sat in the opening, letting my feet and legs dangle down the side of the barn. The lot below looked so far away. When I worked in the hospital before Michelle's birth, I'd seen my share of fall victims and it was never pretty—surgery, pins, rods, physical therapy. I'd have to take a chance and jump when the fire overwhelmed the barn. I thought about Gracelynn. Could I leave her in the barn and try to escape myself? My heart broke as I contemplated my next move.

The fresh air blowing against my face gave me hope until I realized the breeze only fanned the flames below. I leaned back against a nearby bale and began reciting all the things I was thankful for in my life. My children, my health—at least for now. After I jumped, it would be a different story. I was thankful for my amazing best friend, Angie, and that she would soon give birth to a long-awaited baby.

In some ways, I was thankful for Phillip. Without him, I wouldn't have Michelle or Jessie. I wouldn't recognize the difference between a toxic relationship and an excellent one —which led me to Alder. He had flaws that I was sure would be revealed as we continued to learn about one another, but he'd proven himself to have a good heart. What more could I ask?

Wham! Something below me fell and shook the building. I hopped to my feet, nearly losing my balance. Smoke billowed into the loft. I stared at the barn lot below me. Was now the time to jump? I checked the highway, hoping for a car, a truck. I'd even settle for a bicyclist. Someone to see the flames and call 9-1-1.

I had made up my mind. Now was the time to jump and worry about the consequences later. I moved closer to the edge of the opening, closed my eyes, and said a quick prayer. When I opened my eyes, I saw a cloud of dust rising on the gravel. Someone was driving lickety-split up the rutted road leading to the barn. The dust rolled in waves, covering the vehicle, but it didn't matter. Someone was coming. I lost sight when the road curved to the right to make its way behind the barn, but the dust kept expanding, so I took that as a positive sign.

Unless it was Felicity coming back to make sure the barn was still burning with me and Gracelynn inside.

———

I raced downstairs, ready to greet my rescuer. At the foot of the wooden staircase, I stopped. Gracelynn looked so peaceful, like a sleeping princess. Fire inched toward her, toward the hay. Flames engulfed the single door. The two double doors were on fire. If my rescuer could get the other doors open, I could move a few bales and escape.

My only dilemma being the kerosene. Felicity had drenched the bales. If I climbed them, I'd be a human torch if the fire ignited the bales before we got the doors open or if the flames exploded in a back draft when the doors opened. A chance I was willing to take.

I stepped on an end bale and picked my way up the zigzag pile until I was standing on top. A bale in the stack shifted, and down I went, bumping against ragged bales and smacking the ground when I landed facedown on the ground.

A roar filled my ears. I covered my head, certain the kerosene had ignited. Between cowering and praying the end would be quick, I blocked out everything around me and closed my eyes tight. I didn't want to see the fire coming.

"I'm sorry, Gracelynn," I cried. "I'm so sorry."

"Cece! Cece! Where are you?"

Someone tugged my arm and dragged me across the barn floor.

"Gah! I'm choking," I yelled, trying to get myself loose.

"Good grief, you need to cut back on the sweets. Can you help and not be such a sack of potatoes?"

Nancy's voice had never sounded so sweet.

When we cleared the door, she helped me stand. "Are you able to walk? We need to get farther away from the building."

"We need to get Gracelynn. She's still in there." I stood on shaky legs and limped toward the barn.

"Stay here." Nancy propped me up against my van and went back inside.

"Hurry!" Every pulse point in my body pounded.

A few minutes later, she emerged dragging Gracelynn. I ran over to help. We pulled Gracelynn to the adjoining field, me coughing and hacking like I had a two-pack-a-day habit.

A loud *whoosh* exploded. I turned in time to see the entire barn go up in flames, with Nancy's Jeep sitting in a crumbled mess where she'd crashed through the double doors to liberate us.

"Holy crap," I said. "You rammed the Jeep for me."

"I would have used your van, but you locked it." Nancy laughed and threw her arms around me. "Speaking of vans, you better move it. And her car too."

"My purse and keys are on fire in the barn. Hers too, I imagine. Let's just hope it doesn't spread. I can't afford to lose the van."

Nancy frowned. "Yeah, I'll miss that Jeep. I hope you come through with that raise."

"After you rescued me, I don't have a choice. We'd be toast if you hadn't arrived." A sharp dryness brought on another coughing fit, and I choked out a breath.

In the distance, a siren blared, then another.

"Sounds like the cavalry is here." Nancy patted my back. "Are you okay? I panicked when I drove up and saw the barn on fire."

"What made you come out here?" Not that it upset me. She'd saved my life. "Weren't you going to Hunter Springs?"

"I did, but I wanted to be here when you talked to Felicity. Grant wasn't there, so I figured, what the heck, Cece can get mad if she wants, but I'm going, and she can get over herself. Did Felicity set the fire?"

"Yes, after jamming the door so we couldn't get out. She must have had it all planned and doused the hay bales with kerosene. Even had a cooler with water bottles that had some kind of sedative in them. If I had drank that water, both Gracelynn and I would be dead."

Nancy looked down at Gracelynn. "Was she involved?"

"No, Felicity did this all on her own."

Two water tankers, several fire trucks, and a rescue vehicle pulled into the field and started unloading equipment and hoses.

My phone vibrated in my pocket. *Now I have a signal.*

"Ms. Cavanaugh, it's Flick Donovan. I checked the security footage," he said.

"Let me guess, Felicity planted those photos."

"No, Sasha did," he said.

"I don't understand." Now I was confused. Why would Sasha plant the photos? Was she working with Felicity?

"I think it was an attempt to discredit me. Sasha still holds a grudge because I wouldn't commit to her. She had to have taken those photos herself. She knew we would be shooting at the restaurant," Flick said. "But I can't believe she would be involved in Kayla's murder."

"No, she told Felicity about her attempt to ruin your reputation with Glow Girl," I said.

"If those photos were found during the investigation, it would have been all over the news. Sasha hid them the day after Kayla died. I didn't see it earlier because I only went back to the day you and your assistant broke into my studio. I had a feeling that something was off that day. If I had gone back farther, I might have—"

"Don't beat yourself up," I said. "Did she put the eye drops there too?"

"No, that was Felicity," he said.

"Were they together?" I asked.

"No."

"I'll lay odds that Sasha's fingerprints are on that bottle. I bet Felicity waited until the rehearsal dinner to snatch a bottle from her." Felicity set Flick up for Kayla's murder, but when she found out Sasha had a plan to get even with him, it was more than she could handle. Felicity wanted the sole pleasure of seeing Flick squirm for his indiscretions.

"Will you call Detective Zimmerman at Wickford Police Department and tell him?" I dreaded giving information to Zimmerman.

"Will do," he said.

"Flick, can you keep my name out of it? Zimmerman's been on my case, and he won't appreciate my help."

"Sure thing." Donovan disconnected.

I called Phillip next to let him know. When all the dust had settled around this case, I wanted credit. I didn't give him details, because I was afraid Willow would tip off Felicity before the police caught up with her.

My call went to voice mail, and I didn't have to speak directly to him.

"It's Cece," I said into my phone. "No need to call me back. Keep your eye on the news in the next day or so. I can't share the details, but *we* know who killed Kayla and probably Sasha. I wanted to let you know it's almost over. Tell Hazel the Cavanaugh name remains unblemished." Other than the blemishes Phillip inflicted.

An ambulance and a county deputy arrived, and I was glad we weren't in Wickford waiting for an inquisition from Detective Zimmerman.

CHAPTER TWENTY-FOUR

"Again, if Cece had trusted me, she wouldn't have gotten into this mess. The Jeep would still be in one piece instead of smashed into a disaster."
Nancy Lustbader

The fire department declared the barn a total loss along with Nancy's Jeep. By the time they got the fire under control, the barn had fallen into itself and onto Nancy's Jeep. My van survived, with a few scorch marks on the hood and blistered paint where burning embers had fallen.

A paramedic radioed the hospital where Jessie was on duty and asked her to call Michelle to bring my spare key ring from home. I was not looking forward to conversations with my daughters. The paramedic said I didn't need to go to the hospital, and I agreed. Gracelynn had come around, but since we didn't know what she'd been given, they loaded her in the ambulance and took her to the hospital. After the deputy questioned us, Nancy drove me home in my scorched van.

I had just sat on the sofa when the doorbell rang.

"I'll get it!" Nancy yelled. "Stay put."

Footsteps pounded down the hallway, echoing off the tile.

"Where is she?" Detective Zimmerman yelled.

"Great room," Nancy said.

The huge, hulking form of Detective Zimmerman filled the opening between the kitchen and the great room. "What is your explanation?"

I motioned for him to sit down. "I guess the deputy contacted you?"

"I guess the deputy contacted you," he mimicked. "Of course, he did. You practically got killed and almost blew up my case. I have a warrant for Felicity Gaines's arrest. Now she's gone. If you had stayed out of this investigation, like I asked, she'd be sitting in jail. Instead, I had to issue a BOLO."

I cringed. I knew enough from listening to Alder what a BOLO was. Be on the lookout—as in all cars were given a description of her vehicle and license plate. Her photo would soon flash across the TV too.

"You're blaming the wrong person. She called me. You think I chased around the county looking for her, found her at the barn, and confronted her? Guess again." Normally, I would have shut my mouth and taken his tongue-lashing, but I was angry. Angry at myself for getting duped by Felicity. Angry at Zimmerman for being a condescending jerk. Angry at Alder for being on leave.

Zimmerman paced to the fireplace and back to the sofa. "What were you thinking? Oh, wait. You weren't. You were running around playing Nancy Drew. I've got news, lady. You're lucky I don't haul you down to the station and book you."

Tears sprang to my eyes, and I blinked several times to keep them back. I would not let this oaf intimidate me. Despite my determinedness, a tear rolled down my cheek. I swiped it away.

"Jeez, don't do that," he said. "Tears do not work on me."

Nancy walked in with a cocky grin and sat on the sofa. She wore skin-tight leggings and a top so see-through I knew what color her bra was. "I guess you'll want to question me too."

Zimmerman raised his hands in the air in defeat. "Why me? What did I do to deserve this?"

The doorbell rang.

Nancy rose. "I'll get the door." She sashayed out of the room, wiggling her booty seductively.

Zimmerman put an index finger to his head and mimicked pulling a trigger.

An angry voice drifted down the hall. A few seconds later, Nancy returned. "Detective, there's someone in the foyer who'd like a word."

"What now?" Zimmerman growled.

Nancy shrugged. "Something about the investigation."

Zimmerman stomped out.

"What was that all about?"

Nancy grinned. "A little rescue mission."

"Huh?"

More angry voices came from the foyer.

"Can you cut her some slack?" It was Alder.

Zimmerman flung a curse word back.

"Look, Leo, I've overlooked a few of your blunders. More than a few, actually. Cece is not calculating or manipulative. Well, maybe a little manipulative. She was trying to help. Misguided or not, her intentions were not malicious."

Manipulative? Misguided? Wait until I talk to him.

"I need to know what happened today," Zimmerman said.

"I'm not asking you to overlook anything. I'm asking you to give her some time. She'll cooperate. Besides, she has a pretty good intuition."

Ah, how could I be mad at that?

"Alder, you're letting this woman cloud your judgment," Zimmerman said.

"Leo, don't even pretend you know anything about me. My patience level is about a minus ten. Now get out of here and leave her alone. You can get your information tomorrow."

"Oh, I'll get my information," Zimmerman said.

The next words were spoken lower, and I couldn't make out what was said.

Footsteps crossed the front hall.

"Thanks, Alder," Zimmerman said. His entire demeanor had changed. "You tell her I'll be back tomorrow."

"Will do."

The front door open and closed.

A few seconds later, a rumpled-looking Alder appeared in the doorway. His five o'clock shadow looked more like a ten o'clock shadow, and dark circles lay beneath his eyes.

"Are you okay?" Alder joined me on the sofa and put his arm around me.

I nodded and leaned into him, feeling his scratchy chin hair against my cheek. "Yeah, I'm fine, but you need to shave."

Nancy plopped down into a chair and drew her legs underneath her. "Guess you told Zimmerman off, huh?"

"Do you mind leaving us alone?" Alder said.

"Sure." She smirked. "Thanks for calling me, Nancy. Thanks for keeping Cece from getting burned to a crisp. Thanks, Nancy, for crashing your Jeep into the barn," Nancy said with sarcasm. "Sure, I'll go to my room. No worries. I'm just the hired help." She left, waving her arms like a raging lunatic had possessed her.

"I'll have to smooth that over, you know," I said to Alder. "She didn't deserve that."

"I know. I know. I'll bring her a donut from Oppenheimer's tomorrow as a peace offering," he said. "I am glad she called, but she can be so annoying. I don't understand what Grant sees in her."

"I heard that!" Nancy yelled from the kitchen.

"Nancy, please!" I said.

"I will because you asked nicely," she said to me. "But not because *you* insulted me." Those words she directed to Alder. "You get more flies with jelly. Remember that—and I'd rather have a red velvet cupcake."

The door slid shut, and there was blissful quiet in the kitchen.

"Jelly?" Alder burst out laughing.

"It's Nancy. What can I say? But you owe her an apology and a cupcake. Maybe two. That was harsh."

"Let's get back to the reason I'm here." Alder took my hands in his. "Or better yet, what's this about crashing her Jeep?"

"Long story, but she sacrificed it for me," I said.

"We've got time. Tell me what's going on. Nancy's phone call was irrational, but I gathered you and Zimmerman were tangling about the recent murders. Something about cornering the suspect. Which doesn't surprise me in the least."

"That's not exactly the way it happened. The woman duped me. She called me under false pretenses then locked me and her best friend in a barn and set it on fire."

Alder smirked. "Out of the blue, she invited you out to a barn, and you didn't think it was odd?"

"No, she invited me to a photo shoot. I'd said I wanted to see one. It made sense."

"Right. I got rid of Zimmerman for now, but he'll have questions for you. And you better be straight with him."

"I overheard. How did you get rid of him?"

"He's been angling for a promotion. He needs my recommendation, so I told him to back off, and I'd see what I can do."

My heart melted. "You did that for me?"

"I did. But to be fair, he deserves a promotion. He's had a couple of slipups, but nothing detrimental. He's a good guy. Just a little over the top now and then. Enough about him." He leaned in and planted a kiss on my cheek. "Are you okay?"

I nodded. "If Nancy hadn't shown up when she did, I'd be toast."

"I guess we both owe her a debt of gratitude," he conceded. "And I'd say you owe her for calling me when Zimmerman showed up. You'd be knee-deep in trouble if she hadn't."

"Sorry," I said.

He shook his head. "Don't worry about it."

I cuffed him on the shoulder. "How come you answered her call? Not that I'm complaining, but you haven't answered a call from me all week."

Alder rubbed his shoulder. "You got quite a punch for someone who's recuperating from smoke inhalation." His expression turned serious. "Joyce is in the hospital. Becca and I are taking turns staying with her. I was on my way home when Nancy called."

"Oh, jeez. I'm sorry. I didn't even ask about her. Is it bad?"

Alder nodded. "She reacted to the treatment. Took her to the hospital last night."

That explained his appearance. "I'm so sorry. Were you there all night?"

"Yeah. I can't get Becca to leave, so I was on my way home for a quick shower." He raked his hand through his hair. "I need to stop by Becca's place and pick up a change of clothing for her."

"Is there anything I can do?" The stress was wearing on

him. It must have been horrible supporting Becca while juggling the emotions he felt about his ex-wife. What I did not understand was how Joyce could cheat on this amazing man.

He sighed. "There's not much anyone can do."

"I'm here if you need me. How's Becca?" My girls would be a mess. I dreaded the day something happened to Hazel. On one hand, she would no longer be a dominant figure in my life, but Jessie and Michelle would be devastated. I would put aside my ill feelings and do whatever it took to comfort my girls—that was what family did. I empathized with Alder's dilemma.

"Having a tough time. As expected, she and Joyce are close. I worry about her."

"Make sure she takes care of herself. And if she's agreeable, get her to talk to the hospital chaplain. That might help. Take care of yourself too."

He pulled me in for another hug, then stood. "I need to go. When Zimmerman comes back, and he will come back, level with him. That's your best option. He won't arrest you for interference, but you'll go a long way in repairing the damage you've done with him."

I walked him to the door. "What about you? You didn't stick your neck out too far for me, did you?"

He touched the end of my nose with his finger. "Let me worry about me. Weave your magic with Zimmerman so he'll cut you slack."

After I closed the door, I turned around and screamed.

Nancy screamed.

"Jeez, where did you come from?" I asked. "You scared me to death."

Nancy stuck a finger in her ear like she'd pull out a glob of wax. "Yeah, well, I'm deaf now. Thanks. And you're awfully jumpy."

"With a great excuse. Until Felicity is behind bars, I won't be getting much sleep."

"Crazy dingbat. Lucky for you I got a hold of Alder."

"I will still need to answer Zimmerman's questions, but thanks for calling Alder. At least I can put it off until tomorrow."

"Are you in deep dookie with Alder?"

I shrugged. "No more than normal."

CHAPTER TWENTY-FIVE

**"I swear Cece needs to be in custody to protect her
from herself. Since the divorce, she's gone loony."
Phillip Cavanaugh**

The first thing the next morning, before I'd even opened my
eyes, someone was ringing the doorbell. I threw on a robe
and trudged down the stairs. When I flung open the door,
Phillip pushed past me.

"What the hell? Are you okay?"

I rubbed the sleep from my eyes. "Huh?"

"It's all over the news about the fire and that crazy broad
locking you in there." Phillip gestured wildly. "The news
didn't say your name, thank goodness, but they plastered your
van all over the news, so everyone knows the *local woman* was
you."

"Slow down. It's way too early for this." I tugged the belt
of my robe tighter and padded down the hall to the kitchen.
"I'm making tea. Want a cup?"

Phillip cursed. "No, I don't want that sissified crap. Did you throw out all the coffee?"

"It's been a year. Gross," I said. "The house is now a coffee-free zone."

"Even for the cop?"

"He doesn't live here. My house, my rules." I smiled up into his face. "What were you saying about the news?"

"They arrested the woman who killed Kayla and that caterer."

I placed a cup of water in the microwave and pulled a tea bag from the canister. "When?"

Phillip sank onto a barstool. "Last night. She had her car loaded. They caught her before she crossed the river."

"Good."

I grabbed the cup and dunked my tea bag. "Are you here to pay off your debt?"

Phillip blinked. "My what?"

I glared. "Our deal."

"Oh, the money to pay off your van?"

"And?"

He stared blankly.

I snapped my fingers. "Beatrice. You're hiring her outright and getting your mother off my back. And Michelle."

"Yeah, yeah, yeah," he said. "Got it covered."

"Well?" I pushed. "Get out your checkbook."

"Lord, have you always been this pushy?"

"For money, I am. If I don't look out for myself, no one else will. Get to writing, buster." I mimicked signing a check.

He pulled out his checkbook. "I can take the payment by the bank."

"No way. Write the check."

He signed the check and pushed it across the counter. "I added a few bucks for a paint job. That will get Mother off your back."

"No dice. I like it. Without the scorch marks. It gets attention, and that's what I need to get traction for the business."

He snarled. "You may be on your own with Mother then. I'll tell her to back off, but you know her. She has a mind of her own where you're concerned."

"Don't forget Beatrice. Call the agency and buy out the contract. You'll be able to give her a raise, and it will still be cheaper than what Hazel was paying," I said.

"Remember, only until Michelle leaves for college. I'm not supporting your habit for the rest of your life." Phillip slid the checkbook back into his pocket and stood. "Is Michelle still here?"

"Yeah, she was awake when I came downstairs. Go on up. You can give her the good news about not having to be your best girl—if you and Willow patch things up."

"You never quit, do you?"

"Nope."

The doorbell rang. Phillip followed me to the foyer.

When I opened the door, Detective Zimmerman stood there. He did a double-take when he saw Phillip.

"What?" I asked.

"Did you and Daddy Moneybags get back together?" Zimmerman asked.

"Why would you think that?" I asked.

Zimmerman looked down at his watch. "It's barely seven thirty. You're in a bathrobe, and it looks like you just came downstairs with your ex-husband."

I gulped, realizing how it looked. "Get your mind out of the gutter, Detective. I assume you want to talk about Felicity."

Michelle came down the stairs. "Hey, Dad. What are you doing here?"

"Stopped by to ask if you wanted to go for breakfast,

kiddo."

"Let me get my shoes." Michelle scampered back up the steps.

"See," I said. "There is a reason he still comes to the house, and I can assure you it's not me."

"We arrested Felicity Gaines last night. She confessed to the murders of Kayla Martin and Sasha Withers." Zimmerman slid his sunglasses onto his forehead. "She also confessed to locking you in the Whitwer barn and setting fire to it."

"Good."

Michelle zipped back down, grabbed her father's arm, and pulled him out the door. "Let's go. I'm starving. Can we get waffles?"

After they'd gone, Zimmerman said, "I want you to know Detective Alder saved your butt. He is the sole reason you aren't in handcuffs right now. I will ignore your intentional intrusion into my case, but you need to fill in the details I'm fuzzy on."

I motioned to the living room. "Let's sit down."

Over the next hour, I laid out everything I knew about Felicity's involvement, her obsession with Donovan, the hidden camera at Sasha's, and the photos hidden in Flick Donovan's studio. Zimmerman's expression never changed as he listened to me recount what had happened at the barn. I couldn't tell what his next move would be or even if he believed me.

"Well, this is one for the books," Zimmerman said. "I assume almost getting roasted alive will thwart any future plans you have to insert yourself into police business."

I could have told him it wasn't intentional, but he'd never believe me. Instead, I crossed my fingers behind my back and nodded.

Satisfied with my answers, he slid his sunglasses into place and slammed his notebook shut. "You're a lucky woman, Ms. Cavanaugh."

CHAPTER TWENTY-SIX

"It's about time Willow came to her senses. I love my dad, but he's old, and Willow is my age. Ack!"
Jessie Cavanaugh

I nudged Michelle through the front door of Maggie's Salon and Day Spa. Maggie had offered me and Michelle a free visit. It had been a little over a month since the bridal party fiasco spoiled our outing.

This time, Jessie came along. It had been far too long since I'd spent any time with my two girls, and I couldn't think of a more perfect way. We'd also invited Angie, who claimed she couldn't touch her toes, much less paint them. Nancy joined in too. It was the least I could do since she'd saved my life.

"Have your dad and Willow rescheduled the wedding?" I asked Michelle.

"Dunno."

"Last I heard, Willow still wasn't talking to him," Jessie offered.

A year ago, I would have celebrated Phillip and Willow splitting, but then we were married. Today, the prospect of Phillip being single set me on edge. He'd either be on the prowl again, which would embarrass the girls, or he'd be looking to worm his way back into my life. That door was closed, slammed, and bolted shut. I'd learned my lesson the hard way, but it was one I'd never forget.

Sarah greeted us and took us to the mani and pedi stations. Jessie and Michelle opted for manicures while Angie, Nancy, and I sat down at the pedicure baths. It would be a while before I could afford to indulge myself. When Phillip paid off my van, a portion of my financial stress had been relieved. Plus, I'd been able to give Nancy the raise she deserved. Beatrice was free of Hazel's grip but still on borrowed time. I'd have to grow my business before Michelle left for college, unless I figured out a way to make Phillip extend Beatrice's salary.

A week after Zimmerman arrested Felicity, Alder's ex-wife passed. Alder extended his personal leave, and he and Becca had flown to Belgium to settle Joyce's affairs. He and I had talked every night. Their flight was due to land first thing in the morning, and I couldn't wait to see him.

My cell rang. I smiled when I recognized his number.

"Hey, hope you're not calling to tell me your flight is canceled," I said into the phone.

"No, we're right on schedule. Can't wait for tomorrow," Alder said.

"You okay with me picking you up at the airport? I mean with Becca and all." I knew Becca was hurting over Joyce's death, and I didn't want to complicate matters. "If you would prefer to take a rideshare, I understand."

"No. We've had time to talk, so it's time for the two of you to meet," Alder said.

There was nothing I wanted to hear more. He had been

guarded where Becca was concerned. I had never pushed meeting her, but he'd also never suggested it. He knew both Michelle and Jessie, so him wanting me to meet Becca was a big step forward in our relationship.

"I'll be at the airport around seven. Text when you land." I disconnected and relaxed in the chair, ready for pampering.

The nail tech placed cucumbers on my eyes and told me to relax.

"Hey, Cece." Willow's voice interrupted my thoughts.

I removed the cucumber slices from my eyes.

Sarah flew over, apologies written all over her face. "Willow, let's find a stylist for you."

Angie and Nancy exchanged glances, waiting for a brawl to erupt. Michelle nudged Jessie in the side.

I held up a hand to call everyone off high alert. "It's okay. Hi, Willow."

She bent and whispered, "Can I talk to you a minute?"

I looked down at the nail tech removing my polish. "I'm busy right now. Can it wait?"

She shook her head. "No. I'm leaving for Milan in the morning."

That got my attention. "What about the wedding? Have you rescheduled?"

She shook her head again, and tears moistened her eyes.

The chair to my right was vacant, and I motioned for her to sit. "What's going on?"

Nancy and Angie were still gawking. I wiggled my fingers. "Carry on, ladies. I need a minute, okay?"

"You sure?" Angie asked.

"Yes." I turned back to Willow, who had slid into the next chair. "What's up?"

"I've created such a mess, and I wanted you to know how sorry I am." Tears trickled down her cheeks. "My selfishness destroyed your marriage."

A year ago, I would have wanted to punish her for stealing my husband. Today I only felt empathy for her. She was so young, too young to realize the damage she had caused. And she wasn't alone in her selfishness. Phillip played a major role in the breakup of our marriage. And in all honesty, I played a part too. There was a reason Phillip had strayed. I wasn't ready to take all the blame, but I should have seen the signs and at least called him on it.

"You're the only person who can decide what to do with your future. If you want my blessing, you need to understand I am not in a place where I can give it to you."

"When I lost Kayla and Sasha, it made me think about what I want and if I want to tie myself down at this point in my life." Willow swiped at her tears and took a deep breath. "I got word yesterday that I got the modeling contract. I had originally taken my name out of contention, but after everything that happened, I changed my mind. I'm going to Milan to sort through my feelings. In the meantime, I've told Phillip he's free to date whoever he wants. I won't hold him to his commitment."

Whoa! Stop the madness. Is she kidding?

"Is this the job you and Gracelynn were in contention for? The one Flick will be shooting?" I asked. Willow leaving Phillip unattached did not bode well for my mental health. He didn't do well on his own, and I didn't want to be the one he came running to when he figured it out.

She ducked her head. "Yes. I need time away from Wickford and Phillip. This opportunity is perfect. I'll stay busy and figure out what I want. It's not the right time for me to commit to Phillip." Willow pulled her purse onto her shoulder and stood. "I've made my decision. I saw your van outside and wanted to apologize for all the trouble I've caused your family. And to thank you for everything you did for Kayla and Sasha."

She turned and walked away.

"Wait!" I pulled my feet out of the footbath and slid them into my sandals. "Come back. Willow! Don't do this. Stop and think about what you're doing. Running away isn't the answer." Especially running away with Flick. Phillip didn't stand a chance of getting her back. At least, not until Flick dumped her. With his track record, she might be back before the year was up.

Dejected, I turned back to the pedicure chair. This was not good, not good at all.

"What was that all about?" Angie asked.

"The wedding is permanently canceled. She's leaving town," I said. "With the photographer."

"Yay!" Michelle shouted.

Jessie gave her the side-eye and shushed her.

Angie frowned and said to Nancy, "Better buckle up. We're in for a rough ride."

I chuckled. *You got this, Cece.* My friends needed to have faith in me. It was time for me to have an important conversation with a certain detective, and it wasn't Leo Zimmerman.

If you enjoyed Mimosas, Magnolias, and Murder, follow Cece's journey by reading Book 5 - Gauntlets, Ghosts, and Grannies. Find out what happens when Cece encounters a feisty group of senior citizens, a persnickety ghost, and a dead real estate agent.

ALSO BY TRICIA L SANDERS

Grime Pays Mystery Series

<u>Book 1 Murder is a Dirty Business</u>

Between hot flashes and divorce papers, a middle-aged woman reconsiders her outlook on life when she butts heads with a hot detective during a murder investigation.

<u>Book 2 Death, Diamonds, and Freezer Burn</u>

An unwelcome visitor, an unrequited love, and a dead body create chaos in Cece's plan for a productive summer.

<u>Book 3 Pensions, Tensions, and Homicide</u>

A former friend, a runaway mother, and a dead body threaten to spoil Cece's low-key family Thanksgiving.

<u>Book 4 Mimosas, Magnolias, and Murder</u>

Cece wants a day of self-care, mother-daughter time... and anything but her ex-husband's wedding.

The Mattie and Mo Mysteries

<u>Hark! A Homicide (Prequel)</u>

When a dead elf threatens to spoil Pine Grove's Christmas, being on Santa's naughty list is the least of Mattie's worries.

<u>Book 1 Flea Market Felony</u>

These new retirees have just hit the road. Will their first campsite's shenanigans land them both in handcuffs?

A Tropical Cozy Mystery

<u>Candy Canes and Culprits (Prequel)</u>

Financially strapped, Shelby agrees to photograph the wedding festivities for her rival. Will a murder at the posh event land Shelby's mom in jail?

Women's Fiction

<u>Dandelion Summer</u>

Annie Chisholm led the perfect life for more than 30 years -- at least
that's how it seemed to everyone around her. But she and her
husband, Michael, knew the truth about their shattered marriage.

RECIPE - GRETA'S COCONUT CAKE

Cake Ingredients

A white cake mix prepared per box instructions and baked in an iron skillet—you can use regular cake pans, but iron skillets are more fun. Make 2 layers which you will cut in half to create 4 cake rounds. (Greta always makes the cake from scratch, but you don't have to.)

Icing ingredients:

(This is probably more than you need, but...yum!)

- 1 lb. coconut (Use to assemble layers.)
- 1 cup butter
- 1 cup white sugar
- 1/2 cup evaporated milk
- 1 tsp. vanilla

Directions:

1. Melt butter in a small pan.
2. Add the sugar and stir until it is dissolved.

3. Add in evaporated milk and bring to a soft boil over medium heat. Stir constantly to prevent sticking.

4. Boil for 2-5 minutes. If necessary, reduce heat so that icing doesn't burn.

5. Remove from heat and stir in 1 tsp. vanilla.

Assembly Directions:

1. Cut the cake rounds in half to create four (4) cake rounds.

2. Place one layer of the cake on a wide-rimmed plate (the icing will pool and that's the best part.)

3. With a wooden spoon handle, poke holes in the layer.

4. Pat a generous portion of the coconut over the layer. Save enough for the sides and rest of the layers.

5. Next pour on ¼ of the frosting, letting it drizzle over the sides.

6. Place another layer of cake on top and repeat. When you poke the holes don't poke into the bottom layer.

7. For the top layer, pat the remaining coconut on the top and sides. It should stick with all the icing you've let drizzle down the sides.

8. Finally pour the last of the icing over the cake.

9. Cover with foil and refrigerate.

This cake gets better with age.

If you don't like coconut, you can make a stellar pecan cake by substituting chopped pecans for each layer of coconut. When you get to the top, use whole pecans and arrange them in a pretty pattern before you drizzle on the icing. You could even put chopped pecans in the cake batter if you want.

ABOUT THE AUTHOR

Photo Credit: Alecia Hoyt

Tricia L. Sanders writes cozy mysteries and women's fiction with a dash of romance and a sprinkling of snark to raise the stakes. Her heroines are humorous women embarking on journeys of self-discovery all the while doing so with class and sass.

Tricia is a recent transplant to Texas, but she's still an avid St. Louis Cardinals baseball fan, so don't get between her and the television when a game is on.

A former instructional designer and corporate trainer, she traded in curriculum writing for novel writing, because she hates bullet points and loves to make stuff up. And fiction is more fun than training guides and lesson plans.

Visit her website at www.triciasanders.com.

facebook.com/authortricialsanders
bookbub.com/authors/tricia-l-sanders
goodreads.com/Tricia_L_Sanders